"IT'S ALL RIGHT, MRS. WHITNEY."

Cedric smiled charmingly at the white-haired woman. "I'll take this customer." He patted her arm and she bustled off.

Marielle feasted her eyes on him. Among all the sweet little old ladies, Cedric looked very strong and very male.

"What would you like today, Miss Bond?" His voice was slightly taunting and incredibly sensuous. "Peanut butter daisies? Amaretto truffles? Chocolate-covered strawberries? Tiger butter?"

"Cinnamon hearts," she said breathlessly. "I want cinnamon hearts, please." Her own heart was racing madly.

He took her hand and placed the small bag of candy in it. "Enjoy them, with my compliments." He lowered his voice intimately. "I hope every one of those hearts makes you think of me...."

ABOUT THE AUTHOR

A veteran Superromance writer, Christine Hella Cott has a particularly active imagination and a flair for humor. Christine is also known for the interesting occupations she chooses for her protagonists. According to her, half the fun of writing is getting the chance to "work" in various fields. But Christine, who makes her home in Vancouver, British Columbia, still thinks her own line of work—writing—is number one! *Cinnamon Hearts* is sure to delight her many fans.

Books by Christine Hella Cott

HARLEQUIN SUPERROMANCE

These books may be available at your local bookseller.

Don't miss any of our special offers. Write to us at the following address for information on our newest releases.

Harlequin Reader Service
901 Fuhrmann Blvd., P.O. Box 1397, Buffalo, NY 14240
Canadian address: P.O. Box 2800, Postal Station A,
5170 Yonge St., Willowdale, Ont. M2N 6J3

Christine Hella Cott

CINNAMON HEARTS

Harlequin Books

TORONTO • NEW YORK • LONDON
AMSTERDAM • PARIS • SYDNEY • HAMBURG
STOCKHOLM • ATHENS • TOKYO • MILAN

Published July 1986

First printing May 1986

ISBN 0-373-70220-5

CHAPTER ONE

THE YELLOW PORSCHE suited Marielle Bond to perfection. Its racing-style seat hugged her body—a sleek, feline body sheathed only in the second skin of a bright yellow body stocking. As she swung the car door shut, it closed with the wonderful sound of engineered precision, encapsulating Marielle inside. The engine sprang into an eager, throaty purr at the touch of her hand, and the car slid effortlessly away, up the underground parking ramp, through the electric doors and out into the night. Marielle released a sigh of relief.

The day had been a long grind through various disasters. Everything that could possibly go wrong at a health spa had gone wrong, from a customer screaming that her locker had been rifled and her new tennis racket stolen, to the pool's filtering system breaking down completely. Each calamity had been worse than the last. It was almost eleven o'clock on a fabulous warm March evening, and she was just getting off work; she had started at the inglorious hour of six that morning. Owning one's own business wasn't all it was cracked up to be!

But now the smooth, powerful glide of the car under Marielle's fingertip control made her forget her problems. The irritability that had built up over the course of the day crumbled into dust under the car's glittering spoked wheels. She had worked so hard and so long for this car, and it felt great now! There were, after all, compensations for being one's own boss. . . .

Since it was such a beautiful night, Marielle decided, on the spur of the moment, to take the scenic route home. Her health spa was located in downtown San Diego, and it usually took her about fifteen minutes to get to the area called Pacific Beach. But tonight, even though it was already late, she turned toward the mansions of Coronado and sped along the white-gold beaches and all around the lush peninsula, joy-riding, with the radio playing happy tunes and the warm sea wind blowing in her hair.

Homeward bound at last, Marielle had just come onto the Coronado Bay Bridge when she saw a blaze of lights dead ahead. Police cars and ambulances. She groaned in quick dismay.

What appeared to be a catastrophic four car accident, made even more gruesome by the twisted remains of a couple of bicycles, took up most of the road. Flares drew even more attention to the wreckage. Pulling up to a stop, shivering at the ugly scene, Marielle tried not to look too closely at a stretcher that was being hurried past by two paramedics.

Policemen were trying to keep the traffic flowing through the outer lanes on either side of the mess. As Marielle waited her turn in the shuffle, she felt weariness creep back over her. She tried unsuccessfully to stifle a huge yawn. The wail of several ambulance sirens helped keep her alert. Now she wished she had gone straight home, after all. . . .

Then it was her turn. But suddenly one of the traffic cops halted her with both palms up, and she had to slam on the brakes. The next thing she knew, he was leaning in her window.

"Sorry to inconvenience you, miss, but this is an emergency. All the ambulances are full, and a mother-to-be needs a ride to the hospital."

"Oh, of course I'll give her a ride! Which hospital?"

"The closest one. It's—" He told her the name then looked back over his shoulder when he heard a yell from another policeman a short distance away. Shouting back, he confirmed that he had indeed landed a ride for the pregnant lady and to bring her on over. "Do you know how to get to the hospital?"

"No problem." She nodded.

"Now if I could have your name and address, miss?" He scribbled down the information, and then, seeing his fellow officer and the pregnant lady come toward them, he lowered his voice and said, "She seems fine physically—the medics have checked her out—but we're concerned about delayed shock. She doesn't seem to be thinking clearly; she won't divulge her name or address or anything else that's of any use to us. She just keeps repeating that she's eight months, two weeks and two days pregnant!"

"She's probably worried about having the baby right here in the middle of this disaster!"

"Poor kid," the officer said, nodding. "Drive safely, but don't worry about speeding tickets. I'll see you get clearance. Get her there pronto."

"Right!"

Five minutes later Marielle had the accident victim settled into the passenger seat and buckled down. As Marielle drove past the cop, he gave her a salute, and she waved slightly and sped away. The young mother-to-be looked pale. She was slumped down in the seat, her eyes closed. Marielle thought she hardly looked old enough to be having a baby at all! Her sweet, youthful features were scrubbed clean, and her hair was long and limp, a decidedly mousey brown color. Parted in the middle, it hung down in an uninspired fashion on either side of her face.

The girl had told the police that she was precisely eight months, two weeks and two days pregnant, yet she hadn't given them her name. This odd and stubborn refusal now returned to plague Marielle. Anxious about the young woman's condition, she turned on the floor heater for warmth. The open sun roof was letting fresh air in. Then she switched the radio to a station with relaxing music. And then, calmly and casually, she introduced herself and asked her passenger's name.

Finally opening her eyes, the girl managed a wan smile. "I'm Deirdre Wheeler."

Marielle sighed in quiet relief—the accident victim showed no signs of hysteria. Hopefully all danger was past.

"And I'm eight months, two weeks and two days pregnant," Deirdre Wheeler added importantly.

"Yes." Marielle smiled. "I know." Indeed, it was obvious. The slip of a girl in the pretty blue dress was huge through the middle.

Deirdre Wheeler eyed her driver for a moment. "I'm going to have the baby any day now."

"I'd say you're on to something. Are you excited . . . or do you wish it were all over?"

"Oh, a little of both, I think," Deirdre admitted. "I want a boy. I'm going to get one, too. I just know it." She flashed a momentary, happy grin.

"I have a friend who's a doctor, and she says in most cases the mother's right," Marielle agreed, glad to have found a topic of conversation that the girl responded to so well. "Have you picked out names for the baby yet?"

"We-ell . . ." Deirdre hesitated. "Of course it will depend on what he looks like, but I like Toby or Nathaniel or Andrew. If it were Andrew, he'd be called Andy for short, and that's rather cute, isn't it?" Marielle agreed that it was.

"I've always had a secret hankering for Napoleon, or Charlemagne, but—" She shrugged her shoulders by way of explanation, and they both laughed.

"I know I'm not supposed to ask this, but what if it *is* a girl?" Marielle was still smiling.

Deirdre dissolved into sudden tears. Marielle could hardly believe it. The transformation had been so unexpected. She couldn't think of a thing to say. Was this the delayed shock setting in? She sent an anxious glance toward the young woman's stomach. It would take about five minutes to get her to the hospital.

Marielle pressed her foot down on the accelerator. The Porsche sped through the empty streets, sure-footed, tight to the ground, taking curves like a dream. "It's all right, Deirdre," she said soothingly. "We're almost there, and everything will be fine, you'll see."

But Deirdre only burst into more violent sobs.

"What's the matter? What is it? Am I driving too fast?"

With some difficulty Marielle pieced together that the girl was terrified of having a miscarriage. The accident was sure to be bad for the baby, Deirdre said, sobbing uncontrollably. Reassurances that the baby would be fine if she would only calm down had no effect. Marielle began to be afraid that her passenger would bring disaster upon herself by the sheer force of her growing, unreasoning fear.

In a soft but authoritative voice, Marielle said, "Quiet!" Deirdre swallowed on a startled gulp and stared wide-eyed at her. "Calm down," Marielle ordered firmly.

Deirdre sniffed, almost pathetically, and began to dry her eyes with a sodden tissue. "I'm sorry. I'm okay, really!" She let out a long, shaky breath. "I just wish the baby's father would...if only he could be with me I'd feel so much better. I miss him. I feel so awfully...alone." Her soft voice wobbled away poignantly into tearful silence.

Marielle was touched. Normally thick-skinned, she hated to feel helpless while the young woman sat there aching for the absent father-to-be. Soon, fresh tears were flowing.

"Please don't cry anymore, Deirdre. You can call your husband from the hospital. And look, we're here." She pulled the car up to the hospital's entrance and headed for the emergency doors. "There's a nurse waiting for you, see? You can ask her to call him while a nice doctor has a look at you—"

"No!" she cried wretchedly, "I can't! I mean, she won't!"

"But of course the nurse will call him. He'll come and get you and—"

Deirdre wailed. "He's not my husband! I hate him! I love him...I need him... Oh, I need him. Will you get him for me? Oh, please? You'll get him for me?"

"*Me?* But...." Marielle was suddenly at a loss for words. A sense of dread was welling up inside her. She brought the car to a stop and pocketed the keys. "Come along. Let's get out of the car, and I'll go in with you and—"

"Please, please, please!" Deirdre begged earnestly, not moving, her eyes fixed beseechingly on Marielle's face. They were big blue eyes, shimmering now with sad tears. "I haven't anyone in the world but him." The girl's pale lips quivered. "I'm so scared all by myself!" She scrubbed at her tears. "I've never had a baby before, and I'm scared half to death! Will you get him for me?"

"But, uh, but..." Marielle stalled. She really didn't want to get involved, but at the same time she knew she should. She was beginning to despise her impervious attitude. Had she become so hard-boiled that nothing could move her? "But Deirdre, I think it would be better if the nurse called him, don't you?"

Deirdre shook her head firmly. "He has an unlisted number. I don't have it. All I have is his address. I was going there when t-the accident h-happened...."

Moaning under her breath, Marielle fished a fresh tissue out of her purse and without a word handed it to the crumpled little figure huddled forlornly in her passenger seat.

Valiantly the girl tried to blink away her tears and steady her breath. "C-c-couldn't you just drive over to his place quickly? It would only take five minutes! Please? I just know something awful is going to happen if he doesn't get here! I'll lose my baby—I know I will! I know I will!"

"All right, all right, okay! I'll get him!" Marielle couldn't take any more. "So what's his name and address?"

"It's Cedric." Deirdre went on to give her the address on Daffodil Drive in Coronado, where Marielle had been joyriding only minutes ago.

"Cedric what?" Marielle urged, wondering why the name should sound familiar. Already an orderly was opening Deirdre's door, and a nurse was reaching for her arm. Deirdre was being steered away in a hospital wheelchair when, as if afraid that Marielle would simply go home and forget all about her, she called out, "Please go get him for me?" At the note of terror in the childlike voice, Marielle sighed resignedly.

She knew the bridge to Coronado would be a bottleneck because of the car crash. But it would take longer still to drive around the sandspit that circled all the way around San Diego Bay. Marielle practically flew back to the scene of the accident. She was able to drive right up to the policeman who had stopped her earlier. Told of her mission, he led her on her way through the lane that had been kept clear for emergency vehicles, and she was through the jammed area in ten seconds flat.

But the closer she got to the address on Daffodil Drive, the more reluctant Marielle became, and the slower she drove. She wished there was some way out of the situation that had grown sticky too fast. The last thing she wanted to be doing at 11:49 P.M. after a long hard day was to dig up a recalcitrant father-to-be. And from the little that she had inferred about the relationship—they weren't married, they didn't live together, and they didn't even talk over the phone—Marielle had an awful sinking feeling the father was going to be reluctant....

Marielle wished she had a telephone number to call. A phone conversation would be so impersonal, while this.... She simply wasn't cut out for this sort of mission, Marielle thought in silent protest, turning onto Daffodil Drive.

She found the right block easily enough, but the house eluded her. Finally she came upon it. It was the one residence that was invisible from the street and whose identifying number had probably been long buried in the tangle of a wildly overgrown hedge. Obviously, not too many visitors stopped by here.

Huge agaves, pampas grass and bottlebrush were wound together with prickly pear cactus to make a living wall not even a mouse would dare to chance, Marielle thought, shaking her head. She drew the car alongside the curb and surveyed the impressive barrier. It reached up to a surprising height. Creepers and vines snaked along the top and rippled down the sides.

Taking her foot off the brakes, Marielle coasted a few feet to where a rusty black wrought-iron gate stood open. For a couple of yards the glow from a streetlight penetrated beyond the gate, but what she could see was scarcely more encouraging. There was even a prickly pear erupting right out of the middle of the ancient dusty cobblestone driveway.

Groaning to herself, Marielle backed the car up to the curb again and parked it. She would have to walk in, it appeared, and she wasn't looking forward to it. This mission just kept getting worse.

Stepping out of the car, she shivered a little in the cool night air. There was a breeze coming in off the ocean, and it had a keen edge. Hugging her thigh-length jacket closer around the yellow body stocking beneath, Marielle took a long, unhappy look down the lane and stepped in.

The soles of her soft pink ballet slippers made no sound on the cobblestones. The lane continued to the right of the prickly pear, which meant she could have driven in, after all. But she'd gone too far to want to turn back. Right then, she would have given just about anything to be safe and warm at home!

Feeling every bump in the lane through the thin soles of her slippers, ears stretched for any false note in the junglelike darkness, Marielle crept up the driveway. Vegetation crowded in on her from both sides, making the road into a narrow, intimidating tunnel. Only a few jagged slivers of moonlight fell below the overhead branches.

Marielle did not like the way things were shaping up. Cedric Whoever-he-was was badly in need of a gardener. Why anyone would choose to live in such a spooky place was beyond her!

With longing she thought of her pleasant third-floor condominium on the Pacific Beach shore, a place of tranquillity and bright sunlight, where she could listen to the pounding of the surf or the crickets or the birds in the palm tree right outside her kitchen window....

Her own place was divest of knickknacks and unnecessary furniture. This mayhem of a garden offended her in more ways than one. Marielle tread on the cobblestones like a cat unwilling to dirty its dainty paws. Had her hair not been gathered up into one long, thick braid, it would have stood out on end, Marielle was convinced.

The mansion loomed in the darkness. Even Marielle's stout heart quailed momentarily, and she tipped her head back to take a better look at it. Made of stone, it exuded an awesome air in the moonlight, standing tall in the forgotten garden. Straight ahead two dim lights beckoned.

Suddenly there were shallow stairs underfoot, and Marielle carefully felt her way into a grand portico that funneled toward the front door. Once there, she raised a hand to grasp the ponderous tarnished knocker.

It fell with a crash that she could hear reverberating through the house. Appalled at the noise, Marielle pressed her hand over her heart in a vain attempt to ease its mad race. The door slowly creaked open.

Spellbound, but nevertheless on the very edge of frightened flight, Marielle stared fascinatedly at the stooped figure that barred her way. A reedy, sepulchral voice came floating out to her. "Good evening, miss. Whom shall I say is calling?"

Marielle couldn't find her tongue and had to swallow, with some difficulty, before it loosened. She completely forgot to ask whether she had the right house. "I'm Marielle Bond. I must see Cedric immediately."

With a slow shuffle the black figure moved aside. Marielle slid past him into a vast shadowy hall. The black-and-white checkered floor was cold, and Marielle knew instantly that it was made of polished marble. She felt precariously off balance and unprepared.

"Your coat, miss," the thin voice intoned behind her.

Marielle hastened nervously out of it before the manservant could help her. She held the blue jacket out to him at arm's length, noticing the man's eyes had bugged out in astonishment at her costume underneath.

The yellow Danskin, cut high on the thigh, molded every elegant curve and seemed to shine with a light of its own in the dimness. The tight leggings of outrageous yellow lace and the crisscross of pink ribbons above her ankles held the butler speechless.

Finally he cleared his throat. "Follow me," he at last managed, swiveling and bearing left.

Marielle itched to slap on every light in the place. How could the butler see where he was going? Either Cedric was conserving electricity assiduously, or he was a species of mole.

The manservant's bedroom slippers slapped on the cold marble floor. But there was no other sound. Marielle knew the house was near the beach, but not even a whisper of the surf could be heard. How she yearned to be home, luxuriating in her very own private Jacuzzi....

She suddenly found herself in a salon. The light was a little brighter, and she could make out long, heavy velvet draperies swathing the windows. The room was almost unbearably stuffy. And to add to her discomfort, it was crowded with imposing oversize antiques embellished with carved curlicues and fancy inlay. The walls were covered with family pictures in frilly gilt and mother-of-pearl frames.

A thin middle-aged gentleman, who was fidgeting on a stool in front of a piano, captured Marielle's attention first. He looked as if he didn't want to be present; Marielle felt the same way and sympathized.

Next, Marielle noticed a woman, seemingly cemented into an easy chair and as oversize as the furniture. A small fire provided a spot of cheery warmth right beside her, and a television was not more than five feet away. With the remote control unit in her lap, the woman looked as though she hadn't moved in the past century. She held a large silver bowl of chocolates, and Marielle's arrival had stopped the woman's hand en route to her mouth. A chocolate was halted in midair, and the woman's plump lipstick-red mouth, poised to receive the sweet, remained open in surprise.

Marielle didn't see the room's third inhabitant until last. Standing in the shadows behind a love seat, he was a tall, lean figure, a man to be reckoned with, she knew instantly. She tensed.

Decidedly male and very sensuous, his dark Byronic look affected her immediately. While she stared wide-eyed at him, the others all stared, astonished, back at her, and the butler sank into the shadows by the door to watch.

CHAPTER TWO

UP UNTIL NOW, the butler hadn't said a word. He seemed to have an innate sense of the dramatic, Marielle thought. His employer, the young Lord Byron, recovering quickly, looked only mildly curious as he stepped forward, thereby breaking the spell of shocked silence and prompting the butler into speech.

"This is Marielle Bond, Master Cedric. She requested to see you immediately."

Cedric came closer into the circle of light. The better visibility didn't worsen his looks, Marielle found, although it did reveal a certain resolute toughness. He was in evening dress, and that, combined with everything else that had already happened, had the effect of making the whole evening seem surreal. Marielle took an instinctive half step backward as he continued to come toward her. He was devastating in white tie and tails.

"Marielle Bond." He took her hand before she could retreat any farther. His grip was warm and very hard. "I'm Cedric Greenleaf.

Marielle's eyes widened. Now she remembered why, when Deirdre had first said his name, it had sounded so familiar. Hardly more than an hour ago

she had been reading about him in the daily newspaper. That was, if there was only one Cedric
Greenleaf in San Diego. And how many Cedrics
could there be, let alone Greenleafs?

The man in front of her, with one dark, impatient
eyebrow raised, looked like someone who would
donate a fountain to the city. That's what the article
in the paper had been about. Mr. Greenleaf, after a
booming fiscal year at the helm of a world-famous
chocolate and candy manufacturing company,
Greenleaf Sweets, was donating a water fountain to
the city of San Diego. Marielle couldn't fathom why
anyone would want to donate a fountain, but there
was no accounting for some people's crazy whims.
When she had put the newspaper aside and had gone
back to signing payroll checks, she realized it was
probably plain business sense that had prompted Mr.
Greenleaf's flamboyant generosity. What a marvelous tax deduction! And it was a great publicity stunt.
By the time Marielle had signed the last check, she
had come to the conclusion that Mr. Cedric Greenleaf was probably a very shrewd businessman. She
whimsically hoped that one day her own business
would give her enough spare cash to build a glorious
water fountain! And then she'd promptly forgotten
all about the newspaper article.

In the paper, there had been a picture of the pro-
posed fountain as it would look when it was finished—the first sod had been turned that very
morning. However, there hadn't been a photo of the
philanthropist responsible for the sod-turning. So
this was Cedric Greenleaf!

With enough money to build a fountain, one would think he could afford a nicer home, Marielle thought to herself. For the largest part of her life she herself had had to put every effort into finding food to put in her stomach and a roof to put over her head. But now she had a far nicer home than this depressing place! Was this how 'old money' lived? Marielle wondered, wrinkling her nose slightly at the musty smell.

The seconds were ticking away, and Marielle still wasn't ready to speak. To her relief, Cedric Greenleaf, with a faint, impatient sigh, gracefully continued the introductions. Charm personified, he acted as if there was nothing at all unusual about a woman in a yellow body stocking and pink slippers standing on his salon rug at midnight.

"Marielle Bond, may I present Aunt Agatha and her husband, my uncle, Willy Greenleaf."

Everybody murmured how-do-you-do's. Marielle, feeling a bit like Alice in Wonderland, tried to collect her disoriented thoughts and quickly requested to speak to Cedric in private, wondering all the while what on earth a grown man like him was doing with an ingenue like Deirdre. She couldn't help frowning at him. He really ought to know better! And furthermore, if it weren't for him, she'd be luxuriously soaking in her Jacuzzi. Marielle would spend her money on Jacuzzis over water fountains any day. At least a Jacuzzi had some practical value. Pshaw on water fountains, and something a whole lot worse on all fathers who ran out on their families-to-be!

The kind of man who deserted his family was the kind of man Marielle despised most. Her own father had been one of them. In her experience, deserters were either too spineless or too selfish to even say goodbye. One could always, at the very least, say goodbye. And according to Deirdre, Cedric hadn't spared the time.

Aunt Agatha heaved herself laboriously out of the chair, and Uncle Willy sprang up from his stool in a flash. The two older Greenleafs were diffidently leaving the room to give them the privacy she had requested. Taking a sidelong look at the younger man, Marielle wondered at their automatic surrender to him and wondered, too, about the limit of Cedric's arrogance. Not to mention that his aunt's weight problem was probably due to those chocolates he made! Tsk, tsk, tsk! Uncle Willy waited for his wife at the door, and with a faint, uncertain smile and a nervous twitch he was off, his wife following him into the dark hall.

Feeling somewhat dazed by events, Marielle turned back to face Cedric. But once again she was at a loss for words.

"I daresay we could stand here all night staring at each other." There was a subtle sting in his manner. "But I'm tired and I want to go to bed. Please, state your wish."

"Wish?"

"You came here for something other than to look at me as though I were a creature from the Black Lagoon, didn't you?"

"Oh, er, yes. But where should I start?" she muttered to herself, puzzled. It had sounded so easy—go get Cedric. Sure. She sighed mightily and ran a weary hand up over her forehead. "I was on my way home from work when—"

"Where do you work?" Suddenly all laziness and leisure, he sat down on the arm of the love seat.

"Sun Studios; it's a fitness center. Look, it hardly matters!" Marielle cried, anxious to have the ordeal over with.

"I've heard it's the best place in town."

A fleeting smile broke through her serious expression. But she sobered immediately. "As I was saying, this visit doesn't concern me. Not in the slightest!" She remained standing, yearning to be gone. "There was a terrible car accident...." Briefly she outlined everything that had happened to her since she had been stopped at the scene of the accident, including the policeman, Deirdre, and the drive to the hospital.

All the way through her story he listened politely, neither interrupting nor fidgeting. She had his undivided attention.

"Finally I agreed to find the father of the baby and get him to the hospital. Tonight. Deirdre Wheeler only told me that the father's name was Cedric, and then she gave me this address." Marielle took a deep breath. Cedric had turned to stone. The air was heavy; even the fire hardly crackled. Very, very carefully she released her breath. "And you're Cedric...and I'm here."

Cedric looked dangerous. Their eyes held; he was staring her down. She gazed at him in fascination tinged with fright, trying to anticipate his next move.

"And?" he finally urged, not taking his eyes from her.

"And what?" She didn't understand.

"And how much money do you and Deirdre want to keep quiet? Isn't that why you're here? How would, say, fifty thousand sound to you? Twenty-five for you and twenty-five for Deirdre. Or I could give you the fifty thousand to divvy up as you want. Sixty percent for her and forty percent for you, or maybe an eighty-twenty split. What do I care? As long as you're off my back."

"Wha-at?" Marielle gaped at him, big gray eyes round with astonishment. "Are you crazy?" she squeaked.

"I can't think of any other reason for you to be here. Your friend Deirdre Wheeler is in the hospital having a baby and can't come herself. She needs cash to look after her baby. And probably because of that idiotic article in the paper today, she picked on me to supply it! Any man fool enough to have his wealth advertised…well, it is horribly plain, isn't it. I'd sue the paper, only that would get me even more publicity. So why don't you just get out of here, before I throw you out!"

Mouth open, eyes wide, Marielle could only stare at him in complete dismay.

"Go on, get out!"

"Oh, you're even lower than I thought!" she burst into speech. "Leaving that poor girl all alone, in tears, and out to here!'' She indicated Deirdre's enormous size. ''With *your* baby! You ran out on her, you deserted her, and now you have the nerve to accuse her of blackmail! All she wants is to *see* you! Oh, I had an awful feeling all along about you! That poor kid! Crying her heart out for you! And what about your very own child? Don't you care? Don't you even want to see him?''

He shook his head in a disgusted way.

''Oh!'' Marielle cried in astonishment. ''I've never met anyone as hatefully arrogant as you in all my life! Why—''

''Quiet!'' he exclaimed.

No one had ever spoken that way to Marielle. Aghast, she could only stare at him, arrested in the middle of her diatribe. But she was more accustomed to dealing out authority than bowing down to it, and she soon shrugged the order away.

She marched over to where he sat and glared straight into his smoldering dark eyes. Placing her hands on her hips, she spat, ''I might have guessed you'd answer her tears with the jingle of cheap cash! But crying foul play after what you've done really stinks! And now I suppose it's up to me to go back to the hospital and tell that poor kid you're not coming! Thanks a lot!'' She was so angry she was trembling.

''You got yourself into this...you get yourself out!''

''Is that what you told her?'' She turned away, too disgusted to stand the sight of him a moment longer. ''Donating a thousand fountains isn't going to make up for neglecting your baby... not to mention Deirdre! You should be ashamed of yourself!''

"Right now I *would* donate a thousand fountains just to be spared your sermonizing!'' he returned sarcastically.

She tried one more time, in a pleading tone. "She's so young and such a dear. I don't know how you can resist her! Doesn't the memory of her waken even a tiny bit of concern?''

He was looking at her as if she were an alien life-form. Dryly he murmured, "Blackmailers are many things, but they're never dears.''

Her shoulders slumped a little as she turned away. The thought of having to go back to the hospital and face Deirdre's further tears was daunting. Finding the father of her baby had been the easy part; it was getting him to the hospital that had utterly stumped her. She had failed in her mission. Marielle sighed wearily as she headed for the door then turned once to ask shortly, "What's the butler's name?''

Cedric's black brows rose. He didn't move otherwise. "Sylvester.''

"Sylvester!'' Marielle called, leaving the salon without looking back or taking leave of the man therein.

"Yes, miss?'' The ancient butler creaked up behind her. He had been in the salon the whole time, she realized. She looked at him with loathing.

"My jacket, please.''

"Yes, miss.'' He brought it to her.

"There's no need to see me out." She snatched the jacket from him, not wanting him to assist her into it. "Good night, Sylvester."

She watched him shuffle away. With a heavy heart she wondered whether she had tried everything to bring the unwilling father to reason. She had, she concluded, short of physically dragging Cedric down to the hospital. There was just no way she was going to get him there if he didn't want to go.

Sadly she headed for the front door, feeling ineffectual. The marble was cold and slippery underfoot. Why the dickens couldn't they turn on a few more lights, she stormed inwardly. She was angry at all the Greenleafs, *and* Sylvester, though she was beginning to wish she hadn't been quite so hasty in dismissing him. Was she going the right way? Normally, she liked dim, indirect lighting, but this was ridiculous!

All of a sudden, just ahead, were the two dim lamps on either side of the door. Marielle eagerly grasped the oversize knob with both hands and stepped into a place she had never been before.

Instantly a wave of terror engulfed her. She was lost!

Clenching her fists, she tried to orient herself. In front of her was a lawn, and she could make out rose bushes in the moonlight. She was in a neatly tended English garden. It was actually a nice sort of place, Marielle mused, with its close-cut grass and box hedges. Wings of the house continued down either side of the garden. The many windows yawned black and empty.

Shivering, Marielle relaxed a little, feeling foolish for having panicked a moment ago. It was just that everything about the Greenleafs so far had put her off, off, off!

As she turned to re-enter the door behind her, she distinctly saw a flicker of fire darting across a window in the bottom floor of the wing on the right. She stopped with a slight gasp. Fire? It couldn't be. She must have imagined it. The place was creepy and she was dead tired. It could have been anything, she tried to reassure herself. But as she moved again, a lick of greedy yellow flame lit up the entire window.

Marielle, staring at this certain evidence of a fire, groaned in abject dismay. Was she ever going to get to bed tonight? It was as if the evening were jinxed!

Naturally, she had to check the flames out. One couldn't, under any circumstances, walk away from a fire, a potential disaster in a dry, hot area like San Diego. Gritting her teeth, she went to see what in blazes was burning in the right wing....

She broke into a run and upon arriving at the window in question, she peered in. She couldn't see a thing. It was pitch-dark inside. Marielle began to think that she must have been seeing things, after all.

Swinging around abruptly, she bumped into someone. She drew in an audible, terrified gasp and went ice-cold.

"Oh, I daresay now I've frightened you." The figure spoke softly and mildly enough.

Marielle sighed faintly. "Oh—oh, not at all!"

"I don't often get visitors," the voice said interestedly. It was a pleasant voice, and Marielle discerned she was speaking with an elderly gentleman, quite a bit older than Cedric's Uncle Willy. And what he was holding was not some dreadful weapon but an armload of firewood.

"I'm not visiting. I thought I saw a fire." She motioned to the window behind her. "It's a fireplace?"

"Um-hm."

"Oh. Well, thank God!" She smiled weakly. "I'd better be going. I'm sorry to have intruded, but I got lost in the hallway and..." Her teeth chattered faintly. She was chilly and miserable and tired, and now she felt foolish, too. "Good night, uh..."

"Paddy Greenleaf," the nice voice supplied.

"Paddy?"

"It's Fitzpatrick, actually, but that's much too long. Let me return your favor and invite you in to enjoy a spot of that fire."

"I really couldn't—"

"It would only be right to accept a bit of comfort from something that gave you so much *dis*comfort. Come along inside, you'll like my fire...."

He opened the windows—she realized now that they were French doors—and held a door wide for her to proceed.

"I really shouldn't...."

"A fresh hot cup of coffee and a snifter of brandy won't hurt, will it?"

"Er...no." Marielle proceeded forthwith. For some indefinable reason she liked Paddy, perhaps just because he was sane; a welcome change from the other Greenleafs she'd met so far.

Paddy switched on a small lamp to guide their way and closed the French doors behind them. Marielle found herself in a sort of sunroom. Paddy then led the way across to a doorway and held a curtain aside for her to enter another smaller, much cosier room.

She could see how, every time the curtain was lifted, the fire snapping and leaping in the grate opposite them would shine right through to the French doors beyond. At a gesture from her host she crossed the room to sink gratefully into one of the leather easy chairs placed to one side of the hearth.

The mantel of elegantly carved white marble was tall and narrow. There were bookshelves all around, from floor to ceiling, and there were several ladders perched along the walls. A long table was half littered with papers and more books, and a few odd chairs stood around it. Thankfully, there were no heavy velvet draperies obscuring the cut-glass windows.

"It's lovely in here," Marielle responded spontaneously, settling back in her chair and feeling better already. She didn't realize quite how surprised she must have sounded until she saw his smile.

"I like it here, too." Meticulously he stacked the firewood he'd brought in into a large brass firebox. "The coffeepot is at your elbow." His gentle manner was relaxing.

But glancing at the little table between the two armchairs, she was startled to see that it was set for two, and she looked up to gaze at the white-haired man with round eyes, suddenly wary.

He chuckled. "I see I've frightened you again. No, no, I didn't *divine* your coming. The other place is set for my son, Cedric."

"Oh! Well, I really must go, but thank you for the kind invitation." Marielle rose.

"No, no, sit, sit! He's making a few phone calls, and he'll be awhile. And I would like to talk with you. You and Cedric are going to have a child?"

"What? Me?" Marielle cried. "No!"

Pushing a snifter of brandy in her hands, Paddy repeated, "Sit, sit." There was something so easy and soothing about Fitzpatrick Greenleaf that Marielle subsided and took a sip of her brandy.

"Mmm, this is good." She put it down with a tired sigh. Sniffing the reviving aroma issuing from the coffeepot, she picked it up. "Was I supposed to pour?"

"Please." He sat down in the other chair, peering at her over the top of his glasses. To Marielle he seemed rather wise. He had lots of wavy white hair, and it looked as though he was long overdue at the barber. Marielle guessed that his glasses were often halfway down his nose, just as they were right now.

He was comfortably and conservatively dressed, and she figured he had an equally tidy mind. There was none of the grandiose in him, no arrogance or fancy airs. The only giveaways to his financial status were two details that could have gone unnoticed—his high-quality leather sandals and the thin gold wristwatch that quietly indicated good taste.

Marielle noticed these accoutrements because she had long made a practice of noticing such things. It was a habit that came in handy when choosing staff or accepting checks from unknown customers. The details said so much about people.

He was studying her, too, she knew, taking note of her clear gray eyes, her healthy, shining hair and her tanned skin. She was a living, walking advertisement for her studio, and she knew it. In her line of business, she couldn't afford not to be.

"That's really too bad," Paddy murmured into the comfortable quiet of the room. Just beyond their toes the fire snapped and spat.

At his raised eyebrows—he was silently questioning whether she wanted sugar and cream—Marielle shook her head. He smoked a pipe, she was happy to see. Not that she knew why that should make her happy, but it did. And it suddenly struck her that this cozy little visit was every bit as unusual as the rest of the evening had been. "What's too bad?"

"That you and Cedric aren't having a baby. I would like to be a grandfather."

"You mean you know already? But were you— how could you—"

"Sylvester keeps me informed. I must have misunderstood, for I thought—"

"Paddy, I'm not having anyone's baby, let alone Cedric's! I hadn't met him until about fifteen minutes ago, and frankly I don't even like him, so there's no chance, not even a remote one, of our ever making babies together! I don't even want to *think* about it!"

Paddy smiled slightly. "People usually react violently to my son. They either love him or hate him."

"Then it's too bad Deirdre Wheeler had to love him!"

"And who is Deirdre Wheeler?" he asked curiously. "Will you have a chocolate?" he added, offering a silver bowl full of the most delectable-looking chocolates that Marielle had ever seen.

"No!" She hastened to add, "Er, no, thank you. I disapprove of chocolate!"

"Is that entirely wise?"

"Uh . . ." Thrown slightly by his question, Marielle glanced at the temptation in the gleaming silver bowl.

"There's good nourishment in chocolate. You should look into it."

She waved the bowl away. "Deirdre Wheeler is the one who's going to have his baby! She's in the hospital right now. She could be having the baby this very minute. And he doesn't care."

"Suppose it *is* blackmail."

Marielle was quiet for a moment. Her brow puckered; then she shook her head slowly. "I'd expect you to be biased: you're his father. But Cedric should pay attention to what he's doing. He's got trouble on his hands with Deirdre. He should have known that when he got involved with her."

"If he got involved."

"It's simply preposterous to think Deirdre is blackmailing him!" Marielle protested. "You should have been there. You should have seen her tears. She—she's hardly more than a baby herself!"

"If Cedric's old enough to know better then you're old enough to know that it's often the ones who *look* innocent who are the most amoral. There's a law written down about that somewhere.''

''You could be right,'' Marielle murmured, tipping her head back against the chair. She looked around at the books lining the walls. There was something restful about all those books, something wonderful about all that stored knowledge there for the reading. ''But right now, I don't give a damn. I'm just glad that Cedric and his problems belong to Deirdre, and not to me!''

CHAPTER THREE

"ME AND MY PROBLEMS belong only to myself, and I thank God for that!" remarked a deep and definitely surly voice from the doorway.

The damask curtain with its fringed silk tassels made a striking background for the tall figure in the severity of formal black and white. Marielle didn't have to look to know it was Cedric.

Intruding on their cozy fireside chat, he went on, "It's unfortunate, however, that you insist on forcing yourself into the number one spot on my list of difficulties! Just what are you doing here?"

Marielle was momentarily silenced by his unfair accusation. She glared at him, beginning to despise him heartily.

"Now, son, she did me a good turn, and I'm returning the favor. I invited her in. You really should watch that temper. Pull up a chair. You know where the cups are."

"I am surprised," Marielle said finally, in an icy tone, "that someone as accomplished as you admits to having difficulties! One would think they'd be beneath you."

"Now, now, kids," Paddy said placatingly, spreading his hands. They both turned to glare hotly at him. He just smiled, shrugged and said, "Don't mind me. I was only having a nice quiet evening toying with my equation."

"Equation?" Marielle couldn't help asking.

Paddy pointed to a blackboard in the semidarkness behind him. Scrawled from top to bottom was one long math equation. "It's my hobby," Paddy explained.

"Isn't that nice." Doubtfully Marielle pulled her eyes from the equation and placed her delicate coffee cup, ringed in cobalt and gold, down on its saucer with a decisive little click. She rose, and the shadows from the fire jumped onto her yellow-clad figure, burnishing the sleek body that stood effortlessly poised and yet whipcord taut. In the firelight her tan was a richer brown, and her long, thick braid gleamed like the gold that decorated her frail cup. In the flickering light she was a dozen shades of luscious gold.

"Thank you for sharing your fire, Paddy, and for your company, too." She felt genuinely sorry for him for having such a nasty son. "The brandy revived me and your coffee was delicious. But I really must go now. Good night, Paddy, and thank you again."

Cedric, tall and vaguely threatening, stepped into her path. It struck Marielle why Deirdre had sent her, a stranger, to do her dirty work. Were she Deirdre, she would have sent someone else, too. There was something about Master Cedric Evelyn Greenleaf that made one wish one weren't the one fencing with him.

"I'll see you out," he informed her.

"That won't be necessary."

"I want to make certain you leave this time."

His insult took her breath away. Nevertheless, her answering silence spoke volumes. As they measured each other, the charged, unhappy intensity between them grew.

"Goodbye, Paddy!" Marielle tossed over her shoulder. Determinedly she veered around Cedric, a high black and white barrier. His shoulders seemed at least a mile wide, and she much preferred to go around him than insist on a collision course.

"Good night, Marielle! It was a pleasure!" Paddy returned, peering at her over the top his glasses. His gentle smile was lost on her as she hurried from his library.

Cedric fell into step behind her. He was literally hounding her out! Back through the manicured rose garden and all the way down the echoing hall she went, with him on her heels. They didn't exchange a syllable. And every step taken hardened Marielle's heart a little more against him.

The whole matter boiled down to believing in Deirdre or in Cedric. Sweet-faced Deirdre, or wolfish, lean and hungry-looking Cedric. A young inexperienced girl, or a sensuous man of the world. Blue eyes full of helpless tears, or flinty black ones full of contempt.

For a few seconds Paddy's logical reasoning in his son's favor had made her wonder. But no more. It was horribly plain, just as Cedric himself had said. He was simply a thoroughly nasty person, and his nastiness emanated from him with every word and

deed. He had rudely treated her like a criminal, and
everyone else with surly disdain. If she had to choose
between believing in him or believing in Deirdre,
there was really no contest. Paddy could think what
he liked—he should support his son—but she would
die before she did!

Marielle's pace was the rate just two notches
slower than a flat out run; she had to hold her im-
patience to leave in check. She realized that earlier,
when she'd come out of the salon calling for Sylvester, her sense of direction had been confused, and she
had merely gone left when she should have gone
right. Eagerly she pulled at the ponderous front
door.

On the front steps, her slippers crunching in the
dead leaves, she breathed a sigh of relief. The tangled garden was dreary and dark, but it was far
preferable to the ominous quiet inside the cold stone
walls. A shiver caught at her when she heard footsteps close behind her. She hastened down the stairs.

As she started along the lane, the driving force
behind Greenleaf Sweets moved up to walk beside
her. Moonlight fell to the cobblestones through an
overhead grid of branches. As they passed along the
leafy tunnel, it rippled over them, fragmented into a
mosaic of silver lights. He was close enough for her
to smell his cologne; it was fresh and biting. Marielle turned to see him shoving his hands into his
pockets and glancing around, apparently taking
stock.

"Nobody ever uses the front door," he suddenly
commented in an absentminded tone.

"I thought the house never got any visitors."

"It gets precious few." He lapsed into silence, and they walked on, the air growing thick with things unsaid. Finally he said carefully, "Tell Deirdre she's wasting her time."

"You could have fooled me!"

"It's just another money-grubbing paternity suit," he snarled impatiently.

"The pot calling the kettle black? Or just another pat excuse for weaseling out of your responsibility!"

"And isn't *that* just like a woman! You want equality? Then what about her responsibility? Tell Deirdre to accept her equal share of the blame for conceiving an unwanted baby! Miss Wheeler is innocent, is she? Then may I ask, just how did she get pregnant in the first place?"

"It's plain she was seduced. She's young and gullible and probably very foolish. But you, you're none of the above! *You* could probably be accused of cradle-snatching!"

"Isn't it peculiar how, in a case such as this, the verdict is always guilty until proven innocent. I'm damned if I did and damned if I didn't. All some flake has to do is cry and point at me, and presto— even though I might never have set eyes on her, let alone touched her—I'm the father of her baby! And you have the nerve to say it's a man's world!"

Too tired and cranky to refute his arguments, which sounded annoyingly logical, Marielle snapped frostily, "There is no need to see me all the way to my car! Please go back home and leave me alone!"

"Oh, no. I won't rest until I actually see you go. And this time you'd better stay away! I've dealt with your kind before."

"Pride cometh before a fall, or so I've heard!" she muttered.

"Just who gave you the right to spout wise old sayings?"

Marielle bit her lip. It was a habit of hers that she knew she had to break. After all, it wasn't up to her to codify the morals of the world. But at the same time, he was wrong for accusing her falsely. She had no interest in him or his money. All that concerned her was Deirdre's well-being. But this senseless squabble wasn't getting any of them anywhere. Cedric Greenleaf was without a conscience, and people without a conscience couldn't be persuaded to do the right thing by anyone at anytime. Tomorrow would find him no more mellow or receptive. She would wash her hands of him.

Wrapping her jacket tighter around her, partly because of the chill and partly to make herself less vulnerable, Marielle hunched her shoulders. Had it not been too undignified, she would have simply dashed away to the safety of her car.

"Why didn't you drive in?" he now demanded testily.

Gritting her teeth firmly together, Marielle refused to reply. In the darkness he seemed very tall and very powerful beside her. He moved with a lithe assured animal grace. An inexplicable tremor tingled down her spine. It wasn't that she was afraid; something more subtle was happening. Every feminine nerve in her body was vitally aware of his every move.

After what seemed an eternity they arrived at the street. "There's my car. You can go now!"

But he whistled under his breath. "A brand new Porsche! You must be doing well."

"Very well, thank you! So why you think I would want your money, I can't imagine!"

"Does anyone ever have enough?" he suggested with an unpleasant sneer in his tone. "Or maybe you're in trouble with your sugar daddy. Perhaps you need some quick cash to keep that fancy car from being repossessed by the banker."

Marielle smiled sweetly. "The car is paid for. It's mine, lock, stock, and steering wheel. And my relations with my banker are excellent."

He looked her up and down. "Oh, yeah?"

If she had had a gooey custard pie to throw at him, she would have done so with glee, although she generally frowned on such forms of expression. His smug, presumptuous manner caused her wrath to explode. "Oh-h-h-h!" she gasped. "You . . . you . . . you—"

"—are more articulate than you, obviously." He remained unperturbed; even worse, he seemed amused. "You should have invested in an education rather than that car!"

He had, without knowing it, hit a sore spot. Marielle had had no education, hadn't even finished high school. It was her best-kept secret. "You are despicable," she whispered, turning away. It was clear that she wasn't going to have the last word. She decided to cut her losses. Sweeping her braid back over one shoulder, she made a beeline for the bright yellow car parked at the curb. She omitted to take her leave of him for the second time that night. He didn't deserve even that small common courtesy, she thought, hurrying away.

"Good night, Marielle Bond!" he called mockingly to her back. After a pause he added, "Your manners seem even thinner than your vocabulary!"

This last carelessly thrown remark stung even more than the one about her education. Having grown up in a Los Angeles slum, she was streetwise, but her practical knowledge of Miss What's-her-name's *Proper Etiquette for All Occasions* was rather sketchy. She was constantly worried about committing the unforgivable faux pas. For Cedric to be unerringly right on both counts smarted unbearably; he had had both the education and the social training, and he could obviously tell she hadn't had either. It was only with the greatest effort that she kept her mouth shut. She would *not* swear at him!

"Good night? Good*bye*, Mr. Greenleaf," she returned, embarrassed into the sarcastic retort. She would have liked to point out that what *she* owned, she had earned, not inherited, like he, and that she was as much of a business success as he was. But he wasn't worth the effort. However, she couldn't resist saying, "If I were you, I wouldn't make any smart remarks about my manners, not when yours positively reek. Do you accuse every woman you meet of being a tramp? At least I have an excuse for my bad manners; I was born on the wrong side of the tracks. But what excuse have you?'' She smiled faintly, but it was really more like a baring of her pretty white teeth....

Marielle arrived at the hospital to find that Deirdre Wheeler had already gone. Her first reaction was one of intense relief, and she felt a little guilty. But she couldn't have borne any more of the young girl's tears tonight. Deirdre must have come to the conclusion that Cedric wasn't going to show up. Obviously she knew him well!

Bone-weary and fed up, Marielle returned to her car once more and headed for home, fervently hoping she would never see either Miss Wheeler or Mr. Greenleaf again. The combination of Deirdre's helpless tears and Cedric's anger had resulted in jittery nerves on her part. When she at long last stepped in the door, the quiet of her condominium felt like a benediction.

Sparkling clean and fresh, almost Spartan, it was a restful space of white-on-white. White sheepskin rugs lay scattered on a gleaming golden oak floor. White sofas and chairs were soft and big and plush. Her dining room table was made of brass and glass. Matching brass chairs were upholstered in white silk. A few carefully chosen plants provided vigor to what otherwise might have been a too static environment.

On one wall hung a colorful collection of miniature oil paintings; elsewhere, there were a few tasteful limited edition prints. That was all the decoration Marielle had wanted in her living space. There were no knickknacks, no doilies, and certainly no clusters of family pictures: her family had been next to nonexistent.

No heavy draperies obscured her many windows or the fabulous ocean view. Where she needed curtains for privacy, she had installed louvered shutters of plain golden oak, oiled only enough to bring out the natural beauty of the wood, not to change its soft, rich shade.

The condo was her first real home. She loved it and it showed. Everyone else who saw it liked it, too. Surrounded by sumptuous pristine white, they never dreamed of the filth and neglect Marielle had grown up in. But that was long ago, she told herself staunchly. Cedric Greenleaf's sneers still smarted deep down, but there was a blithe smile on Marielle's face. He could keep the dark, cluttered Greenleaf mansion in Coronado with her blessings!

And then, with effort, she shoved him and Deirdre right out of her mind.

THE NEXT MORNING it was work as usual. Marielle was up at five, at her studio by six. The nightly cleaning crew had already come and gone. She made her regular rounds of inspection, checking the various facilities—the whirlpools, the saunas, the showers—to ensure everything was sparkling clean and in order. Her staff knew her as something of a martinet. By the time she reached the weight-lifting room up on the third floor, Rusty had joined her.

Rusty Devon was her sidekick, or so her friends had begun to call him. A popular ex-football star, he was a main attraction at Sun Studios. Women automatically adored him, and men joined him at the barbells in droves with the aim of looking just like the affable, handsome blond giant.

He owned a ten percent share in her company, which she figured he had earned over the years through his sheer hard work and dedication. There was no way she wanted to lose him, and her unprecedented, generous gift of the ten shares guaranteed that she wouldn't. He really was invaluable to her. Steady, reliable and honest, she could trust him to execute her orders to the letter, though at times she wished he had more brains to go with all his lovely brawn. But he made up for his lack of scintillating wit by being a genuinely nice fellow.

What was more, they had a good rapport. He never undermined her position as boss, never wasted her time in argument or tried to second-guess her. Loyal and devoted—she knew very well he adored her—he lived happily under her rule.

But while she and Rusty had truly come to care for each other, they would never fall in love. They were too comfortable together, too good at being pals, too needed by each other as the family neither of them had had. What everyone else thought of their close association—a matter of much speculation—was of no consequence. They knew gossip was inevitable, and sometimes it was actually rather handy. They could both tout the other as a ready excuse for getting out of tight spots. Rusty seemed to get into more of these than Marielle.

''Oh, by the way,'' he said now, straightening a stack of fifty-pound barbell discs as if they were poker chips, "if a girl called Nancy wants to know what I'm doing tonight, you and I have a heavy date, okay?"

"Uh-huh. Except don't get caught like you did last time, out dancing with Sue. You'd better stay home tonight. Anyway, your account's overdrawn. In fact, your whole paycheck is spent already!"

"Aw, Marielle...."

"Your capacity for spending money is only exceeded by your inability to retain it!"

"Aw, Marielle, c'mon!"

"I'm serious, Rusty. Once your overdraft is paid, you have about one dollar a day until next payday!"

He frowned and scratched his head of tousled blond curls. "We-ell, how about an advance?"

"No way! If I gave you an advance, what would you use to pay your overdraft next payday?"

"We-ell..."

"Rusty, how much money did you have when we first met?"

He squirmed. "Aw, Marielle, you know I didn't have the change for a bottle of beer."

"Not only that, but you were in debt up to your eyeballs! Star quarterback for the Raiders! You made millions! Where did it go? What did you do with it all?"

"Don't bug me, Marielle." He polished away a tiny spot on the chrome handlebars of an exercise bike.

"Okay, fine, but just tell me what you're worth today!"

"Well, lemme see, I own the beachfront condo underneath yours; I own my car, a Corvette; I have a small investment thingamajig—"

"It's called an investment portfolio."

"That's it. And a ten percent share in this company!" He beamed. "And, oh, yeah, there's fourteen dollars left over from today's paycheck, you say."

She nodded.

"And I know I have you to thank for it all. I know that! The smartest thing I ever did was make you my financial adviser, huh? So, if you won't give me an advance, how about a loan?"

Marielle groaned. "You already owe me fifty bucks! Okay, what for?" she demanded after a long sigh.

"Well, see, there's this girl—"

"No! Take your dates home and feed them pizza and beer, Rusty. That's all you can afford! If that! As it is, you'll probably be eating at my house for the next two weeks! No more advances, no more loans, and I suggest you consider cancelling your overdraft privileges at the bank. Until you learn to live within your budget, you're not getting one more thin dime out of me!"

"You're a hard woman, Marielle!" he complained.

"And proud of it!"

The pool's heating and cleaning systems didn't break down that day, and no customers raged over stolen tennis rackets. But a newly signed-up guest burned his hand while dousing the sauna rocks with water. Exactly how he had managed to inflict the injury on himself was unclear, and Marielle deduced he had been horsing around and wouldn't admit it. Sending him immediately to the fully qualified nurse on staff took care of that emergency. The rest of the day passed in relative calm.

On the average, she herself held two half-hour exercise classes and two aerobics classes each day, as well as one hour-long class in advanced weight lifting. The last course was for women only. Between these duties, she supervised her staff, a carefully chosen team of highly trained instructors, and looked in on classes in session to encourage the huffing and puffing clients and caution the overzealous.

Beyond that there were other departments to look after, all under the roof of Sun Studios—the specialized sportswear shop and sports equipment store, the book, music, and video shops, the beauty salon, the weight control program, the juice bar and now, the snack bar.

All the administrative work was hers. That included ordering towels and laundry services and keeping track of the hundred-and-one lotions her inhouse salon stocked. Then there were servicemen to call for broken-down machines and interior designers and carpenters to consult with about various additions and alterations. Presently she had to interview a string of cooks who wanted work in her newest brainchild. The idea that had started out as a simple snack bar was rapidly expanding into a fullservice restaurant on the main floor.

There was a constant stream of decisions to be made. Should she carry a certain line of new sportswear? What about a line of vitamins that was the current rage? Should she put in six more racquetball courts, which meant taking out another loan? Hire a karate instructor? Should she fire the new receptionist for talking on the phone for hours or merely issue him a fourth warning? In the latter case, Marielle decided in the end on one more warning and if that had no effect on his work habits, he would simply have to find himself a new place of employ.

A whole week flew by. Most nights Marielle was far too tired to go out. Instead she would lounge around in the delicious quiet of her home to read a good book or watch a movie on video with Rusty sprawled on her couch, the ubiquitous bottle of beer in his hand. It was her beer, naturally, since he had no spare change left with which to buy his own.

She pored over travel brochures. Her two weeks of holidays were coming up soon, and she still hadn't settled on a destination. With no man prominent in her life, she would be alone, so the choice was proving difficult. She really wanted to go to Paris, but...

The following morning, having a precious hour to spare at work, off she went to the travel agency for more brochures. But the closer she got, the worse the traffic became.

Inching closer to the major downtown crossroad at which the agency was located, she peered around cars and pedestrians to finally see that the whole intersection ahead was torn up. Bulldozers roared, and men at work bustled about. Marielle cursed her luck.

She leaned out her car window to ask a passerby what was going on.

"Don't you know? Where've you been? It's the Greenleaf fountain!"

Her informant hurried off. "Darn it," Marielle muttered to herself, thoroughly vexed. "Trust so-and-so's lousy fountain to be a pain in the neck!"

Eventually she got her brochures and got back to the studio, half an hour later than she had expected. Coincidentally, when she arrived back, there was a message waiting for her from Deirdre Wheeler. Marielle was supposed to call her in the hospital as soon as possible.

Curious as she was to find out what was up, Marielle couldn't convince herself to return Deirdre's call right away. She didn't quite know why she felt the need to stall. Was she afraid of being sent on another fruitless mission? Or was it just the prospect of more tears and more hard-luck stories that stayed her hand?

But her conscience wouldn't let her forget the big blue eyes full of helpless tears, the sad, beseeching voice. If Marielle seriously wanted to do her part for her fellow man, was it enough to stick a few impersonal dollars in an envelope to send off to some charitable organization? Shouldn't she lend a hand where and when it was needed? What about the people who had helped her over the years? They hadn't depended on others to show kindness for them, had they? They had been there when she needed them, even if all she had needed was an encouraging word.

But Marielle postponed returning Deirdre's call for just a little while. And then she postponed it again. And once more. In the business of her day she almost forgot about it, but in a far corner of her mind her neglect of the girl gnawed at her.

The most powerful deterrent to picking up the phone, she knew, was a certain queasy premonition that she couldn't come into contact with Deirdre without somehow coming into contact with Cedric Greenleaf, too....

CHAPTER FOUR

AT HOME THAT EVENING, Marielle finally picked up the phone with a reluctant sigh to call Deirdre. But she was spared both hard-luck stories and hysterical pleas—Deirdre was in labor. Marielle was advised to call back on the morrow for more news of the mother and child. Thankful for the reprieve, Marielle started going through her new batch of travel brochures.

With the sun and sea her constant companions and a palm tree within reach outside her third-floor window, she had no need to seek out a vacation comprised of these elements. In the end she boiled down the long list of possibilities to Paris. She was dying to see Paris and to take a few of her hard-earned dollars and buy some fancy new clothes.

She decided to spend a week of her holidays on a cultural tour of the famous French city, during which she would see its art, hear its music, taste its wines and take in a history lesson or two. Cedric's barb about her lack of education still hurt. She told herself she hadn't gotten where she was today without a willingness to learn....

So half of her holiday would be spent as part of a group, and during the last half, by which time she would hopefully be fairly comfortable with the

French language, she would be on her own. She was a little doubtful about committing herself to the rigid schedule of a tour group, but her agent assured her that many people made use of tours these days, and she would be placed with diverse types of people whom she would be sure to find interesting. Also, the tour allowed for plenty of freedom within the busy schedule.

Her decision made, down she went to the agency the following day to book her reservations. But on this occasion, Marielle jogged instead of taking her car, since only twenty-odd blocks separated her studio from the agency. Normally she loathed jogging, and certainly she was against jogging in traffic. The thought of pumping all that car exhaust into her body disgusted her. Besides, running on pavement wasn't healthy. But she didn't have time today for a leisurely stroll, and she refused to be stuck in the bumper-to-bumper madness that prevailed.

"Now you're sure about this?" her agent repeated. "If you change your mind, you forfeit the entire down payment. And it's half the price of your whole vacation!" She repeated the figure Marielle owed.

"I'm sure," Marielle affirmed, anticipation making her smile as she wrote out the check. Flashbacks of times when she couldn't come up with enough money for a loaf of bread sped through her mind. She looked at the sum she had written on the oblong piece of paper, and for a second it shocked her. She had an attack of panic about spending so much money so frivolously. Then, with a sigh, she pushed her check across the counter. She was committed. She would go to Paris come hell or high water!

As Marielle left the agency, she wondered whether Deirdre had had a boy or a girl. Ahead of her, the intersection was torn up into mounds of dirt. On one side there were piles of granite blocks, and on the other, stacks of pipes of all sizes. The Greenleaf fountain. Workmen swarmed over the sight. She almost expected to see Cedric conducting the finely tuned production in person.

There across the street was the venerable edifice that housed the Greenleaf Sweets Company, Incorporated 1883. The letters were carved in the stone capital high above the massive pillars. The building was a historical landmark in downtown San Diego. It was the original Greenleaf company building, Marielle knew—a further article in the paper had gone into finer detail of the candy business and its heir, Cedric Evelyn Greenleaf.

She smiled a little over the name. How old-fashioned! But it did go well with the grandeur of the building opposite. She had never been inside. Years ago she hadn't had the money to afford costly sweets, and lately, candy went against everything she believed in. Constantly preaching the evils of it to her customers, she could hardly indulge in it herself!

But she paused for one more second, curiously eyeing the elegant brass and glass doors. A steady stream of people went in and out, and those that came out all carried white confectionery bags. Her curiosity was getting the better of her. The story in the paper mentioned how lovely the chocolate shop was inside. . . .

Feeling certain that there was no danger of bumping into the master of the establishment, since he surely did not mingle with ordinary mortals, Marielle stepped off the curb and picked her way through the torn-up pavement and piles of earth toward the candy store, careful lest she get a smudge of dirt on her pale green running shoes. She hurried up to the impressive double doors, and with a glance up and down the street to make sure none of her clients happened to be watching, in she went.

The rich aroma of chocolate enveloped her the instant she was inside. With the delicious aroma accosting her with every breath, Marielle hovered uncertainly close by the door, torn between leaving that instant or pausing to stare at everything.

High oak counters, mellow with age, circled three sides of the shop, their marble countertops shining. Big glass jars ranged along one side, colorful with an assortment of penny candy. Behind the counters, serving the eager crowd, were a number of white-haired older women, all in black dresses and frilly white aprons. Behind them was another wooden counter, and above that were shelves that reached far up to the ceiling. The shelves were lined with big jars, each one full of something tempting and intriguing. It boggled Marielle's imagination. On the far side of the shop, in an exquisite cut-glass case, was row upon row of little chocolate pyramids.

The shop was very old-fashioned and had been kept original right down to the huge brass cash registers. It was an utterly perfect candy store, the epitome of every child's dream. Marielle gazed in happy amazement and could do nothing to stop her mouth from watering profusely.

The final perfect touch was in the sunbeams that radiated through flower bedecked windows to become gleams in the crystal chandeliers above the marble counter. The heavy crystal, multiplying and separating the sunlight into a million brilliant drops, sent the light sparkling around the shop and reflecting in all the polished glass jars.

Marielle had never seen the sun work this particular bit of magic—and in a city where the sun shone almost all the time! While this antique shop was a counterpoint to her modern spa, she noted that there were nevertheless ideas here she could use to enhance her own place of business. Was there a way to incorporate some of this magic of sunshine and crystal in her modern decor? She couldn't help but admire Cedric's obvious business acumen. Even if he wasn't responsible for the design of the candy store, at least he had had the good sense not to redecorate!

A deep, impatient, unfriendly voice right behind her suddenly demanded, "What took you so long?"

Marielle jumped. She swiveled to face Cedric. He must have just walked in the door. And her startled reaction startled him, for as soon as she jumped, what looked like blueprints started slipping out of his clasp. When the first one hit the floor, they both bent to retrieve the scattering rolls.

"What are these for?" she asked automatically, not thinking.

He was caught between staring at her jogging out-fit—another Danskin, this one a shimmering pale green with a fuchsia zigzag slashed dramatically across it—and scooping up the blueprints. "I'm opening a new store in New York," he answered her, just as automatically.

"Do they all look like this one?"

"As close as can be arranged." Now he was taking in the pale green running shoes. "Some are even prettier."

"I don't believe it!"

"You like it, then?"

Caught up short, unwilling to admit her admiration, she hedged, "It's suitable for a candy store."

As his dark eyes traveled all the way back up her slim length, Marielle discovered that her heart was thudding as if it had tripled in size.

"Why are you dressed like that?" he asked her, a doubtful frown between his thick, well-defined brows. "You wouldn't be advertising, would you?"

"I jogged down from the studio!" she bristled, picking up on his intended slight. The memory of his remark about a sugar daddy had a flood of anger coursing through her veins once more. "And as a matter of fact, I am advertising—for the studio. What better advertising can there be than for the owner to look fit and trim and healthy!"

"You forgot to mention beautiful." He studied the intricate French braiding of her honey-colored hair. "The...owner?" he echoed cautiously.

Her satisfaction at his surprise was immense. It was worth being caught in his shop just to see his chagrin. She couldn't stop a small smile of triumph.

"Well…" It seemed he didn't know quite what to say. "Excu-use me!"

"Apology accepted."

"But if you're jogging, why aren't you wearing jogging shoes? Isn't one supposed to wear running shoes to run?"

"Individuals are supposed to choose the correct footwear for their personal body type. And these are running shoes; they just don't look like them. Anyway, I don't usually jog."

"Neither do I."

"Oh?"

"I have a black belt in karate. That's how I get my exercise." He paused. "And there are other ways."

She knew she wouldn't blush, but her heart did skid to a complete stop. She might not have caught on at all—his tone didn't suggest anything more than climbing a mountainside, really—and yet she knew very well hiking was not what he had on his mind as he looked down at her, his blueprints safely tucked under his arm once more.

Suddenly more distant, Marielle delicately cleared her throat and asked, "Have you been to see Deirdre in the hospital yet? She's had her baby."

"Statistically there must be around a hundred women in San Diego at any given moment having their babies. I don't go to see any of them; why would I go to see her? Can't you get it through your thick head that I don't know her, that I've never known her, and that I don't care to know her!''

"What did you mean by 'What took you so long?''' Marielle's gray eyes narrowed.

"I expected to see you the very next day . . . with a concrete demand for fifty thousand dollars for the poor little mother. Now that she has actually had the baby, is it to be a hundred thousand?'' The sarcastic bite was back in his voice.

Marielle spared a second to wish that he weren't so darkly handsome, so physically attractive. His looks had been poor Deirdre's downfall, she surmised. At the same time she tried to tell herself that his appearance had no effect on her; she knew better than to let mere looks influence her. Haughtily she raised her chin. "Deirdre wants *you*, she doesn't want your money. Can't you get *that* through your thick head?''

"So what did she have, a boy or a girl?''

"Uh, um, I don't know, actually. I haven't been to see her yet. . . .''

"Aha! The Good Samaritan is lapsing, is she?''

He was smirking the smirk that drove her crazy. And dammit, he was right again. She should have at least called Deirdre by now. "You seem to forget, it's not up to me to see her!'' she snapped disagreeably.

Suddenly she wished she weren't in her Danskin, leggings and runners. It put her at a distinct disadvantage. He was simply and utterly elegant from head to toe in pale gray linen, and Marielle wondered what madness had possessed her to come into the candy store in the first place. And if she had had to come in, why couldn't she at least have done so in a dress and high heels!

"I have to go!" she muttered quickly.

"Why did you come?"

"Curiosity, I suppose, never having been here before. I had business across the street, and since I know a sour truth about Greenleaf Sweets, I couldn't resist coming over for a look." She smiled while she delivered her final sally. Most likely she would never see him again so she could afford to be free with her smiles. "Cheerio, Cedric!"

He had reached over to the counter in the meantime. "If you won't take a hundred thousand dollars, how about a hundred cinnamon hearts?" He dropped a small bag into her hands, and with a one-sided smile and a last penetrating look straight into her eyes, he vanished through a door in the wall behind him, leaving Marielle to stare after him, dumbfounded.

THE LITTLE BAG of bright red cinnamon hearts plagued her the whole way back to the studio. Should she throw it away? But she couldn't do that; it was too pretty with its paper lace and red ribbon tie. Besides, her frugal soul couldn't throw away something that had cost somebody good money.

Neither could she keep the bag of candy. Never once in all their years of association had Rusty seen her with candy. He would ask her why she had it. She would have to tell him why, and how, and where.... Why she had gone to the candy shop didn't even make sense to *her*, so how could she tell her sidekick about it? Especially after she had told Rusty how much she despised men like Cedric. He would think it odd, wouldn't he, that she had more or less searched him out? And he would think it even more curious that Cedric had given her a present. It occurred to Marielle that she was probably making a mountain out of a molehill—or a double chocolate fudge sundae out of a one-calorie red candy heart! One Hundred Cinnamon Hearts, it said on the bag. One Calorie Each. Hot and Spicy.

Marielle smuggled the bag into the spa and threw it in the back of a drawer in her desk. No one ever went through her desk, so the bag was safe there. Later she would decide what to do with it....

A little later that day, taking a moment to call Deirdre at the hospital, she pulled open the red ribbon tie. Her office door was shut. She sniffed the contents of the bag. The sweet, enticing smell of cinnamon tickled her nose. It couldn't hurt, could it, to try just one? Marielle slid one bright red heart onto her tongue and waited for Deirdre to come onto the line.

Hot and spicy was an understatement! She sucked in some air to cool the cinnamon burn on her tongue, her lips puckering up. It was delicious!

"It's a boy, Marielle!" Deirdre's glad voice burst upon her. "A perfect baby boy! I'm calling him Cedric! After I thought about it, I knew I really couldn't call him anything else!" Marielle winced to herself at this news, while Deirdre's voice bubbled on. "Oh, I just knew you'd call. You're ever so kind!"

Now Marielle felt embarrassed. She was anything but kind! It was only her conscience that had finally made her call, and after the call, it was guilt that made her go out and buy a huge bagful of baby clothes and toys. From what Deirdre had said, she didn't have much and wasn't expecting many visitors at her bedside.

She and the baby were being kept an extra few days in the hospital for observation because the birth had been a hard one and the baby had been born prematurely. It was the same hospital that Marielle had taken her to after the car crash—a private, expensive, rather exclusive place. While any hospital accepted emergency accident victims, this one wasn't the sort she would expect a penurious person to book themselves into. While Marielle wondered who was paying for the very likely astronomical hospital bills, Deirdre didn't volunteer the information, and Marielle didn't pry, although she did think it odd.

Deirdre didn't volunteer one word about her family or background, either, and this made Marielle wonder whether, like herself, Deirdre had no family. Perhaps she had none that she was close to. It occurred to Marielle that her parents may have disowned her upon discovering she was going to be an unmarried mother. Having a family could be worse at times than not having any relatives at all, Marielle knew. She couldn't help feeling sorry for Deirdre.

Face scrubbed clean, blue eyes shining, Deirdre leaned, weak and exhausted, back into her pillows after the excitement of opening all Marielle's presents. "Oh, everything would be just absolutely perfect, if only..." Her girlish voice trailed away while her fingers played with the ties on a tiny knitted blue bootie.

It didn't take a lot of guesswork to figure out what—or whom—she was talking about. Marielle's heart ached for the girl, and Cedric—senior—sank a few more degrees in her estimation. She tried to change the subject to talk about Cedric junior, whom she had only glimpsed behind the glass partition.

"Yes, isn't he beautiful? Not ugly at all, like most of them. But then, look at his father. No baby of Cedric's could possibly be ugly!" Deirdre even managed quite a cheerful smile. Then she asked longingly, heart-wrenchingly, "How is he?"

"Er...um..." Marielle was as uncomfortable as she could possibly be. All she could think of was how, in the candy store, Cedric had said she was beautiful and had hinted in a very roundabout way that as far as they were concerned, all things were possible. And here was his discarded lover, alone and lonely, in a hospital bed, having just given birth to his baby. It all but made Marielle sick to her stomach. "Um..."

"No, really, how is he?"

"I don't know. It's not like I see a lot of him!" And she would see even less of him from here on in, she would make sure of that! Then Marielle took a deep, fortifying breath, and plunged into what she felt she had to say. "He refuses to acknowledge the baby as his, Deirdre." She repeated the words, for they didn't seem to be sinking through. "He totally and completely refuses. He says he's never heard of you, or seen you, let alone touched you." Some small lingering doubt made Marielle keenly watch for Deirdre's reaction to this unpleasant information.

A huge tear formed, spilled over, and slowly trickled down the girl's pale cheek. Marielle felt absolutely dreadful. The last thing she wanted to do was make her cry! Again!

"I don't know what I did to make him hate me so!" Deirdre wept. "Oh, God, I wish I'd never ever seen him. I wish I'd never taken that job at the candy store!" The tears came faster. "B-but I needed the money so badly!"

Marielle stared at the girl in horror. Something inside her had fallen, like a heavy weight. "You worked at the Greenleaf store? Here? In San Diego?"

"Where else? I packed chocolates in boxes. Day in and day out, all day long. I had to wear white gloves, and a stupid baggy white smock and an ugly hair net! I hated it! And you've no idea how sick one can get of chocolates! Although, gee, I'll bet I ate ten pounds that first week! They let you eat as much as you want, you know, because if you stuff yourself you do get sick of it eventually. That's where I met Cedric, of course. He...asked me to work late one night, and...then after everybody had gone, he told me to come up to his office. And then, he, he— there's this great big plaid couch in his office, roomy enough for two, and it's ever so soft...." Tears overcame her.

Marielle was utterly disgusted. Cedric could sink no lower. Some of Paddy's calm logic had gotten to her; for she had hoped against all reason that Cedric Evelyn Greenleaf had been telling the truth. And Cedric himself had been rather convincing on his own. But *now*!

She couldn't find words to describe him. And he had said he'd never seen Deirdre, had never heard her name! He must have heard the name at least a few times, if only to sign her paycheck!

Marielle did her best to stop Deirdre's tears and to perk her up a bit. But it was a difficult afternoon where despair outweighed everything else. The mere effort to try and redirect the girl's mind toward a happier future without a certain tall dark man, just had her melting into tears over and over again.

In the end, Marielle had actually managed to cheer Deirdre to the point where she was blowing her nose and giggling. But leaving the hospital, Marielle herself felt despondent enough to start weeping. Which was crazy, for she never cried. At least, she hadn't since she was nine, when her father had deserted her.

After getting into her car, Marielle just sat there for a moment then put her hands on the steering wheel and her forehead on her hands. Right then, the world seemed a sad, mean, ugly place. She was tough and mean enough to handle it, but how would someone like Deirdre cope? How could that poor soft, sweet-faced little chit of a girl deal with someone as heartless as Cedric? And what a shame it was that someone who looked so much like Prince Charming should really be just an ordinary cad.

She remembered how he had looked yesterday in the store, all elegance and assured masculinity. In her mind's eye she could see the one slight wave in the dark hair and the eyes glittering with vitality. He was as tough as she was. More so, probably. But at least she still had some heart left.

Lifting her head, Marielle inserted her key in the ignition and sped away. All she could do to help Deirdre was to be her friend.

And Cedric? If she saw him again she would spit in his eye. The liar! The cheat!

It was too bad she still couldn't throw that bag of cinnamon hearts away, though. The candy was too delicious, the wrapping too pretty. She slipped out a small shiny red heart every now and then.

She told Rusty all about her visit to the hospital, but she never mentioned the tiny red hearts that were so hot they made her lips pucker up for a cool intake of breath....

CHAPTER FIVE

MARIELLE DIDN'T SEE DEIRDRE over the next few busy days, though she called the hospital a few times to chat. The girl remained despondent. Even over the phone Marielle could envision her thin shoulders drooping as she struggled not to cry while asking yet one more time whether Cedric was coming to visit her that day.

Deirdre's plaintive repeated queries and Marielle's continual assertion that Cedric didn't confide in her regarding his daily schedule began to sound like a stuck record. Marielle had to hold on to her temper on the fourth day. She wanted to snap at the new mother in sheer aggravation. Swallowing bravely, she said instead, the soul of kindness, "Why don't you ask him, Deirdre, instead of me?"

"But I don't have his number!" she mourned.

"Then telephone the candy store!" Marielle was losing her patience.

"But his secretary always says he's not in."

"Leave a message!"

"He won't call back." Deirdre sniffed.

"That should tell you something!" Almost all Marielle's forbearance was gone by this point. "I don't know why you chose to get involved with him,

Deirdre, but you should know by now he is not concerned in the least about you or little Cedric. You're going to have to make your life without him. You can sue him for support of his child—but you can't make him care.''

And Deirdre was crying again.

Marielle groaned to herself. This continual weeping was getting on her nerves. ''You have to get ahold of yourself, Deirdre! You have a baby to care for now. You can't sit around crying all the time! If you didn't want the baby, you should have taken the proper precautions! There's no excuse!''

''But you don't understand! He told me we were going to get married! I was in love with him, and he was in love with me! He said he'd never met anyone like me and that he couldn't live without me!'' Deirdre sobbed. ''Then, six months ago, when I told Cedric I was pregnant, he just dropped me. Bang! H-he said he would pay for an abortion, but that was all he would do. He didn't want to marry me anymore, and I couldn't...I just couldn't have the abortion....'' Her small voice quavered to a stop, and Marielle assumed she was scrubbing at her tears, a habit of hers that made her seem twelve years old. ''I just *couldn't* go through with it! I had hoped that once the baby was born and he saw it, he would change his mind. Now what am I supposed to do? S-snap my fingers and fall out of love?''

''That would be a good place to start,'' Marielle said firmly, although she felt unkind while she said it. Cedric's sins were mounting by the day. If Deirdre did take him to court for support, the jury would surely string him high!

"You've obviously never been in love or, you would understand!"

"You're probably better off without him!"

"I have nothing! Nothing! And if I can't have him, I, I just want to die!" Deirdre avowed.

Marielle rolled her eyes skyward, glad Deirdre couldn't see her. The girl was beginning to sound like a melodramatic movie! When she replaced the telephone receiver soon after, Marielle wondered whether there was some way she could bow out of this unfortunate affair entirely, without her conscience acting up.

Although she considered herself well-off these days, the many years when she had had nothing weren't forgotten. Nor had she forgotten the handful of people who had been supportive and constant. There was a bit of a debt to be repaid to society. Well, she was certainly willing to repay that debt, but did it have to be to someone who cried all the time?

Rusty, surprisingly, had a simple solution to her dilemma. When they were both up to their necks in the whirlpool after the club had closed, easing out the day's aches and pains, he pushed his wet blond curls off his forehead and suggested, "Go visit her one more time while she's still in the hospital. If all she does is whine, then tell her if that's all she's going to continue to do, you won't see her again."

It was with this plan of action in mind that Marielle, with a lovely bouquet of cheerful daisies, went to the hospital the following day. Deirdre and Cedric Jr. would be released the next morning, the nurse at the front desk told her. Going up the elevator, she wondered where the young mother planned to go with her baby. She supposed Deirdre had a home somewhere. Strange that she never talked about it, or about her family, or friends... or anything, really, except Cedric. Senior, of course.

Just before she stepped into Deirdre's private room, a familiar voice stopped her short. There was no mistaking the deep, velvet voice with the sarcastic edge. Carefully Marielle peeped around the corner to see Deirdre, in bed clutching her baby, looking small and defenseless. Then Cedric came into sight, pacing around the foot of the bed, his hands in his suit pockets. He looked grim and decidedly impatient.

Deirdre was crying again, which wasn't too surprising. And although Marielle couldn't make out what Cedric was saying, a great sense of relief gripped her. Surely everything would be all right now that the parents were finally together. She could thankfully bow out of the whole mess. From now on, Cedric would be the one handing Deirdre tissue after tissue to mop up her tears.

The baby started to cry, too, and Marielle hastily decided to make herself scarce. Handing the daisies to a nurse, Marielle asked her, "Will you give these to somebody who needs them?" And she went downstairs to wait in the lobby. When several long minutes later Cedric finally appeared, she hurried out the front doors after him. He seemed to be angry, striding along at an unchecked pace, looking neither left nor right. He was going so fast that she practically had to run in her high heels.

A warm breeze blew some long, silky strands across her cheek, and she raised a hand to free her eyes. Finally catching up with Cedric on the stairs, she remarked happily, "Cedric! You came!"

He didn't look very surprised to see her. "I've got my fair share of curiosity, too," he retorted, continuing on down the stairs. In the full sunlight she noticed that his hair was a dark, rich mahogany brown, with a slight hint of red in it.

She hurried after him. "Will you give me a minute—slow down! I refuse to break into a gallop!"

"What do you want?" he snapped, abruptly pivoting around. His stop was so sudden that she bumped right into him. Quickly he reached out to steady her. His grip was warm and hard.

"To know whether you and Deirdre have come to some agreement!" she gasped, stepping back. "You've no idea how relieved I was to see you two together!"

He took in her dainty high-heeled sandals and simple pale pink cotton sun dress. "Why? You expecting to hear wedding bells? Or Deirdre the ring of a cash register? When will you understand that I don't know her?" He was quietly furious. "That I have never seen her before today!"

Marielle was taken aback for a second; then she exploded, "Oh, come off it! She worked in your candy store! How can you stand there and still pretend not to know her? What good is it doing? For heaven's sake—"

Grasping her wrist, he pulled her forcefully down the hospital steps after him, toward the parking lot. Sputtering, Marielle twisted and turned, but his hand was like iron. He hadn't been kidding about that black belt, she was sure now. He stopped in the parking lot. He'd obviously wanted to ensure that their row remained private.

"For heaven's sake," she went on from where she'd left off, "you don't have to see her again if you don't want to, but you do have to take some responsibility for your son! Cedric Evelyn II, I believe, is his name!"

"I'll kill her!" he ground out, in seemingly genuine amazement.

"You mean she didn't tell you?"

"Of course she didn't tell me she gave *her* baby *my* name! I doubt even you would have the gall to say something like that to my face . . . would you?" He bent his head down a little to look her right in the eye.

As his eyes bored into hers, she kept leaning backward to put more distance between them, but his hold on her arm didn't lessen and stopped her from going very far. Heavens above . . . was it possible he was telling the truth? And that that sweet little chit of a girl in the hospital bed was nothing but a nasty, sneaky con?

"Well, um . . ." Marielle couldn't begin to understand him. He was either mad or incredibly selfish . . . or innocent. "Well, um, sure I would, if the baby was yours!"

With a throttled groan he dropped her wrist, as if her touch had suddenly burned him. "Don't tell me now you're pregnant, too!"

She took a few hasty steps backward and inadvertently stepped over a curb and lost her balance. Just as she cried out, he reached out to grab her. He caught her securely within his arms. Surprised at the sudden close contact, she stared up into his eyes. He seemed just as startled. The abstract idea of making babies still lingered forcibly in the air, and what with the sudden reality of their bodies so perfectly aligned . . .

Quickly they parted company. It seemed now neither had anything to say, and the anger of a minute ago was gone.

"I-I have to go," Marielle murmured shakily.

"Goodbye, Marielle Bond." He sighed, "I swear I hope never to see you again!"

"That was my line!" she spat, stung into the childish retort. Then, her wide skirt ruffling, she swung away and made for her car. Damn him anyway, she kept repeating over and over to herself.

Though she had hurried to get to her yellow Porsche, once she was inside and the door was shut, she just sat there, immobile. Should she get out of the car and go have her visit with Deirdre, or have done with the girl once and for all?

What with all her tears, Deirdre alone was enough trouble. But with Cedric, the situation became entirely too difficult to handle! And by continuing to see Deirdre, the plain truth was, Marielle would keep bumping—literally—into Cedric.

She was going to wash her hands of the whole mess. She didn't feel terribly guilty about it; for now there was an element of self-preservation involved. Not that she totally understood what it was she felt exactly....

The car sprang to life, and the gears shifted smoothly, effortlessly. Marielle rolled out of the hospital parking lot.

Just before she reached the street, she saw Cedric stalking in the exit, back toward the hospital. He stopped some little way in front of her, and at first she was going to ignore him and drive on past—it was going to be a gesture much like thumbing her nose at him. However, she brought the car to a gentle stop instead without really knowing why. Perhaps the time for childish gestures had passed.

"I'm having trouble with my car." Looking thoroughly fed up, he took a backward glance over his shoulder at a huge, antique Rolls-Royce. Its two-tone paint job could best be described as milk chocolate and dark chocolate. "Are you on your way home?" At her nod, he continued, "Then will you give me a lift to La Jolla? I have an appointment, and I'm going to be late...."

She could hardly believe it! Him, requesting favors! And after he had only just sworn he never wanted to see her again! After a fractional hesitation, she offered coolly, "Sure, hop in. I live in Pacific Beach, so it's no trouble."

Pacific Beach and La Jolla were side by side, La Jolla farther north of the city center. It was only a little out of her way. She was intensely gratified as she watched him circle the front of her car. There was his grand Rolls-Royce, out of commission, while here was her little Porsche, sweetly purring, music to her ears. It was difficult to keep a smirk off her pretty pink lips as he got in with a black look in her direction that seemed to say, Don't say anything, just don't say *any*thing!

Before she could shift the gears again, however, he challenged vocally, "If you're going to preach at me, I'd rather walk!"

"I'll stay off the subject of Deirdre," Marielle promised, realizing with a start that not more than two minutes ago she had vowed to stay away from Deirdre *and* Cedric. And now here he was. And her heart was misbehaving again, racing along as if it was in a tremendous hurry to get somewhere. Abruptly she queried in a brisk and businesslike manner, "Where exactly do you want to end up? Downtown La Jolla?"

For a fleeting moment their eyes held again, and he finally said, "You know the street, Camino de la Costa?"

Marielle had the strangest feeling his destination was not what was on his mind. "Um-hm, it's not that far from my place."

"Yes, I know, you live on Goldstone in Pacific Beach." A sharp-edged half smile taunted her. "I . . . looked you up in the phone book."

"Oh . . ." Marielle wondered about that. She took a deep, steadying breath, assuring herself that for whatever reason he had looked up her name, it wasn't important. Then she smiled inwardly at their polite tones. Was the rest of the ride going to be like this? "What's the matter with your car? I thought a Rolls was never supposed to break down!"

"It's my father's car, but Uncle Willy has been driving it and not maintaining it, apparently. Nothing works indefinitely without maintenance. You should know that."

She couldn't resist saying, "You're still driving your daddy's car?"

He flashed her a quick look but wasn't quick to reply. "I take it that was a dig."

"Well..."

"Since you're expecting me to parade my wealth, I'll inform you that I have three automobiles of my own." That sting was back in his voice. He was daring her to despise him just because he was wealthy. He'd obviously experienced such judgment before, probably often, if the cutting edge she heard was any indication. She was sorry now that she had poked fun at him. While she had meant her words to tease, she suddenly understood that she had hurt him instead. Perhaps she had meant to hurt him all along, but now that she had succeeded it was an empty triumph, and she felt like a foolish and spiteful human being. And what made the silly little incident that much worse was that she suddenly realized he had expected her to understand....

She could feel his eyes on her face and braced herself for a scathing, hurtful rejoinder, but he only said, pointedly, "And...my father simply *gave* me the Rolls yesterday."

"Poor Uncle Willy," she jested lightly, easing out a long-held breath. "What's he to do now?"

"He walks!"

"You'd let your own uncle walk while you have *four* automobiles at your disposal?" she protested, appalled.

"That's right! How about this for a wise old saying: 'Give a beggar a donkey, and he'll ride it to death!' If Uncle Willy—" Abruptly he changed the subject. "You know the difference between getting and earning, I suppose?" Perhaps what he had been about to say was too personal for her to hear. She wished he would have gone on about his Uncle Willy, though....

"Of course I do. I certainly earned this car!"

"Mm-hm, and yet, paradoxically, I'll bet it's a lot more important to everyone around you than it is to you."

She gaped at him in amazement. "But I really do appreciate it!" she ascertained.

"Why?"

"We-ell, for one thing, it's good for my business. In this car, I'm automatically assumed to be a success, therefore my spa is a success, therefore people want to go there."

"Yet some people will hate you just because you own the car, and they don't. Didn't you have friends that were suddenly too busy to see you after you bought it?"

"Well, ye-es," she admitted reluctantly. She took a tight turn on the typical curving La Jolla road with the unthinking precision of a race car driver. She realized that he was intimating that in some ways they were the same.

"So?" he prompted.

"So I decided that if a car was so important to them that it negated our friendship, then they weren't very good friends to begin with." She was still a bit bitter.

"The wise old sayings are unfortunately all true. It's lonely at the top...."

"Mmm. I'm a long way from the top, and I still don't have many friends!" She sighed.

Marielle realized he was gazing at her askance, and she could have bitten her tongue! What on earth was she doing, confessing to him that she had no friends? Had she gone crazy? She wished she hadn't agreed to give him a ride! And why on earth did her heart have to beat faster than it did in aerobics class whenever he was near? It seemed that all he had to do was to come within a foot of her, and her entire system went slightly awry.

"I'm sorry," she said shortly. "I should hardly be burdening you with my troubles." Was she blushing? Her cheeks were feeling mighty hot!

"No, no, please, go on," he returned politely, continuing to eye her with his compelling big brown eyes. "I'm just a little surprised all that perfection is actually human."

"I never said I was perfect!" she cried.

"No, but you damn well act like it."

"That's unfair! I just don't think that any good comes by shirking our responsibilities! Perhaps you view Deirdre as a millstone around your neck, awkward to have to explain to your family, your friends...or a fiancée. But you should have thought of that when you first asked her to work late that night. Because it's too late now!"

Rather than insist that he didn't know the girl, he asked instead, "What's Deirdre to you? You keep saying you don't know her. Then why are you fighting for her as if she were your wronged baby sister?"

"Maybe it's because you're the top dog while she's the underdog. Somebody has to stand up for her."

"What's the matter with her?"

"You've seen her! She couldn't stand up to a puppy dog!" With a deft spin of the wheel, Marielle turned the car onto Camino de la Costa. "Where to?"

Cedric directed her to a secluded adobe house on what seemed at least a double-size ocean-front lot. "I'd invite you in—this is my home—but since you see me as Bluebeard, I really don't dare." His sarcastic tone sent a shiver down Marielle's spine.

He smiled softly at her, his eyes fastened on her face. "Thanks for the ride. I hope to return the favor sometime."

"I hope not!" She smiled an acid smile, trying to bait him. Then she added impulsively, "I thought you lived in Coronado!"

"No."

"Goodbye, Cedric."

"So long, Marielle." A tall, enigmatic figure, he watched her drive away.

Marielle wondered whom he had an appointment with. Who would be meeting him at his home? Just when the question occurred to her, a car zoomed past her, going in the opposite direction. Slowing down, she watched the newcomer park on Cedric's driveway. A slender fellow, dressed in a white tunic and slacks with a black belt slung around his hips, bounded out of the car. Cedric's karate partner, she guessed. Turning her head for another look, she recognized him as one of the instructors at a martial arts studio several blocks from her spa. Mark Tanaka.

Pulling away, Marielle remembered that Tanaka had been in the last Olympic Games, and rumor had it he would be showing off his talents in the newest Hollywood outer-space movie. It occurred to her that an instructor of his stature would contribute even more prestige to her spa. Moreover, his other engagements, such as the movie, would be fantastic advertising. But just how expensive would he be?

Marielle wrestled with the pros and cons of this idea that had, in fact, been incubating for quite some time. She hadn't been enthusiastic enough before to make it work because she had been unable to think of a satisfactory leader for the project. She wondered how to tempt Tanaka away from his present employer, beyond offering more money. Perhaps she would open a martial arts division rather than simply hire one instructor to come in part-time. A small division that could operate right alongside the studio, in the same building. The old warehouse, which she had bought when the price was right, still had plenty of room. Mark would be the department head, and under him, maybe four more instructors.

Marielle had been heading toward home. In midstream she whipped her car around and made for downtown San Diego instead. Her banker had a habit of working late. She would have a talk with her and see what she thought of lending capital for the plan. Marielle, threading through the rush hour traffic, marshaled her arguments for the banker: even if the new division lost money the first year, it would still be a tax deduction, and not only that, but the addition would put at least five more jobs into the economy, and—

What she had been lacking in enthusiasm before, she made up for now. It was curious that she came up with these grand ideas every time she saw Cedric. Was it just because, as a fellow business person, he ignited creative sparks? If only she had met him some other way than through Deirdre and Cedric II! She would have loved to vet Cedric regarding Tanaka, and she would have liked, too, to talk to him about how to incorporate old-fashioned crystal into a modern decor. He would also be able to advise her on the pitfalls of opening other studios; he would know all about franchising and branch offices. Here her mind was teaming with possibilities and problems that Rusty, certainly, wouldn't comprehend....

A few minutes later Marielle was in her office with the company books spread out before her, waiting for her banker to come on the telephone line. Marielle sat drumming her pen against the scratch pad and wondered suddenly why Deirdre had been driving to Coronado the night of the car accident. She had said she was going to visit Cedric, but he lived in La Jolla! As his lover, wouldn't she know where he lived? And even if she did know, how could she have guessed that he would be at the family mansion for those few hours that night?

Marielle made a mental note to ask Deirdre about that the next time they met then remembered that she had determined never to see her or Cedric, ever again, and this time she was going to stick to her guns! She really was!

CHAPTER SIX

SUN STUDIOS WAS DECORATED simply but beauti-
fully. While her condo was white-on-white, the spa
was a soft, easy panorama of grays. Neither sex
could take offense to such a neutral color; it was
macho enough to suit the men and tasteful enough
to please the women.

The spacious lobby was paved with warm terra
cotta tiles. Soft dove gray walls rose to a twelve-foot
ceiling, and areka palms, weeping figs and several
splendid dragon trees flourished. There were four
huge matching Italian leather couches in dove gray,
with the palest of orange piping around each cushion. Such simplicity never went out of style.

Marielle's fifth-floor office was perhaps the most
luxurious spot in the whole spa. She had her own
private bathroom, as big as the office area, plus a
walk-in dressing room and a cosy sitting nook. Her
office was more of a suite, really; a home away from
home. After all, she spent so much time there.

It had been the last area of the studio to be decorated. Even Rusty's office had been renovated from
warehouse status long before hers. For years she had
had to put up with bare cement floors, a knock-about
desk and an old steel chair. Secondhand lockers had

comprised her closet, and although she'd always had
a private bathroom, it had been spartan.

When she finally had the spare cash to spend on
her own space, she found she had so much that she
could order the best of everything. And she'd made
do with next to nothing for so long that now she
wanted everything. Needless to say, anyone lucky
enough to gain entry into her office was impressed.

Marielle was tough, but she had learned long ago
there was no point in looking tough. She could be as
aggressive as she wanted to be without relinquishing
her femininity. Nowhere was this philosophy more
immediately evident than in her office suite.

The office, while undisputably feminine looking,
was still properly businesslike and held scarcely a hint
of the lady's boudoir just beyond. And while it
maintained the clean and uncluttered approach, it
exhibited more character than the rest of the spa.
Here, gray combined with soft peachy pink on the
walls. There was an expansive golden oak desk cen-
tered in the room, a fabulous antique. The only antique Marielle owned, it had a dozen drawers and
countless pigeonholes. Not only was it efficient, but
its stately, authoritative air duly impressed whoever
was on the other side of it.

In the salon, dressing room and bathroom, the
peachy hue predominated, warming the space in
several shades. The accent color, the palest of sun
yellow, added airy freshness. Although there were no
frills, ruffles or flowery wallpaper, the area was un-
abashedly and unapologetically feminine in its colors
and textures and lines. There was a bit of an ab-

stract design in the accordion-cloth blinds on the windows, windows that looked down over the city.

It was late the next afternoon when Marielle, having finished the last of her exercise sessions, was enjoying a bit of respite. Wrapped in a pale saffron robe after a shower, she was lying comfortably stretched out on a chaise lounge. The frame of the lounge was sculpted out of translucent plastic, so that it looked as if she were floating in midair on the peach cushion she rested against. She was catching up on the news in the morning paper.

A small article near the bottom of the front page reported on the progress of the Greenleaf water fountain. Immediately absorbed, she skimmed through the write-up with interest. A tiny uncomfortable feeling in the pit of her stomach warned her that she shouldn't be so interested in Cedric's doings. Why did she have this lingering wish that the liar in this affair would be Deirdre? And why was she still thinking about that unpleasant business when she had sworn to herself that she was going to put both characters out of her life for good?

Anyway, Cedric couldn't possibly be innocent. Deirdre looked as if she could hardly tie her own shoelaces! The girl couldn't possibly mastermind and execute a sinister blackmail plot! The thought was absolutely ridiculous.

In any case, the foundation and the plumbing system of the fountain had been started. There was a delay at the moment because a shipment of granite had by accident been rerouted and lost. If the head of Greenleaf Sweets decided not to wait for the granite to be found, different stone was to be used. And if different stone was to be used, the article read, perhaps the design would be changed, and so all work had been temporarily suspended.

Continuing on to the next story that caught her eye, Marielle absentmindedly issued a welcome to a knock on her inner office door. She was expecting Rusty, for no one else was ever admitted into her outer office without prior warning from her secretary. It wasn't Rusty who stepped in, however, but Cedric. With parted lips she stared vacantly at him over the top of the paper.

"Good afternoon," he said, full of urbane charm. His dark eyes took her in with a lazy sweep.

Standing upright, her bare feet sinking into the thick pile of the peach-hued carpet, she yelped, "Who the hell let you in?"

He grinned, and it dawned on her that it was the first time she had seen him smile out of plain old amusement.

Subsiding, she sat back down and asked coldly, "What can I do for you?"

"Deirdre has disappeared, just when my lawyer needed her for a statement. But I knew you would know where she is."

"Disappeared?"

"She was released from the hospital at eleven this morning, and after that she simply vanished. Not that I mind particularly, but since she started this charade, I want her detailed statement of how, where, when and *why* our liaison should have happened. I'd like to think she's gone for good, but things have a habit of getting worse before they get better, and so I mean to find her.''

''Surprise, surprise, Cedric, you're wrong for once! I don't know where she is.'' Marielle pulled a little more of the robe over her thigh, and his eyes belatedly rose from the length of tanned, bare leg to meet hers.

Suddenly furious, he demanded impatiently, ''Why are you shielding her? If she has a claim to make, let her put it down on paper!''

''I'm not shielding her! I don't know where she is! I'm beginning not to care, either!'' Marielle sprang up to face him, his anger infecting her. ''I've jolly well had enough of the both of you!''

The fierce confrontation had them both backing down as quickly as they flared up. They stood in silence, taking stock of each other.

''Why did you have to come here?'' Marielle grumbled, turning away, breaking the tension. ''Wouldn't a phone call have been quicker?''

''I was in the neighborhood.''

''Well?''

''Well?''

''Well, what do you want now?''

He walked over to where she was standing. Towering over her, he bit out, ''You're rude!''

''Oh, come now, surely not everyone bows and grovels when you come by!'' Marielle was not used to people invading her space—they usually kept a respectful distance. She was very annoyed.

''God help me! What have I done to deserve you!'' he exclaimed, puzzled.

"You're alive, aren't you?"

"I do believe we finally hit bedrock!" He chuckled suddenly, maneuvering to confront her again. This time the breadth of his chest hemmed her in. "Don't tell me you're a man-hater." With the lightest possible touch, taking her completely by surprise, he reached out and pulled her satin robe farther closed to cover the shadow of her cleavage. And she knew that he knew she was nude underneath. For some reason, that shook her.

She froze, and for several taut seconds more, his fingertips rested lightly on the yellow satin, creating a subtle heat against her skin. As their eyes held, she took a long, faint, shaky breath. They were so close...he had insinuated himself easily within kissing range....

Before she could warn him off, however, his hand had dropped, and he had casually moved away as if nothing had happened. She couldn't call him to task anymore, she perceived. She should have done it right away. The moment had passed, and to tell him now never to touch her again would seem far too...pushy.

So Marielle said nothing, but her eloquent gray eyes, flecked with green, warily followed his every step. He meandered around the furniture, making himself at home, as though getting to know her territory.

Desperately Marielle wanted him to go. In her feminine boudoir, he was simply too male, too virile, too viscerally attractive. There, she finally admitted it! This man, who aroused her contempt, aroused all sorts of other feelings in her, too.

Poor Deirdre! She hadn't stood a chance against someone as potent as he. Deirdre would have been easy pickings for a smooth operator like Cedric E. Greenleaf....

"Let me congratulate you on your place of business. If it runs as good as it looks, you've a winner on your hands."

She accepted his compliment gracefully. "It runs efficiently now, but then it should. I've had eight years to learn."

"Some people never learn, not even in a lifetime."

She wondered to whom he was referring. She watched him inspecting an art nouveau glass bowl full of glass fruit. It was the only article in the boudoir that was purely decorative, and it was a magnificent work of art.

"I admire your taste." Carefully he replaced a bunch of grapes in the bowl.

"Need you sound so astonished? Just because I wasn't born with a silver spoon in my mouth like you doesn't mean I don't appreciate good quality!"

"Perhaps you appreciate it more?" he returned soothingly, pleasantly. "You don't have to try so hard to get into society, Marielle; you're already in. You've got what it takes—looks and money. Your background doesn't matter; it's what you make of yourself that counts. And you've turned yourself from a street urchin to a lady of property, means and...power. An American success story. And a pretty formidable one at that."

"How do you know what I was?" she cried.

"I happened to run into a mutual friend. I believe your banker is my next-door neighbor." He smiled at her again, a full barrage of Greenleaf charm.

"And she told you—" Marielle squeaked in rage.

"Nothing personal, don't worry. She just happened to mention that you earned the money to open your first studio by performing skateboard tricks down on the beach.

"Well," she said, slightly mollified, "that's common knowledge."

"So I was told." Then one dark eyebrow quirked up a fraction of an inch. "Do you still skateboard along the beach?"

She shrugged impatiently. "Sometimes I go roller-skating. Since I hate jogging, it's a good alternative. Or else I just walk."

"You must be proud of your accomplishments. From performing acrobatics on the sidewalk...to this." A wave of his hand encompassed the beautiful room.

"Not that proud—I stole that original skateboard! And that's *not* common knowledge."

"Now I feel privileged." Gently he laughed at her.

"Do you want a tour of the studio?" It was an unpremeditated offer. For one thing, she wanted him out of her boudoir. The room was too personal, too intimate. Yet she didn't want him to go away entirely. Despite everything, even his flattery, which she mistrusted, she was enjoying his company.

And the more she talked to him, the more she doubted that he was lying about Deirdre. He didn't act like a guilty man. And why wouldn't he admit to the baby if it was his? Of course, there might be some hidden reason that she couldn't possibly guess. She didn't know very much about him at all, in fact....

"I'd like a tour very much. You'll have to visit the chocolate factory soon. I'll be happy to oblige you with a tour in return." A shadow of a smile was lurking around the corners of his mouth, and there was a hint of a twinkle in the dark eyes as they keenly watched her.

Had she wronged him terribly, shouting accusations at him like a banshee? But if he was innocent that meant that Deirdre was guilty, and that was impossible, too. Undecided, Marielle politely offered Cedric some refreshment then excused herself and disappeared into her dressing room.

A critical look in the mirror had her thinking immediately that she wasn't his type. She knew that she was good-looking, but still, she loved rock concerts, whereas his women friends probably went to the opera. While she was content to stroll the beach and snack on cheese-covered nachos, his lady friends probably nibbled on escargots and caviar on yachts. Not that she couldn't do those things if she wanted to; it was just a matter of style.

Quickly she donned lingerie and a short terry tunic in bright aquamarine. Thin leather sandals went on her feet. When she rejoined him a few minutes later, her hair was loose and flowing down her back.

Honey-blond in color, the glossy mane reached right down to her waist.

As he closed her office door behind them, it struck her as decidedly odd that she should be offering a personally guided tour to someone she despised. But then, perhaps she didn't exactly despise him anymore. As they started out together, she stole a sidelong look at him. Deep down, she knew she wished that Deirdre lived in another solar system. But she couldn't allow her personal leanings to shade her judgment. She really shouldn't have anything to do with Cedric, she told herself for the umpteenth time.

But where *had* Deirdre gone with her baby?

"Oh, I'm sorry!" Marielle apologized a moment later, for she had been lost in thought while Cedric's question had gone unanswered. By this time they were in one of the large classrooms, where general workouts, aerobics and dancercize classes were held. "The carpet is made of a special anti-bacterial fibre. Underneath it is a high-density compressible foam underlay and underneath that is a suspended sprung wood floor. No client of mine is going to end up with damaged knees from no-give cement floors! It pains me to see people jogging for miles and miles on pavement. And they think it's good for them!"

Marielle was getting into the spirit of the tour. "A lot of people don't like mirrors everywhere, but here, part of our program is to teach self-confidence." Marielle waved at three walls of the room, which were mirrored floor to ceiling. "I tell them 'If you don't like to look at yourself, then something's wrong; let's right it!' That's a ballet barre, of course, handy for warm-ups and stretching. I hold every kind of class imaginable, including special ones for pre- and postnatal women. The sound system is acoustically engineered, and my music director plays energizing, upbeat tunes—I have an aversion to sloppy love songs and tearjerkers!

"Now we're entering the weight-training division..."

Rusty could barely contain his surprise when Marielle introduced Cedric to him. He made it clear that he had heard about him before this meeting: he almost didn't shake the hand that the candy manufacturer held out to him. Only Marielle's commanding glare had Rusty grudgingly thrusting out a paw the size of a ham. Then he looked at her as if to say, What in the hell is this jerk doing here? Marielle honestly didn't know.

Cedric wanted to explore every nook and cranny of the spa, and Marielle, who loved to show off her pride and joy, gladly did so. She was proud of the fact that she could, in fact, lead a spur-of-the-moment tour; for there wasn't one neglected nook or disorganized cranny anywhere.

The whole time Cedric behaved well. His manners were perfect, although he did have a way of standing too close to her. And sometimes it seemed as if his eyes were registering more than her words. They would travel all over her face and throat and hair and then became fixated on her mouth.

When he finally left, her physical relief was so intense that she felt as though she'd been allowed out of a pressure cooker. He had the power to melt all reason into simple joy at his nearness. It wasn't fair that he could do that without actually doing anything! She had no weapons against his brand of subtlety, and nothing to accuse him of. What a strain it had been, the whole time, to remain cool and distant!

Retreating to her office, she'd just barely sat down at her desk when Rusty came to see her.

Straightaway he demanded, "What was that jerk doing here?"

Looking up from the pile of papers, Marielle smiled. "Looking for Deirdre."

"That's a switch!" Rusty grabbed a chair, swiveled it around and sat saddlewise on it, his arms comfortably propped up on the back.

"She's disappeared." Marielle then went on to tell Rusty what Cedric had told her, and added what she'd garnered later during their tour. "The address she left at the hospital is a false one, and apparently she paid all her bills in cash, so there's no record of her bank checks. She's gone." Marielle sighed hugely, not wanting to admit how confused she was. "I don't really know whether I'm glad that she's gone or not."

"Be glad. She sounds like a drip. I feel sorry for the baby, myself."

"Yeah. You know, I'm beginning to think Cedric didn't do it."

"What? Don't be stupid!"

"Well, if he did, why not admit it? It would be a lot less bother in the long run."

Rusty frowned, running a thoughtful hand through his tousled curls. "Maybe he just didn't want to admit it at first, and later couldn't backtrack. How can he say now, 'Oh, gee, by golly, the kid is mine, after all!' He'd be the laughingstock of San Diego! That just might be it, you know."

"Yeah, that could be it. If he had a twin brother, of course, that would solve everything!"

"How so?" Rusty looked confounded.

"Then we could blame everything on his twin, and Cedric would be free and clear!"

"You want him free and clear?" Her partner was astonished.

"Well, um, what I meant was, er, it's not important . . . just forget it!"

"Strange . . . a guy like that . . . all that money and class, and he's still nothin' but dirt!"

"I gather you're not impressed by our Mr. Greenleaf." Marielle smiled whimsically.

"Huh! I'll bet you ten bills he has a gold toothpick!" He snorted. "Say, talking about money, can you lend me a hundred?"

"A hundred what?" she asked disapprovingly.

"I'm going out with the guys tonight, and it's my turn to cough up for dinner. I'll be darned if all I have is some change!" He looked injured, as if his money had crept out of his pocket when he wasn't looking.

"Rusty," Marielle began.

"Aw, Marielle, don't start on me now, huh? You've got that sermony look comin' over you again."

"You need a sermon! Do you realize that your paycheck—" she tapped a stack of partially signed checks that she'd been working on when he'd come in "—is spent already? The whole thing! On top of that, you owe me two hundred and thirty-five dollars!"

"Thirty-five dollars?" His brow knotted. "What was that for?"

"That was the week you were economizing. You spent that on the yogurt-maker. You were going to make your own and save. Have you made any yet?"

"I never made it through the instruction booklet—it was like the manual for a 747! So I took it back."

"So you got your money back?"

"Not exactly." Rusty looked sheepish. "I bought a kite instead."

"A kite? A thirty-five dollar kite?"

"Oh, but you should see it, Marielle! It's a beauty! Awesome! And it came complete with—"

"Never mind, never mind! Salesmen must drool when they see you coming. Oh, Rusty! Is all my lecturing in vain?"

"I swear I'm getting better, Marielle!"

"Oh, all right!" Marielle reached into a drawer for her purse. Too late, she realized that she was also pulling out the half-empty bag of cinnamon hearts. The little bag spilled its contents all over the top of her desk.

Marielle smiled casually. "Breath mints," she lied, hoping Rusty couldn't tell the difference.

Before she could scoop them all back into the bag, however, Rusty took three or four of the fiery little devils and popped them all in his mouth at once. Marielle sat tight and waited for him to erupt.

"Have you seen my next client yet? She just signed up today. Tall, gorgeous, with legs!" His eyes grew suddenly round, and he pursed his mouth in protest. Rising out of the chair, he sucked in great quantities of cooling air and then, espying her wastebasket, rushed over to it and spit the cinnamon hearts out. The spiciest thing Rusty indulged in were peanut butter and banana sandwiches.

Laughing, Marielle said, "The, er, breath mints work on the principle of burning your mouth right off!"

"Yech! They're awful! Phooey!"

"It's an acquired taste...." She was still smiling as he hurried from the room—with his hundred smackers—in search of cold water. Marielle wondered idly if Cedric was an acquired taste, too. If so, she'd better not be seeing too much more of him....

CHAPTER SEVEN

IT WAS SCARCELY a week later when, purely by accident, or so it seemed to her, Marielle saw Cedric again. It was at a karate meet, where she'd gone to see Mark Tanaka work out. She had found a spot in the bleachers of the high school gym, and in jeans and sweatshirt, she blended in with the students who made up the greater part of the crowd. She didn't particularly want to be noticed, not while she was busy looking over recruits.

However, it seemed Cedric didn't have any trouble spotting her at once. He came right over to where she sat and wedged himself in beside her. "Hi!" He smiled casually, as if they had agreed to meet.

"H-hello," she echoed weakly, gazing at him in wide-eyed dismay. If she kept on seeing him, there was no telling what might happen. He did look wonderfully good to her right then . . . too good.

And she felt terrific, sitting there beside him. Her whole afternoon suddenly brightened. Indeed, the sun outside was shining brightly. Coming through the windows, it fell in solid beams to the gym floor below. The white mats, spaced out on the floor, were the focus of much buzz and activity, but Marielle's mind was elsewhere. . . .

"Have you found Deirdre?" she asked.

"No . . . have you?"

Squeezed in together, they touched all along one side, and the possibility of kissing when they turned their heads was downright alarming. "No."

His dark gaze was taking in the curve of her mouth, and Marielle's knees suddenly felt weak. She was glad she was sitting down. Suddenly she divined that he didn't believe her. He really thought she was lying! It took her by surprise because people invariably believed whatever she told them . . . she had the most sincere gray eyes. Plainly, he didn't agree.

"Honestly, Cedric, I haven't seen her, I haven't talked to her, and I haven't received any letters." Now he really didn't believe her, she realized. Her protestations were making it worse! Marielle sighed.

"Yes. Well. Let's deal with that some other time." For another moment he studied her strong, sculptured profile, the clean sweep of her jawline, the high cheekbones. "Your pet gorilla told me where to find you."

"My . . . ?" Of course, she knew he meant Rusty.

"I'm surprised he told me. I expected him not to."

"I always get my messages," she replied evenly. She kept her head turned away from him, eyes fastened on the warm-up exercises going on down below. Keenly she watched the interaction of the contestants.

This was a landmark event, she thought, with an excited flutter in the pit of her stomach. Cedric had obliquely asked whether she was involved with Rusty, and she had, equally as obliquely, answered no. While it was very much the truth, saying so was more than a mere statement; it was an invitation, an invitation she wasn't sure she wanted to make.

She turned to face him, chin raised, and her eyes met his. She wanted hers to say "don't touch." It was therefore a shock to encounter only soft, enigmatic velvet eyes with a taunting invitation of "I double dare you to touch me!" in their depths.

Marielle quickly dropped her lashes, cutting off the intimate contact, and tried to concentrate on the real reason for her presence at the karate meet. With a loud bell, the competition began.

She had made a checklist for herself of qualities deemed necessary in her instructors, and as the minutes went by, she made small marks on a page.

Cedric watched her with great interest. After a little while he identified the sheet. "Your shopping list?"

Aggravated, Marielle looked at him with eyebrows raised. Undaunted, he continued, "What is it you're looking for?"

"Ability, attitude, ambition, consideration for others, sense of self."

"Anybody in particular?"

They both watched in arrested silence as, down below, Tanaka flung one attacker off his shoulder to the mat, cut the next one to his knees with a lightning kick to the side and heaved the third one backward with a shoulder chop gracefully executed, using a flying rotation of his whole body.

"Wow!" Marielle said, smiling. "This is exciting, isn't it!"

"Especially for the four of them," Cedric nodded down toward the mat.

Smiling a little wider, Marielle asked, "What's your personal opinion of Tanaka?"

Discussion of the various contestants took up the rest of the meet. Toward the end, Cedric happened to mention that he was seeing Mark Tanaka and another acquaintance of his, a screenwriter, over dinner that evening. He had brought the two together, and they were now in the process of preparing to film a space-karate flick. Tanaka was to star in it. Marielle wished at once that she were invited to dinner, too. She couldn't help the feeling of disappointment that washed over her when, with a casual smile, Cedric left her as quickly as he had come, with no invitation forthcoming.

The disappointment continued to well up after he had gone. She sat there, surrounded by the noisy mob of students and feeling very alone. Not the least of her disappointment was due to the fact that he hadn't come to the meet to see her but had come with his screenwriter friend to see Mark Tanaka, which was a pretty silly reason to feel so letdown.

Now, conversely, she wished Deirdre would reappear. If only the truth would finally come to light! Then she could get off the horrible seesaw of emotion, first believing one, then the other. The uncertainty hung like an ugly pall overhead, coloring everything in a negative light.

She had been meaning to go home right after the meet, to enjoy a long stroll on the beach before the sun set. Instead, not wanting to go home in her restless, foul mood, she went to work and carefully composed five letters to five contestants she had picked from the assembly seen earlier. Her letters expressed the desire for an interview to further the development of Sun Studio's new karate division.

Leaving the letters for her secretary, Marielle said good-night to Rusty and left the closing of the spa to him. If she hurried, she just might catch the last glow of sunset down on the beach. She sped her Porsche judiciously all the way home.

Once home, Marielle flung off her office clothes, leaving them in an uncharacteristic heap on the floor. With a quick look to check on the status of the waning sunset, she put on a cozy gray jogging suit and ran barefoot out her door.

As soon as her toes hit the pale powdery sand, she relaxed. Thrusting her hands into her pockets, she breathed the salt air in deeply and went ambling down to the water's edge. Arriving just in time to see the sunset's last triumph, a final blush of ripe crimson, she stood and watched with several others until the hue was a darkening magenta. As soon as the others wandered off, she bent to roll up the legs of her pants so that she could wade in the water along the shore.

A briny tang permeated the crisp air. Marielle passed some die-hard surfers who had only just relinquished the ocean to the night and were peeling out of their wet suits and packing up their gear. Along the beach, in between the condos and cottages and hotels, the open restaurants were swarming with people and humming with music. The boardwalk was populated with joggers, roller skaters and cyclists.

The royal blue sky turned navy blue and then quickly black, and a full moon emerged. It bathed the sand with silver light and lit the whitecaps on each incoming, cresting wave. The rhythm of the breakers was the only solace to be had sometimes.

At the water's edge, here and there, were clumps of sea grass and scraps of seaweed that had been tossed forth by the surf. In the imprint of each retreating wave, one could see an abundance of mica, sparkling like gold dust. The water roared and crashed in its ceaseless ebb and flow. A roller burst onto the beach and left behind hundreds of tiny silver-painted grunions, flapping on the sand like winking silver exclamation marks. They danced magically until the next wave swept them back out to sea. In this peaceful atmosphere Marielle finally pulled her thoughts out to examine them.

Deirdre had disappeared, a curious thing for her to do after she had made all that fuss. Why, now, would she up and vanish? It was completely confusing.

And she had vanished so efficiently! She'd done it without anyone's help. It was as if she'd never been or didn't want to be found.

Perhaps she really had wanted only Cedric himself and not his money. Maybe when it finally became clear to her that he wanted no part of her, she had decided to leave for good. That scenario was certainly possible; whether it was plausible was another matter entirely.

On the other hand, it was even easier now to think that maybe Deirdre was a con. Finding Cedric too difficult to handle, perhaps she had judged it wiser to make herself scarce than to push her luck.

Or perhaps Cedric had scared the girl so badly that she hadn't stopped running yet. Marielle didn't doubt that he was capable of frightening the daylights out of some impressionable, giddy young thing like Deirdre. Of course, he didn't scare Marielle, not in the slightest....

Walking farther, Marielle remembered coming face-to-face with Cedric Evelyn Greenleaf for the first time. A moody, brooding Lord Byron in the flesh in that spooky Coronado mansion. Then later, they'd met again in his father's wing of the house. That walk in the moonlight back to her car was still vivid in her mind. It was a night very much like this night, except the wind had been stronger then....

Given the law of averages, Marielle figured she stood a fifty-fifty chance of being wrong in her choice of person to believe in, no matter whom she chose. She was beginning to be more disposed to give credence to Cedric's terse rational statements than Deirdre's copious tears—despite the initial bad impression he had made on her.

There were things about Deirdre that weren't adding up. Marielle ticked them off on her fingers: why had she been on her way to Coronado that night instead of La Jolla? Why had she no family, no friends, no background? People didn't pop up like mushrooms overnight . . . she must have come from somewhere! And how could she afford a lengthy stay in an exclusive private hospital? And finally, why would she disappear without a trace?

Marielle wondered whether wishful thinking was swaying her opinion rather than a clear-minded inspection of the facts. After all, when one party was absent and couldn't voice their side of things, their point of view did tend to get lost. Marielle was well aware that she was swaying in Cedric's favor; that didn't worry her so much any more. What worried her was, Why?

If the present state of affairs was to continue, there was every likelihood of her swaying altogether too far. There was something about the ''candy man'' that made Marielle appreciate the moonlight more, made her lonely for his company when she hadn't yet decided whether she even liked him. Ruefully she thought of her glib statements to Paddy concerning the impossibility of her ever appreciating his son.

She had never been in love and didn't want to be now. Love had always struck Marielle as a rather uncomfortable state. She didn't want anything to do with the sticky emotion. Especially not with some kook who donated water fountains. And for all she knew, he could be juggling a dozen trusting girlish hearts! The last thing she needed was that kind of trouble.

Musing onward, she thought briefly of Paddy, Cedric's white-haired father, perpetually engrossed in his books and his mathematical equations. She would like to pop in on him sometime, just to say hello and to sit awhile in that lovely library. She wondered whether he would enjoy some company.

Did Cedric visit him often? How was Uncle Willy faring without a car? Even though she was relieved Cedric didn't live in that gloomy mansion, she envied him his family, curious as they were.

The bottom line was that she was too chicken to have an affair with him, yet she didn't want to let go entirely, either. Nevertheless, she *had* to let go. There was no earthly reason to hang on, no good reason to clap eyes on him ever again.

Marielle had a light supper at one of the restaurants and then turned slowly homeward. The lonely feeling wouldn't go away; it was ever present, a gentle irritant robbing her of peace of mind. It was the first time in a long time that a walk alone on the beach hadn't cured her ills and left her restored.

Damn that Deirdre for disappearing! The mystery of the baby's father could forever remain a mystery. Would Marielle always be tortured by his identity, always be wondering? Why couldn't she just forget all about the whole mess?

Just before going inside, Marielle stood for a moment at the water's edge in front of her condo, contemplating the moonlit impression of a sand dollar. She looked up—right into the eyes of the object of all her thoughts, Cedric.

"This must be my lucky day," he murmured with a faint smile. Lord Byron was in a good mood. Dressed in shorts and a sweatshirt, he looked long and lean, tanned and powerful. The wind was ruffling through his thick dark hair, and he looked at home among the elements. This was a new view of him. In her mind she saw him dressed in an elegant suit, speaking in civilized turns of phrases. She juxtaposed the new image on top of the other, and suddenly a very primitive yearning was unleashed within her.

"Aren't you supposed to be having dinner with Tanaka and what's-his-name?" she asked, as if she would rather he hadn't shown up.

"I already did. At the moment they're in my living room, arguing over the height of a brick wall Tanaka is supposed to leap in the second scene. Tanaka wants a realistic six feet; Fred wants a glitzy ten feet. It was getting dull so I decided on a walk instead of sleep. Marielle, no matter what you might think, moonlight does not turn me into a werewolf. What are you looking at me like that for?"

"I-I'm just surprised to see you here, that's all...." Weakly she defended herself, but a rampant blush was sweeping over her cheeks. She was so glad it was dark! Her desires threatened to overtake her.

"I live a mile down the beach," he said, sounding a trifle annoyed. "What *is* surprising is that we've never met here before! Although I usually walk the other way." He paused.

"Then that explains it. So what are you doing here tonight? Slumming?"

Right after she had said it, she had a nasty feeling that she shouldn't have. It was rude. It just proved once again that she had no manners. She didn't even know why she should have wanted to provoke him. He kept silent, a bad sign. A little nervously, Marielle shifted her bare feet. She was teetering on the verge of an apology when he turned away.

"Good night, Marielle," he said softly.

His words echoed with a remoteness that made her wince. She could have told him to stay away from her in kinder terms. She reproached herself silently, watching him walk away. Her embarrassment kept her rooted to the spot, though she felt she should apologize before it was too late. She should run after him and say, Kiss me, Cedric, hold me, love me—

Marielle clapped her hands to her cheeks in chagrin and attempted to cool their feverish burn. Quickly she turned toward her condo, anxious to reach its safe confines before she did something even more foolish....

A WHOLE WEEK PASSED with Marielle constantly thinking that she had forgotten something or misplaced something, and every time she felt this way, she ended up thinking of Cedric.

So she worked harder, each day adding something new to her plate. By Saturday she was leading the morning five-mile run through Balboa Park, two hour-long weight training courses and three aerobics sessions.

Marielle was tired through and through by the last aerobics class. With an inward moan, she considered that at least it was an easy beginner's course, and only a half-hour long.

"Hands behind the head, arms flat, press the small of your back to the floor and bicycle...touching elbow to opposite knee each time." Marielle led the class enthusiastically, talking all the while. "Get those knees up, Norma...two, three, four... Keep

those arms flat, Gwen . . . Don't let your elbows hug
your ears, Tom . . . six, seven, eight . . . C'mon, let's
go . . . eight, seven, six . . . Don't forget to breathe . . .
three, two, one! Bring your legs up, tuck the left one
under, keep the knees bent and roll up to a stand.
Stand tall and stretch up, left, right, left, higher,
higher, left, right . . .''

Marielle began to pant from the exertion. ''Running on the spot, make sure your heels touch the
floor. Hands push up and out and up and out.
C'mon, Bruce, no cheating, get those arms up there!
Try to smile . . . this isn't so bad. Think of all the
wonderful things you're doing for your body. . . .
Think of how gorgeous you're going to be! Change
to swing arms side to side . . .''

Marielle's Danskin on this occasion was a dramatic plain white. She wore white leggings, too. Only
the slippers were pale pink. Her hair was held close
to her head with French braids caught by a delicate
barette just above the neck. From there on down it
was loose and flowing.

Her hair was a shimmering golden cascade of
movement, her body a sleek fluid line of healthy
feminine grace. At least half the men in the class were
watching her blissfully, automatically playing fol-
low-the-leader. A generous pink mouth and big, sincere gray eyes spurred them on. The women were
encouraged by her straightforward warmth and genuine wish to help them attain the best possible fitness level and figure.

"Jumping jacks, two, three, four, just do your best, six, seven, eight...some days you feel better than others, but just keep going...."

Marielle always tried to keep a sharp eye out for anything unusual, and when Cedric came striding into her classroom, looking like wrath supreme, she sensed disaster and immediately started instructing her class, "Keep jogging to the music, relax and enjoy. Cross arms to the front and back. Keep going until I get back."

Cedric's dark eyes consumed her, and when she reached him, his hand locked around her wrist in a deadly grip. He pulled her from the room, to everyone's gaping interest, and she took a sidelong glance at his grim profile but said nothing. Furious though he might be, she was unbelievably happy to see him.

But she almost had to run to keep up with Cedric's angry strides. Luckily they were already on the fifth floor of the spa. Not wasting a second, he marched her right into her private office and then shut the door quickly behind them. Marielle was a little frightened. She began tugging at her hand for him to let go.

But he held her for a quivering moment longer, with scant inches between them. His eyes razed all the way down her tense figure to the pink slippers and all the way back up to the braided golden hair. Then he let her go, almost a bit too suddenly.

"Why did you do it?" he growled, turning his back on her as if he couldn't bear to look at her a moment longer. Raking his hands through his hair, he paced a few feet away. "Why would you do something so vindictive!'' He swung around to face her again, looking angrier by the moment. Right now she was sure he wanted her reduced to ashes....

CHAPTER EIGHT

"WHAT DID I DO?" Marielle said cautiously, edging farther away from him. Her heart was thudding in an adrenaline rush. She was physically exhausted from the activities of the day but now felt a curious exhilaration. The sight of her might give him agony; the sight of him gave her sweet pleasure.

"Don't play games with me!" he bit out. "You put Deirdre up to it! You knew all along where she was! You're either in with her or just plain neurotic!"

"None of the above!" she cried back, stung by surprise, fighting to steady her breath. Her gray eyes widened. "What on earth are you talking about?"

"Don't give me that!" His fury was palpable, with her the brunt of it. "You've been hiding her all along, and then you sicced her on the house. Why in God's name you should want to do such a thing is beyond me! What were you hoping to accomplish? Couldn't you at least have sent her to La Jolla? Why use my family to get back at me? Why did you do it, Marielle?"

"But, but I—"

He didn't give her a chance to defend herself but raged on. "Did it give you your jollies to think how

Deirdre would upset my uncle and aunt? Showing up on their doorstep with a surprise package in diapers! In tears…and in her arms, a wet Cedric Evelyn junior, screaming his little head off! Thanks to you, my Uncle Willy had a heart attack! Thanks to your meddling, he's lying in a hospital bed right now! I'm amazed at your unlimited vengeance! For something I didn't even do!"

"But I didn't do anything! I didn't sic her on anybody! What a terrible thing to suggest!"

"What about the terrible thing you *did*!" he exploded.

"I didn't *do* anything!" she yelled back.

"Say, Marielle." Rusty stuck his head in her office door. "Did you call?" His overly casual tone didn't fool anybody. He came in and sauntered slowly toward Cedric. "There isn't anybody making a nuisance of himself, is there?"

Marielle had a dreadful mental flash of heavyweight quarterback Rusty Devon taking on C. E. Greenleaf, black belt. She hastened to plant herself between them. "It's okay, Rusty; everything's all right! Back off. I will not have you starting a fight. You can do me a favor, though. Would you please finish my aerobics class before they all keel over in a faint?"

Rusty was successfully diverted, although he gave Cedric a long, suspicious look before he turned to leave.

"At least he comes with a leash!" Cedric murmured, a disdainful eyebrow arched at Rusty's broad retreating back.

"You touch her and you're mincemeat!" Rusty spat from the doorway. "You ain't nothin' but dirt—an' don't you forget it!"

Marielle was so surprised that words escaped her. Cedric, unflinching, stared back at her sidekick with a level challenge, not backing down one iota.

"Please go, Rusty!" Marielle gasped. "My—my class will be collapsing on the floor!"

With a meaningful sigh Rusty left, his eyes focused on Cedric's face to the last possible second. Finally the heavy oak door swung shut. Shaken, Marielle looked from the closed door to Cedric's face to find him studying her narrowly.

"Do you allow him on the furniture?" he asked softly, with that wicked sarcasm back in his voice.

Speechless, Marielle said nothing for a few seconds, simply too surprised by the events of the past few minutes, by Cedric's anger, Rusty's adamant blowup and now, by Cedric's unprecedented gall. Because, of course, he was asking if Rusty was allowed in her bed....

"How dare you!" she shrieked. "What on earth makes you think you have the right to put down somebody who is my friend, my partner in the business, somebody who has never, ever, let me down! How the bloody hell dare you!" Now that he wasn't in a fury anymore, she was. "You can insult me all you want but don't take your nasty, arrogant, lousy mood out on him!" She'd gone behind her desk, where she could assume a position of power. Placing her hands on the desk and leaning forward for emphasis, she finished, "*You* talk to *me* about manners!" And in place of a more colorful expletive she cried, at her wit's end, "Pshaw!"

"You are going to tell me why you sent Deirdre to Coronado," he announced coldly. He had turned his back on her again to stare out the windows.

Marielle had to catch her breath after her outburst. She frowned at his broad back. "I didn't send her anywhere! I haven't seen her since…since the day I gave you that ride home. And even then, I only peeked in at her from around the corner because you were there!"

He too leaned over the desk on the opposite side. "At least tell me why you persist in tormenting me with this Deirdre Wheeler!"

Marielle was about to retort but instead she said nothing and bit her bottom lip. The more she protested, the more he didn't believe her. She realized they were both in the same boat. Each utterly refused to trust the other. But it was painful to be disbelieved! Marielle wanted to keep on protesting strenuously. So she did, saying, "I didn't do it, Cedric. I did not do it!"

Taking a deep breath, he straightened. He drew his hand through the ruffled dark wave over one eye and pushed it back with an impatient gesture. "Then who did?"

"How should I know?"

"You have to know; you're her friend!"

"All I did was give the girl a ride to the hospital one ill-fated night!"

"And what else?"

"I *might* have been her friend, given time, but Cedric, I hardly knew her! And honestly, I'm not sure I liked her all that much! Our entire association consisted of a couple of visits in a hospital ward! I felt sorry for her. I bought her a few baby clothes and called her up when I couldn't spare the time to go to the hospital. That's it! And when she asked me for advice, I told her to forget you. What are you questioning me for, anyway? She didn't work for *me*!"

That stopped him short. He repeated incredulously, "She worked for me?"

"She said she did! Do your chocolate-box packers have to wear white gloves, white smocks and hair nets?"

"Well, yes, of course."

"Aha! She worked for you, all right!" Marielle snapped grimly.

"And what's that supposed to mean?" He scowled at her, his dark brows lowering like ominous storm clouds. "I have forty-four stores. I don't know the name of every single person on my permanent staff, and I certainly don't know *any* names of the temporary help. If you're thinking what I think you're thinking, you're wrong! There could have been a dozen Deirdre Wheelers working for me at any one time!"

"You're telling me to my face that you've never even heard her name? You must at least have signed her paycheck!" Marielle said accusingly, crossing her arms on her chest. "Running a business, I know that much, anyway!"

But he just shrugged. "As a matter of fact, that's Uncle Willy's job, signing paychecks. He can't make a mess of that. But he can't even do that now!"

"I'm sorry about your uncle, Cedric, I really am. Please, please believe me, I had nothing to do with anything. My whole crime was that I went joyriding when I should have been going home to bed!" At his quizzical glance, she explained, "That's why I was over in Coronado that night. It was late when I got off work, hadn't had a break all day. So I went for a spin...." Her voice trailed away. A sudden sinking feeling told her that no matter how hard she tried or what brilliant arguments she devised, he would not believe her.

"You know, I'm beginning to believe you." A whimsical smile suddenly curved up one corner of his mouth.

Nonplussed, she waited for him to continue. She could hardly believe he had actually smiled! After his cold wrath, it was like a lovely ray of sunshine.

"It's so much easier, and it feels so much better. I *want* to believe you."

"You...you sound like you're trying to talk yourself into it."

"I am."

A faint, answering smile was born on her wide pink mouth. She wanted to believe him, too....

Then he asked, "What did Deirdre give you as the reason for our supposed separation? I never did get to that part of the plot."

"We-ell...you had promised to marry her, but when she told you she was pregnant, you offered to pay for an abortion instead, and when she wouldn't go for it, you bowed out. She was banking on the hope that seeing the baby would change your mind."

"Banking on? Is that a Freudian slip?"

"Why are you so sure she wants money?"

He looked at her as if she was hopelessly dim, and that, more than anything else, made her think she might have made a terrible mistake in choosing Deirdre before him. He went on, "At the hospital she *told* me it was that first article in the paper about the water fountain that prompted her to look me up. Never again am I going to have anything to do with blasted water fountains! So far, that thing has been one painful disaster after another!"

A grin slipped out before she was fully aware of it. "Are you some kind of a megalomaniac?"

For a second he looked at her in annoyed astonishment. Then he spread his hands. "You see? Everybody thinks I'm at least slightly insane just because I want to build a fountain."

"You must admit, it's a little unusual."

"It seems pretty straightforward to me."

"But then I'm sure you don't care if the whole world thinks you are cheerfully nuts!" She smiled and leaned with one hip on the corner of her big antique desk. "There's a lot of Paddy in you."

On a prowl around the office, Cedric stopped at the windows. Looking out at the view of city streets and docks below, he said offhandedly, "It's not the world that counts, only a handful of people. I care what they think of me...not the rest. There's no point in trying to please the public."

Absorbing his words, Marielle slid up onto the desk to perch there more comfortably. She studied Cedric's profile while he stared out over the city below. "How's Uncle Willy?"

"He'll be okay... in time."

Marielle felt dreadful about poor Uncle Willy. "He'll walk and talk and everything?" she checked anxiously.

"Oh, yes. It's going to take a few weeks, though, before he's on his feet again." He paused. "My uncle and aunt knew nothing about Deirdre. I didn't see any reason to let them in on it. So it came as a... a rude surprise to be introduced to Cedric junior. They are... old-fashioned."

"Oh," Marielle said softly, nodding. She envisioned the scene as it must have happened at the front door of the Coronado mansion, with Deirdre in tears and the baby squawling. Well, she had wanted Deirdre to reappear, and she had. "Since you live in La Jolla, why does she keep going to Coronado?"

"I was going to ask you the same thing." He eyed her, smiling faintly. Then his gaze dropped slowly, and he began to take in all of her. His dark eyes moved from her throat down to where the white clingy material molded her shoulders and breasts... down to the narrow rib cage and the indent of her waist, which emphasized the curve of her trim hips, and then down farther along the smooth thighs and calves and delicate ankles crisscrossed with pink ribbons, ending in pretty, dainty pink ballet slippers. He seemed totally wrapped up in his perusal of her.

The adrenaline rush returned to quiver through her veins. Marielle tried to ignore it. She cleared her throat. "Did, um, did Deirdre say why she disappeared in the first place?"

"After the ambulance left with Uncle Willy, I found myself with Aunt Agatha and Miss Wheeler—and of course, the baby—in the salon. Basically, this is what she said: After being discharged from the hospital and having too much pride to hang around where she wasn't wanted, she bravely tried to make it on her own. But after three weeks of struggling without friends or food, she came seeking help. And what did she have in mind? In return for a roof over her head, she would wash floors and scrub potatoes!" He finished vexedly, "It's right out of Dickens, for crying out loud!"

"That's what she said?" Marielle all but gasped.

"That's about it, verbatim. I wanted to kick her out, but it's not my house. And—are you ready for this?—Aunt Agatha invited her and the baby to *stay*! Far from being treated like the maid, she's being pampered like visiting royalty! Since I won't look after her, Aunt Agatha said, *they* would! For some reason, my relatives think I'm guilty, too. Just like everyone else. Just like you."

She met his eyes and saw an angry spark therein. Marielle sighed. She was very glad that she wasn't Deirdre. "But it's Paddy's house, too! Where's Paddy?"

"In Philadelphia. Overseeing the opening of a new store for me." This time he ran both his hands through his mahogany-colored hair, pushing it back off his high forehead, but the heavy, silky hair immediately fell back down. "At least my dad gives me the benefit of the doubt."

"Were you there when she arrived?"

"Aunt Agatha called me at the office. I got there just in time to see Uncle Willy being driven away in an ambulance."

"So...so you mean to tell me Deirdre is actually moving in with your aunt and uncle?" Marielle questioned in wonderment.

"Amazingly enough, yes. She's there now. I left her and Aunt Agatha cooing over the baby!" He sounded so disgusted that Marielle almost smiled. But she shouldn't; the situation was too serious. With Uncle Willy in the hospital and Deirdre insinuated at the house, the whole complexion of the case had changed.

Marielle wondered whether Deirdre might not be exactly the opposite of what they had all supposed—too clever and cunning for anyone's good but her own! "Where has she been for the past three weeks?"

"She didn't say."

"I'm curious to know."

"I've been toying with the idea of hiring a private detective to do a little research for me. It might be the fastest way to find out what I'm dealing with."

"That's not a bad idea." Marielle was surprised to discover how much she liked it. She desperately wanted to get the question resolved. For if Cedric was the father of the baby, then she could happily forget all about him; but if he wasn't.... Well, the possibilities were piling up. She would like to go for dinner with him...and a sail...perhaps a stroll on the beach. She would like to try a kiss. Marielle knew instinctively that kissing him would be divine. If he was going to be free to play, she thought, she would love to!

"How are you going to choose the detective?" she asked curiously. "The phone book?"

"I'll ask around. Have you ever used one?"

"No."

He nodded and sighed, rather wearily, she thought. For a second she had a vision wherein she soothed his fevered brow, held him close and ran her hands through his hair, gently kissing away his worries...but she blinked away the daydream.

"I should go," he said, rubbing his nape. "I suppose I've taken up enough of your time. Sorry for interrupting your class, but I must admit, I thought you were responsible for Deirdre's grand entrance. I'm, uh—" he paused, his dark eyes again drifting intimately down her lithe shape "—relieved you didn't do it!"

Marielle felt as if she'd been physically touched, and the feeling he inspired made her want to stretch and purr for more. She slid from her perch on the desk, saying briskly, "So long, Cedric."

Her cool tone held him back for a second, and he searched her face. "By the way, Uncle Willy is in the same hospital that Deirdre was in." He walked toward the door. Marielle wondered with a pang what he was going to be doing for dinner that evening. "Bye," he said, smiling, and he was gone.

Again there was that welling of disappointment inside her. If only Deirdre weren't in the way, she sighed. He might have kissed her by now. And if not, she would have kissed him! She was dying to know what it would feel like to be kissed by him. And she hated the empty feeling he always left behind.

Disconsolately she wandered through to her private chambers. There was a knock on her door a few minutes later. Rusty, no doubt, with some questions. "Come in," she called, trying not to sound impatient. She came out of her bathroom, tying a thick terry robe, to see Cedric standing in the middle of her sumptuous boudoir.

"Did you forget your hat?" she said, smiling.

He came right up close to her, and his gaze slid over her wide, gray eyes and the soft, full mouth, then farther down the long, sensuous curve of her neck to the neckline of the robe. "I was wondering...that is, once this paternity suit is out of the way, I'd like to see more of you...."

He was impossibly disagreeable at times, yet other times he managed to be genuinely charming and sweet. One second she wanted desperately to be rid of him, and the next saw her melt in a warm glow of happy anticipation. "Um, well..." Marielle stumbled uncharacteristically. He was standing close to her and looking steadily into her eyes. She trembled a little. Every cell seemed to sense his proximity. The velvety brown eyes were fastened on her intently.

Nothing would escape those eyes, she knew. There was no point in pretending she wasn't interested. Heavens, she was fascinated!

But if she did want to say goodbye, now was the time to do it. He was forcing her to make a conscious decision, to take a stand, for or against him. It was clever of him to get the question out into the open like this. She admired his courage. He had sacrificed his own pride. How very gentlemanly of him. . . .

"Marielle, I want to see you again." His low, soft voice persuaded her almost before she knew it.

"Well," she replied, sounding as casual as she knew how, "I suppose we could. Keep on seeing each other, I mean." Faintly she smiled up into the dark eyes. "We could . . . have a game of tennis or something. . . ."

"Or something," he agreed.

For a second longer neither of them moved; then he made for the door. When he reached it, he turned to look at her once more and then he broke into a wide smile. Shoving his hands into the pockets of his immaculate cream linen suit, he was off, and she could hear him whistling Beethoven on his way through her office. The closing of the outer office door shut out the last of the cheery tune. Marielle stayed exactly where she was, staring off into space in a blissful reverie.

But she soon found herself thinking of Deirdre again, and she came back down to earth with a thud. Trying to be impartial, trying not to let her own interests interfere, Marielle had to admit the girl had tremendous nerve to show up on Uncle Willy and Aunt Agatha's doorstep. Especially if Cedric wasn't the father of her baby. Could she really be brazen enough to try such a risky bluff? And if so, why would she attempt such a tricky maneuver? Was she hoping to be bought off? Perhaps she had gone to Coronado rather than La Jolla because she knew Cedric wouldn't let her in his door.

But it was difficult to think of poor little Deirdre with the limp hair and scrubbed face as brazen. She hadn't asked for a penny. Instead, she wanted to be allowed to scrub the floors! The request was almost funny, hardly brazen. It revealed desperation, Marielle thought, sighing.

Deirdre's actions kept saying that she was the wronged party in this whole mess. On the surface, anyway, anybody would take her side and naturally assume Cedric was guilty of desertion. So, unless she was extraordinarily deep and devious...

Once again, there were two voices in Marielle's mind, clamoring to be heard. She wondered if Rusty was right, and Cedric simply didn't want to be so undignified as to backtrack on his earlier statements. But no, that was too preposterous. He was too much of a man for that sort of cowardliness.

But one of them was telling the truth, and one of them wasn't. It would be as hard to pick the right one as it would be easy to choose the wrong one. She had to try to make the logical, intelligent choice.

If only she weren't yearning for Cedric to sweep her into his arms and kiss her passionately! Her desire kept interfering. She really did want to believe him, just like he wanted to believe her. But she was so afraid that believing him would prove to be a terrible mistake, a far worse mistake than doubting him could ever be....

She definitely wanted to have an affair with him. That she knew. She did *not* want to fall in love. She was afraid that this time she had more than a casual interest, however. When the mere sight of a man turned her to liquid fire, something unusual was afoot, and Marielle was not sure she liked it. To crave for a kiss was dangerous and lunatic.

The trouble was, Cedric was slick, smooth and polished. She was afraid he would very likely find her, like Deirdre, easy pickings.

CHAPTER NINE

MARIELLE DIDN'T APPRISE Rusty of the fact that she had more or less agreed to date Cedric once Deirdre's case had been settled. He would think she'd lost her mind. And it was very likely she had, she thought wryly. She didn't even want to think about the future, for when she did, her body went into a state of delicious shock in anticipation of Cedric's lovemaking.

Neither did Marielle want to think any more about who was guilty, Deirdre or Cedric. The seesaw was beginning to make her dizzy. Rather, she preferred to pretend the whole affair was none of her business, and that sooner or later it would blow over and be gone. Of course she acknowledged that in her heart of hearts she had chosen to take Cedric's side. She was reasonably convinced that her choice was a logical one, not one based on mere emotion. After all, his arguments were sound and his words and actions not those of a man with something to hide. What did she know about Deirdre on the other hand? The girl seemed to have a one-track mind devoted to Cedric Senior. She did an awful lot of crying over him, and strangely, seemed to have no existence outside of her association with him. And what was one supposed to make of her long disappearance and her equally mysterious reappearance, the reappearance that had caused Cedric's Uncle Willy to have a heart attack? Then, there was still the fact that she kept going to Coronado while Cedric lived in La Jolla. And who had paid her hospital bills?

She might very well look innocent, but she certainly didn't act it; whereas Cedric looked anything but innocent, yet his actions bore him out. In his story, there were no discrepancies, no unanswered questions, no curious voids....

THE FOLLOWING DAY Cedric came sauntering into the lobby of Sun Studios while Marielle was conferring with the carpenter hired to build the counters and booths for her restaurant on the main floor. When she saw Cedric, she stopped in midsentence, her arm raised to point at a valance she wanted removed.

"Um...uh..." She looked back at the carpenter, blinked and then remembered what it was she wanted to tell him. His sparkly blue eyes were full of admiration for the feminine beauty before him, crisply issuing instructions. She finished with "Get right on it, okay?"

"Yes, ma'am!" he said happily.

With a quick parting smile, Marielle turned once again to see Cedric waiting for her impatiently.

His appreciation was less blatant than the carpenter's; nevertheless, he didn't take his eyes off her. He contemplated the chic beige shift and the long length of bare leg ending in cream high-heeled sandals. He decided he liked the effect of her hair swept up into a chignon, and he also decided he wouldn't move; she would have to come to him.

Marielle was completely conscious of the subtle power play, and she had a tart line all ready for him, but he managed to get the first word in. "How about lunch?"

This was not what she had expected, and she stared blankly at him. Because of her high heels, she didn't have to tilt her chin up as much as usual, and she liked that. She echoed uncertainly, as if she might have heard wrong, "Lunch?"

"Since I didn't think you'd consent to a weekend in Vegas, it's lunch, yes." A spark glimmered in his dark brown eyes. "I've a picnic basket in the car and the spot already chosen."

Marielle felt her muscles tense. Breathless excitement rose in her chest. Carefully she licked her suddenly parched lips. "But Cedric, I—I thought…that is—"

"I realize the paternity suit isn't over yet, but it could take a while. In the meantime, we might as well get to know each other." He smiled like an angel, but there was devilment in his dark eyes. Marielle was suddenly struck with another attack of wild and crazy desire. When she didn't immediately agree, he went on, "I promise I'll have you back to work in—" he checked the slim gold watch on his wrist "—exactly two hours."

"*Two* hours?"

"It's not healthy to bolt your food."

She eyed him a moment longer and then decided that she simply couldn't resist the tempting offer. "Okay, let's go!" She sighed. "How's your uncle?" she added as they walked together to the front desk to collect her purse.

"Much better, thank you. He'll be pleased to know you inquired."

She directed a look at him, wondering, startled, whether Uncle Willy would care one way or another. "Do you think . . . will he get visitors?"

"I'll be dropping in every night after work…about six. Dad will help him wile the hours away and, of course, there is Aunt Agatha…." A shadow of a frown touched his brow, as though he doubted a visit from Aunt Agatha would cheer his uncle up. "I'm sure he'd love to see a fresh face if you cared to go and see him."

By disclosing his estimated time of arrival at Uncle Willy's bedside, he really left the decision of whether she should visit or not entirely up to Marielle, with no strings attached either way. How, Marielle wondered, was she to withstand the charm, deviousness and quick mind of one C. E. Greenleaf! She was hopelessly fascinated by him.

Over the past few days she had found herself wanting him for a friend at the oddest moments, like when she was brushing her teeth in the morning. At other times she longed to kiss him—like right now. And she had just consented to a picnic alone with him in some shady glade! She *had* lost her mind! Marielle was consumed with curiosity over just what sort of a place he had chosen for their picnic.

Marielle checked herself "out for lunch" at the front desk, and with a call to the weight-lifting division, let Rusty know she was off—but not with whom. Cedric's hand settled lightly on the small of her back as he opened the door for her on their way out.

Out on the sidewalk in front of her establishment, an elderly chauffeur stood waiting to open the back seat of the two-tone chocolate-colored Rolls-Royce. He was smiling hugely.

But she queried critically, "Does it run? I won't think it amusing, Cedric, if you leave me stranded way out in the boonies!" Actually she was wishing for an arrangement whereby his hands would have to be kept on the steering wheel.

"Does it run, Schwartz?" Cedric smiled beatifically at the man.

"Like a dream!" Schwartz, beaming, bent to open the car door with a flourish. Inspecting the chauffeur for a lightning moment, Marielle thought, of course, the trusted servant, aiding and abetting everything that was about to go on in the back seat!

"Do you play the violin?" she asked him coolly as she stepped into the car. Short of making an undignified dash for the safety of her office, there was nothing she could do but get in.

"Violin?" Schwartz gazed at her vacantly. "Violin? Boss!" He swung to face Cedric, spreading out his hands in appeal. "You never said nothin' about playin' a violin!"

Cedric waved airily. "She's having you on, Schwartz! Actually, she's having me on!" He slid in beside her and shut the door behind him.

Marielle settled into the plush, creamy chocolate leather seat and looked somewhat warily at her fellow businessman. Schwartz set the gleaming regal car into motion.

Marielle was on tenderhooks. She knew she wouldn't allow Cedric to touch her, but she wondered whether she could resist touching him. Her fingers itched to feel his hair, his cheek, his lips. She longed to know whether he felt as good as he looked. She shuddered inside at the unaccustomed wanton feelings coursing unbidden through her veins. She was so starved for love, so hungry for one little kiss that it was going to be hard not to make a fool of herself.

Beginning to stare at him with something akin to consternation, she wondered which had come first, the yearning for a little romance in her lonely world or her meeting Cedric Greenleaf. It was a little like the eternal question of the chicken and the egg. She couldn't remember which event had preceded the other, and that frightened her, for that meant she wasn't in total control of the situation anymore.

"Cedric," she began urgently, "Cedric, I don't think—"

"Marielle," he cut in, "I didn't set this up!"

"Oh, sure!" She laughed. "You've seen to everything—except the violin."

"Marielle, *darling*—"

The sudden silence was profound. He held her eyes for a searing second. While privately he'd been thinking of her in such intimate terms, he hadn't meant to reveal that at this juncture.

Marielle was inwardly thrilled. She felt as though it were Christmas, Easter and Thanksgiving all rolled into one! But she was also stricken with panic at his use of the word "darling." Things were happening a bit too fast. She cleared her throat delicately, choosing to sidestep the issue. "So, tell me, how is your fountain coming along?"

A wry smile slanted his mouth. He said nothing for a moment but studied her profile. He sighed faintly.

"The granite's been found." His tone now was conversational, controlled. "It was in Idaho. It'll be arriving in town later tonight."

"Well, that's marvelous." Marielle was equally polite. "You must be delighted."

He shrugged. "Now that the stone is here, the stone mason has gone. His Italian grandmother is getting married, and the whole family has gone to Italy for three weeks. I'm probably going to have gray hair by the time this water fountain is finally finished!"

His endearment seemed to remain hovering provocatively in the air between them. But he didn't even so much as move a muscle toward her. She didn't know whether to be relieved or disappointed. She decided she was very happy not to have to fend him off.

The spot Cedric had chosen turned out to be the quintessential picnic spot—a gently sloping hill cushioned by an emerald lawn. For shade there was a small grove of craggy gum trees, and the city sprawled below their feet. Marielle's relief was genuine.

It was a particularly pretty spot, open and yet private, with vivid red geraniums along one side of the roadway and wild ice plants on the other. It was a spot where just about anything was possible—except X-rated love scenes!

Schwartz spread out a blanket as Cedric helped Marielle out of the back seat of the Rolls. A moment later she leaned on his arm while she slipped out of her high-heeled sandals. She sank her bare toes gratefully into the soft cool grass. Their physical contact was casual yet totally conscious, and the clasp lingered just a little bit longer than was strictly necessary....

They were side-by-side on the bright Mexican blanket, and with Schwartz acting as master of ceremonies, the meal began. Cedric's general factotum had a wonderful knack of being on hand when needed, and he disappeared seemingly into thin air the second he sensed his presence was superfluous.

A light consommé was followed by a romaine salad with sliced mushrooms and grated Italian cheese, served with a vinaigrette of lemon juice and olive oil. While they were enjoying that and small loaves of crusty French bread, Schwartz was busy with a portable barbecue. The grilled chicken breasts were served over asparagus spears topped with a light lemon-and-egg sauce. Icy cold mineral water in fluted wineglasses accompanied the repast.

"So Schwartz can cook, too?" Marielle was full of admiration.

"Judge for yourself." Cedric indicated her plate.

"I hope he's well paid!"

"Extremely!"

"Do you cook?"

"I can handle the basics. The only thing I'm really good at, though, is chocolate."

"Then you really enjoy what you do? I mean, you didn't just follow in your father's footsteps?"

"I think I must have chocolate in my veins instead of blood," Cedric replied simply. "And why do you do what you do?"

Marielle thought carefully for a moment, wanting to give as concise a reply as he had. "Well, because I can." That didn't seem clear enough, however. "I wasn't born into the best of circumstances, but I was determined not to end up waiting for handouts on a street corner. I couldn't afford a formal education, so I decided my occupation had to be something I already knew how to do.

"Well, I could have become a professional thief— I was already a pretty good one. You see, I excelled at acrobatics partly because I spent so much time dodging the cops." She grinned an urchin grin, and the dancing lights in her eyes proclaimed the truth of her words. "But I got tired of running and hiding. Gymnastics came naturally, and I wanted my own business. I also liked working with people, and that was the third factor that contributed to the idea of opening an exercise studio. I scraped and saved and opened my first studio in a rented corner of the warehouse I now own. I built Sun Studios all by myself...and hot-diggety if I didn't do it straight! I mean, honestly.''

"So...that Porsche means more to you than I thought it did.''

"We-ell, yes and no. Like I said before, it's a tool, a useful one. But when you're standing on a street curb, the idea of owning a fancy car is absurd. So as soon as I could afford it, I bought one." Again that mischievous grin lit her face.

Cedric looked at her closely. His gaze drifted over her choker of fine pearls and the delicate pearl earrings. She might have been born in them. A few blond strands, eased free of the chignon by a teasing wind, fell over her cheek, and she brushed them away.

"I had been snubbed by shop clerks so many times. Salespeople can be cruel if they think you've no money," she explained.

Cedric merely nodded and waited, a shadow of a smile in his eyes.

To make sure he wasn't laughing *at* her, Marielle checked his expression keenly, a little nervously, ready to vanish inside her shell on the instant. But the dark velvety eyes were warm, and she could have drowned in them.

Quickly she blinked. "Where was I? Oh, yes, well. I put on my most tattered blue jeans, a cheap T-shirt and a pair of old rubber thongs—you know, the ninety-nine cent variety? And then I walked into the car dealership. Do you know, they almost threw me out? Oh, you can't imagine my joy in seeing that snooty salesman's jaw drop when I said I intended to pay cash! He was terribly mean. All the salesmen were gathered around with silly smirks on their faces. There was only one who wasn't sneering—so I asked him whether he could afford to turn down the commission on a fifty-five-thousand-dollar car. When he quickly said no, I said, very high and mightily, 'Consider the car sold.' Whooppee!'' She chortled in remembered glee.

"I had to do it, Cedric! Normally I don't believe in revenge, but I had to do that for me and for all the people who had ever been snubbed by salesclerks!''

"Bravo!'' One corner of his sensuous mouth lifted in a contemplative smile.

And Marielle began to wish their picnic spot were more private, after all....

Two small strawberry tarts with dollops of whipped cream on top and a steaming pot of rich, delicious coffee finished the luncheon off. Marielle had eaten everything that had been dished out, and she'd also discovered that Cedric was a thoroughly charming host. She was so relaxed that she didn't want to go back to work at all anymore! She had also discovered that intimate details could be shared easily over a picnic lunch; things that would never have been said in a restaurant were said with ease under a tree.

A bumblebee hovered around Marielle, and she froze as the insect buzzed just past her nose. Cedric brushed the bee away with a wave of his hand. It took the hint and droned slowly off.

"He looks like he's weighed down with honey." Marielle smiled and turned to look at Cedric. Coming to her aid had brought him nearer, and he didn't return to his former position on the blanket but stayed where he was. Her heart skipped a beat. She carefully moistened her lips with the tip of her tongue and hoped he couldn't see her apprehension. She was yearning for his touch, melting with a dizzy feeling.... She should suggest returning to work.

But he merely continued nonchalantly, "Do you have any family?"

She blinked and tried to refocus on the pink and yellow ice plants shimmering with shocking brilliance in the noonday sun. Her heart seemed to be banging against her ribs. "Um, no. I ... my father took off for good when I was thirteen. I went to his funeral almost a year later." She shrugged a noncommittal shoulder. "I don't remember my mother, and I didn't care for my dad."

"What happened then? Did you go to a foster home?"

"Oh, no. I had quit going to school by the time he died. The authorities never caught up with me." She wished he would move back a little. His nearness was preventing her heartbeat from slowing down. When she glanced at him, she had to lower her eyelids. He seemed rather too fascinated by the thick sweep of lashes and the expression that they veiled. She tried to take a deep, steadying breath. "Your family, er, seems very ... nice." It wasn't quite a lie.

He laughed. "Very... *nice*, eh? Very peculiar, to say the least. But they're my family. What can I say? I do care a great deal for my Dad," he admitted thoughtfully. "I'm sorry you never had anyone like him to grow up with."

"Cedric," she began uncertainly.

"Um?"

"Why do they live in that ... house? I mean ..." Now she hesitated, a bit embarrassed.

"You don't like it? You don't think it's wonderful?" He looked faintly surprised.

"Wonderful?" she echoed. "Er...um...gee..." She really didn't want to hurt his feelings, but she thought the Coronado mansion horrid.

"Go on. Speak your mind, Marielle, because I'll probably know if you don't!"

She believed him. "To tell you the truth, I think it's ghastly! Paddy's corner is exempt, of course. It's warm and cozy there, but still ..." She shuddered. "The rest is so dark and stuffy... and dusty and gloomy: all that dark, heavy, old furniture; that cold, unfriendly stone exterior. It reminds me of a Hitchcock movie."

"I don't like it much myself!" He chuckled, amused. "My great-grandfather made wonderful chocolate, but he was no architect. The place is far too big, far too austere. I suppose he wanted grandeur, but he ended up with a train station, and not a particularly nice one." He frowned momentarily. "If you had a choice, would you want to live there?"

"*Live* there? Heavens, no!" Marielle exclaimed. "It might very well be in Coronado, and it's probably worth a fortune, but it is... ugly, isn't it?"

"Mildly speaking, it's atrocious. As for my father, I don't think he minds living there; he's off in his own world most of the time. I don't think he even sees it. And when he does, it's probably full of pleasant memories for him. Uncle Willy doesn't care. And Aunt Agatha? She thinks it's just perfect! But you—you wouldn't live there under any circumstances?"

Marielle gazed at him searchingly, wondering what he was driving at. "Perhaps at gunpoint," she suggested.

A gentle wayward ocean breeze blew the one loose blonde strand across her face, and he reached out and with the lightest possible touch pulled it away from her eyes. His fingers wafted across her cheek, almost not touching her at all. Marielle lost her breath completely. Mutely she gazed at him with big gray eyes, and he held that electric contact for a timeless moment longer.

"You're one of the few women I know who wouldn't give their right arm to live in that Coronado mansion," he said, then lightly changed the subject. "Have you ever been in love?"

"Wha-at?"

He smiled at her astonished expression. "I have, twice. It didn't work out. Both women were completely different, but they both wanted me more for my money than my good looks, it turned out." He grinned crookedly. "It came as a rude shock, both times."

Marielle rapidly put two and two together. "And did they both want to live in the mansion?"

"Like crazy!"

"And that put you off?"

"It's a nice place to visit, but, like you, I wouldn't want to live there!"

"Hmm. Frankly, when I discovered you didn't live there, I was relieved!" The second she had said that, Marielle thought she shouldn't have. Had she given too much away? Would he be able to guess her state of mind? Would he know she was all but suffocating in the sultry sweet heat of desire? "What I mean is, my opinion of you improved considerably." She laughed breathlessly. "From being pegged a species of mole, you moved right up to just somebody I didn't like."

"A mole? You thought I was a mole?" He seemed puzzled and a little dismayed.

Hastily she explained, leaning closer to him in concern, "Because of the dark! There are hardly any windows. Moles live in the dark, don't you see?"

"Er . . . yes. Well, I suppose I should be thankful for small favors. At least you didn't think I was a worm." He leaned a little closer to her. "Where do I stand on the ladder now? Or should I ask?"

"Uh . . . um . . ." Frantically she scoured her mind for something neutral to say. Quivering inside, she slowly eased backward to gain another inch or two between them. "I-I've never been in love, thank heavens!" Her voice echoed her inner turmoil, wavering faintly. "I steer clear. It seems like too much trouble altogether. Look what it got you. Two heartbreaks. And, most likely, a massive distrust of all womankind."

"The third time is supposed to be the luckiest."

"Good luck!" She shook her head and sighed ruefully, refusing to meet his eyes.

"Thank you," he returned gravely. A quick glance of hers noticed a dancing twinkle in the far depths of his brown eyes. "I'll need it!"

For a long moment there was silence, a soft, lazy, and yet absorbing silence full of things left unsaid, feelings half revealed. The sun bathed them in hot golden radiance. Far off, the sea sparkled like a sequined gown. When he suddenly took her hand, she gasped audibly in sensual alarm; she couldn't help it. But he only stood up and pulled her with him. "Your two hours are up, Miss Bond." He smiled down into her eyes, keeping her next to him for a few seconds more.

She felt somewhat dazed. She didn't want to go back to work, back to the ordinary world. She wished this golden afternoon could go on forever. The grass tickled her bare toes, and she yearned to be carefree and crazy. Cedric was just tall enough for her to lean comfortably against his shoulder if she chose to do so. And for an insane instant, she was undecided. Should she, or shouldn't she? God only knew how much she wanted to. But sanity prevailed in the end. She tugged at the hand he still held. Rather reluctantly, it seemed, he let her go.

Cedric returned her to the spa in precisely his allotted two hours. He hadn't kissed her, and she hadn't kissed him, and nothing had been said or done in that regard. Over the course of the afternoon, Marielle found herself imagining how the first kiss would happen. Who would kiss whom, and how, when and where.... She played out endless variations that all ended the same way....

Unfortunately she seemed to be running out of the hot, red cinnamon hearts. But she knew where to get more, and she was dreaming about how to go about getting more several hours after her picnic lunch, with her feet propped up on her desk and her hands linked behind her head.

"You're not listening!" Rusty said for the umpteenth time, Marielle was sure. He grabbed one of her pink satin chairs, straddled it and leaned toward her. "What's gotten into you?"

"Who, me?"

"I don't believe there's anybody else in the room, Marielle! I've been trying to talk to you ever since you came back from lunch, and you keep wandering away! What's going on? Say..." He paused suspiciously. "What did you do at lunchtime?"

"I had lunch." She smiled airily.

"Oh? With who?"

"Whom."

"Don't know him."

Marielle giggled. "With *whom*, silly. That much grammar I do know!"

"What are you talking about?" A frown knit his handsome brow.

"Nothing, Rusty, darling, never mind. I went to lunch with Cedric." She smiled at him again, unapologetically.

"What happened!" he exclaimed.

"Why...nothing happened, Rusty!"

"That low-down dirty double-dealin' dog!" Rusty muttered under his breath.

Marielle stared at him in surprise. "Oh, now, wait a minute! Rusty, nothing happened! And anyway, what if it had?"

"The whole damn city out there is full a' guys, and you had to go and pick *that* one? You've lost your mind!"

"I haven't picked anyone!"

"The hell you haven't! You don't fool me, Marielle. You'd never part with your time unless.... Why do women always go for the bad guys? Tell me that!"

"But I don't think he is one of the bad guys, Rusty! I know it's crazy, and I'm not saying that Deirdre's the bad one, either, but...something is very funny about this whole thing."

"I don't see anything funny about you going out with a guy like that!"

"I don't mean funny, ha-ha, I mean funny, peculiar. Cedric said that Uncle Willy and Aunt Agatha took her and the baby in. She's actually staying at the family mansion in Coronado! Now, isn't that rather strange?"

"Strikes me it's obvious to everyone but you that Cedric ran out on the poor kid! At least his family aren't that mean!"

"That's how it looks, yes." Marielle sighed. She'd been brought back to earth with a rough bump. She was beginning to feel very deflated. "I was going to see Uncle Willy in the hospital, after work, but maybe I'll drop in on Deirdre and see if I can find out what she's up to, instead."

"Well, you just watch it. I don't like that guy. He's trouble. He's been trouble right from day one. And you know how you feel about people like that! You're always saying to me, 'Rusty, if some guy gives you a hard time in the first five minutes, he's going to give you a hard time the rest of your life.'"

"Well, yes, but—"

"So what's this? This is different?" Rusty's hands and eyebrows went up in exclamation as he rose from the chair. He put it back in its place, and with a look that seemed to say "Grow up, will ya!" he left her office, letting the door bang shut behind him. He was back in a minute to tell her what he had come to talk to her about in the first place. He had another complaint to lodge against the new receptionist, the one who talked to his friends for hours on the telephone. The receptionist was a perfect example of Rusty's point, and her sidekick's smug expression said as much.

Several hours later Marielle was walking down the overgrown Greenleaf lane, Rusty by her side. His Corvette was getting a tune-up at the dealership, and she was giving him a ride home. Marielle suspected that his car was only part of the reason he was tagging along; he was probably just plain curious to meet some of the people she had been talking about for almost two months!

Sylvester opened the front door with an ominous creak, and Rusty stared at Marielle with questioning round eyes. Smiling a little, she shrugged and led him into the house.

"Oh, how I've missed you!" Deirdre cried exuberantly, throwing her arms about Marielle's neck. "It's so terrific to see you! I need to ask you about a ton of things, and—"

Marielle was glad Deirdre had quit crying, anyway. By this time, Aunt Agatha had come hurrying, huffing and puffing, from the salon. She had the baby in her arms. Cedric II, in baby blue lace and white velvet, was asleep.

His mother was well-dressed, too, if not quite so splendidly. She was looking sweet and particularly innocent in a flowered print dress that, at first glance, looked ever so simple but on closer inspection appeared to be of very high quality. Marielle glanced at Rusty and wasn't overly surprised to see him looking full of sympathy.

She made the introductions. Both women, Aunt Agatha and Deirdre, were very much impressed by Rusty Devon, she could tell. Deirdre chattered excitedly as they all walked back to the salon.

"—so then, of course, Aunt Agatha took little Cedric and me shopping this morning. Oh, we had the most wonderful time! Doesn't he look fabulous?"

"Mmm, yes," Marielle agreed. "Just like the heir to the throne."

"Is it any wonder, with a father who looks like Prince Charming?" Deirdre pointed out. Marielle thought she heard Rusty snort. She even winced a little herself. Deirdre went on, "Aunt Agatha's been ever so kind! I was all out of diapers, you see, and when we went to the shopping center for diapers and formula, there was a baby sale on and then—" She disclosed that Aunt Agatha had bought her the dress she was wearing and had even taken her out to lunch at one of the fancier establishments in town. And after all that, they had gone to Aunt Agatha's beauty salon, where Deirdre had had her hair cut while Aunt Agatha watched the baby.

"Your new cut is lovely," Marielle complimented her. It was a big improvement. Shorter, her thin hair had more body, and it swung cleanly off her shoulders. She still managed to look barely thirteen years old, though. Marielle wondered—uncharitably perhaps—how she had ever caught Cedric's eye! "Did you manage to squeeze in a visit to Uncle Willy?"

"Oh, yes! Poor darling! I can't help thinking it was all my fault, but I was desperate! I didn't know what to do or where to go! I had tried so hard on my own.... After it finally sunk through my thick head that Cedric didn't love me anymore, I knew I had to try to make it on my own, just like you said. And, well, I was doing okay, and then...and then..." Her voice wobbled.

"Please don't cry!" Marielle hastened to say.

"Dirty double-dealin'..." Rusty muttered under his breath.

"I promise I won't cry! I know you hate it, and I don't want to do anything that's going to make you angry with me!"

"There, there, dear," Agatha interrupted from up front, "You go right ahead and cry if you want to. It's healing to cry. Lord knows you have enough cause!" There was a trace of bitterness in her voice.

"Just go on, Deirdre," Marielle prompted. "What happened?"

"Well, first my landlord asked me to leave because other tenants were complaining about Ricky's crying at night. I call him Ricky, short for Cedric, you know. Anyway, I finally found a new place that didn't mind children, but it was so expensive, and I couldn't manage! I couldn't find a job, and day care costs a fortune, and when I didn't even have enough money for milk... well, I knew I had to swallow my pride and ask Cedric for a little help. I felt so awful, to come begging, but... but..." Her small voice quavered.

"Poor kid!" Rusty muttered to himself.

Even though her voice shook, Deirdre forged on. "Uncle Willy and Aunt Agatha invited me in, and then Uncle Willy had his heart attack. Can you imagine—Cedric hadn't told them anything about me! Not a thing! He treats me like I don't exist!"

"What did I tell you!" Rusty growled.

"Cedric came just as the ambulance was leaving. After Uncle Willy had gone, Cedric blamed me! Suddenly it was my fault he had the attack, and he said—" she quickly took a ragged breath "—he said to my face that Ricky wasn't his son!"

"What a terrible thing to say," Marielle murmured dryly.

"Nothin' but dirt!" Rusty added.

"And then he suggested I go, without even hearing me out! He offered me money to go! Fifty thousand dollars, I think he said, if I agreed to clear out! I was horrified!"

Marielle remembered being horrified, too, when he had offered her fifty thousand dollars. The memory saddened her, and the last rosy afterglow from lunch departed. If, as Cedric kept saying, Deirdre was after money, why hadn't she taken the fifty thousand he'd offered? And would he have offered it if he weren't guilty? Maybe Rusty was right. Maybe the man was trouble.

But maybe he was worth a little trouble.... Perhaps, with his offer, he had been trying to entrap Deirdre, just like he had tried to trap Marielle into admitting blackmail that first night....

But, on the other hand, what if Cedric really was a dirty low-down double-dealin' dog....

CHAPTER TEN

THE SALON WAS EXACTLY as she remembered it. The fire crackled, the television was on and the bowl of chocolates was full.

"If it hadn't been for Aunt Agatha—and Uncle Willy, of course—I don't know where I would be right now!" Deirdre's impassioned exclamation made Agatha pause while she fussed over the baby, who was lying in a bassinet on the couch.

"There, there, it's been lovely having you, Deirdre. We had a good time shopping today, didn't we? Don't know when I've done so much all in one day!" She chuckled merrily, and Marielle, shifting uncomfortably in her overstuffed chair, looked over to Rusty, wondering whether he was thinking the same thing that she was. That Aunt Agatha seemed remarkably cheerful for a woman whose husband had only just had a heart attack. True, it was only a very mild attack, and he was out of danger, but still, the poor man was in the hospital! But perhaps it was glad relief that brought the smile to the normally pouty mouth....

"It's been a long long time since I've had such fun," Deirdre readily agreed, sounding so much like a deprived child that Aunt Agatha reached over with a plump hand to pat her cheek.

"When I think of what you've been through!" Agatha shuddered, all two hundred pounds of her. "Why you didn't come to me sooner, I can't imagine!" She rang the bell for Sylvester to return, and with careful deliberation, chose a chocolate from the bowl. "Men are such brutes!"

Marielle's sidekick shifted awkwardly on the dainty parlor chair. He looked pleadingly at her; he'd obviously seen enough. Meanwhile, Cedric's aunt switched television channels every time a commercial played and dourly talked about bosom friends of hers who had been cheated in various ways by men. All the while, she ate chocolates and drank more coffee.

Marielle ignored Rusty's pleas for a little while longer. She was too busy studying the interplay between Deirdre and Agatha. She didn't see much hope of getting a chance to talk alone with Deirdre. That would have to wait. The questionnaire she had planned for the girl would only work if Deirdre was completely unsuspecting, so she could hardly drag her off for a little chat. Anyway, she'd get more out of her if the girl believed she was on her side, so this visit was important in its way....

Presently Agatha was on about some encyclopedia salesman. It struck Marielle that Uncle Willy might view being in hospital as a pleasant break. Small wonder Cedric didn't rate his aunt as big on laughs. But she finally had an audience; Deirdre sat listening raptly, her big trusting eyes fastened on the older woman's face.

A whole new aspect of the situation suddenly presented itself to Marielle. If Ricky was Cedric's son, it meant Cedric had been Deirdre's lover! Jealousy slammed into her, and she suddenly found herself hating the slight girl for looking so helpless, so sweet—so happy.

Her violent feelings made her sick with worry. Marielle's new demon brought even greater fears that she was losing her grip. Jealousy was a dangerous emotion, she knew; it made people do foolish things and sometimes it wrecked lives. She could already feel it casting its evil spell.

And then it occurred to her that the solution to the complicated mystery of Ricky's parentage was sure to be an unhappy one, no matter who the guilty party turned out to be. If it was Deirdre, Aunt Agatha would mourn losing the baby; if it was Cedric, Marielle herself would be in mourning.

While everyone was bent over the awakened baby, cooing and remarking over his pretty dark curls, Marielle slipped, largely unnoticed, from the room. Only Rusty saw her go, and he gave her a dismayed look at being left alone with the two women. But with an answering gesture that meant "Stay put!" she went off to see Paddy.

This time she knew the way, and she sped down the hall unerringly and out the doors into the neatly tended rose garden. In minutes she was drawing aside the damask curtain at the doorway of the library where Paddy gently welcomed her.

Win "Instantly" right now in another way
...*try our Preview Service*

Get 4 FREE full-length Harlequin Superromance books

Plus this handy, compact umbrella
(a $10.00 retail value alone)

Plus a surprise free gift

Plus lots more!

Our love stories are popular everywhere...and WE'RE CELE-BRATING with free birthday prizes—free gifts—and a fabulous no-strings offer.

Simply try our Preview Service. With your trial, you get SNEAK PREVIEW RIGHTS to four new HARLEQUIN SUPERROMANCE novels a month—months before they are in stores—with near 10%-OFF retail on any books you keep (just $2.50 each)—and Free Home Delivery besides.

THERE IS NO CATCH. You're not required to buy a single book, ever. You may even cancel Preview Service privileges anytime, if you want. The free gifts are yours anyway, as tokens of our appreciation.

It's a super sweet deal if ever there was one. Try us and see.

EXTRA! Sign up now—automatically qualify to WIN THIS AND ALL 1986 "Super Cele-bration" PRIZE & PRIZE FEATURES...or **watch for new prizes and new prize features NEXT MONTH at your favorite store.**

Harlequin *Superromance™* Free Gifts–Free Prizes

YES I'll try the Harlequin Preview Service under the terms specified herein. Send me 4 free books and all the other FREE GIFTS. I understand that I also automatically qualify for ALL "Super Celebration" prizes and prize features advertised in 1986. I have written my birthday below. Tell me on my birthday what I win.

WIN A GREAT PRIZE

▶ If you are NOT signing up for Preview Service, DO NOT use seal. You can win anyway.

FILL IN BIRTHDAY INFORMATION BELOW

MONTH   DATE

This month's featured prizes—a dream come true MINK or FOX jacket, winner's choice + as an added bonus, a world renowned delight, Godiva Chocolates for 101 other winners.

134 CIS 2020

PLEASE PRINT

NAME

ADDRESS   APT #

CITY

STATE   ZIP

PLEASE PICK FUR JACKET YOU WANT ☐ FOX ☐ MINK. Gift offer limited to new subscribers, one per household, and terms and prices subject to change.

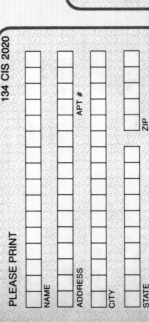

Harlequin
"Super Celebration" Sweepstakes
901 Fuhrmann Blvd.
P.O. Box 1325
Buffalo, NY 14269

PLACE
1ST CLASS
STAMP
HERE

"Hi," she burst out, delighted to see the old man again. He looked delighted to see her, too, as if she were a breath of spring air.

"Hello." With sharp eyes and a faintly indulgent smile he watched her pace restlessly about, checking that things she had noticed on her last visit were still there. All the while she made small talk, until she simply ran out. She sighed, exhausted.

"What is it, Marielle? Did Agatha and Deirdre give you a bad five minutes?"

"A bad two months is more like it, and it isn't necessarily Agatha and Deirdre's fault. That's about how long I've known your son!"

He chuckled softly.

"What do you think of Deirdre moving in?" she asked curiously. Paddy Greenleaf did not look unduly disturbed by recent events, she noticed.

He hesitated and sobered. "It might be a good thing. It might hasten an end to this affair. And Agatha is so taken with that child. She always wanted a baby, and that was the one thing Willy couldn't give her. However, that young woman has more nerve than any of us gave her credit for. To show up on the doorstep!"

"But her story sounds so plausible. She had Aunt Agatha and Rusty eating it up!"

"Does she have you eating it up, too?"

"I take it meeting her hasn't changed your mind?"

"I'm willing to bet you she has big dollar signs etched in back of her big blue eyes." Paddy's own blue eyes suddenly twinkled. "How much do you want to bet? One dollar?"

"What would be the point? We'd be betting on the same horse. But if she wants money, why didn't she take the fifty thousand Cedric offered?"

"Perhaps she sensed it wasn't an offer, but a trap. Maybe she's holding out for more."

"Well, okay, but ... but ..."

"But what?"

"I'm so scared, Paddy." She sighed. "I was hoping it would all blow over, but instead it's getting worse."

"Young women with babies don't just blow away."

Marielle smiled slightly, then shook her head ruefully. "I figured she was gone for good when she disappeared. I didn't like it, but I'd learned to live with it. Now she's back. And we're still no closer to finding out who the father of her baby is!"

Paddy didn't say a word but was attentive without being judgmental. He made a good listener, as Cedric did—or was it the other way around....

"Each time something new happens I have to make a decision again. And every time I make a decision, it's harder because there's more riding on it."

"Of course you're afraid of making the wrong decision?"

"Yes. Scared to death. Paddy, Deirdre has really moved in!" Marielle waved her arm in the direction of the salon. "She looks right at home, curled up in front of the fire, munching chocolates with Aunt Agatha. It's ... it's eerie. Her nerve, I mean."

"Allow Cedric the benefit of the doubt, Marielle. Give him that much." Paddy's voice was soft but very serious. His words went right to the core of her problem. "No matter what happens, promise me you'll always allow him that."

Marielle nodded slowly. "I'll try—but I can't promise anything." She enjoyed watching him thoughtfully fill his pipe.

Marielle resumed her pacing again and said, "Assuming that Cedric is telling the truth means that Deirdre just plain isn't. And if she can be a liar, she can also be a crook. And if this is, in fact, a get-rich-quick paternity suit, do you really want her living in your house? Do you lock up your gold earrings at night?"

"Dear Marielle, I've worn many things but never earrings! And assuming it is a scheme, she wouldn't do anything to jeopardize her new pampered position here. No, I have no fear of Deirdre trying to steal the silver or poison my soup. She may have gained an advantage, but so have we. We can observe her at close quarters and wait for her to make a mistake. And sooner or later, she's going to make a mistake."

"First she tried her tears on Cedric," Marielle mused, "and when that didn't work, she tried the same thing on his family, and it worked! So maybe she meant to come here this time around."

"What do you mean?"

"Have you ever wondered why she keeps popping up here instead of Cedric's house in La Jolla?"

"Ah, yes, I see. I hadn't thought of that. Interesting...."

"She's lucky you didn't answer the door!"

"Isn't she! But a baby is a difficult thing to refuse to shelter, and she knows it. And the simple fact that she *is* in the door means she's being accepted as Cedric's mistress, and Ricky as his son. Which, naturally, makes Cedric look more guilty than ever. It's a brilliant, calculated move. As a mathematician, I can appreciate it. Cedric gave me to understand the girl was dim-witted. I think she's probably had a good laugh on all of us by now. Don't forget, she tried her tears on you first."

"I fell for it all, every word."

"You see how talented she is at enlisting support?"

"Well, yes, but...something's not quite right. Why would she pick on Cedric? Just because she once worked in the store? And just because one day she picked up the paper and saw the water fountain story in it? Is that enough reason?"

"To choose a 'mark'? I don't know. Perhaps. One would assume, even if she is an amateur at this sort of thing, that she would have researched him a little before going ahead. She must have, at the very least, ascertained that he has enough money to make it worth her while. It's really only a standard blackmail plot, changed into a paternity suit. It will be interesting to see whether she actually risks a court battle. It'll be even more interesting to hear her eventual demands."

"Interesting? Dreadful is more like it!" Marielle shuddered, feeling suddenly anxious for Cedric's well-being. "But if she must, I wish she'd get on with it! Midnight tonight isn't too soon to have this over with!'' She smiled at Paddy slightly, suddenly feeling good for ''going public'' by admitting to being on Cedric's side. ''Anyway, I have to go to Rusty's rescue. I left him with Deirdre and Aunt Agatha.''

''Rusty?''

''Devon. My business partner.''

''The name sounds familiar.''

''He was quarterback for the Raiders.''

''Yes, I remember now.''

''Would you like to meet him?''

''Yes, yes, I would! I'll walk back with you.''

''But why does she have to look so sweet?'' Marielle muttered as they left the library together.

''It's effective,'' Paddy pointed out, pointing his pipe stem at her. ''Disarming, for one thing. Agatha thinks she has two babies to care for.''

''I've just thought of something.''

''What?''

''Oh, it's probably nothing, but the coincidence bothers me. Coincidences always make me suspicious....''

''What are you talking about?'' Paddy asked with a confused glance.

''Deirdre and Uncle Willy both going to the same hospital.''

Paddy seemed even more confused.

''Well, it's not unusual that Uncle Willy is there, is it? That's where your family physician practices, right?''

''Yes, that's right. Cedric was born there.'' A reminiscent smile flashed across his aged face. Then he quickly returned to the present. ''Oh, I see what you're driving at, yes. It's a private hospital, and it's expensive. If Deirdre is as penniless as she would have us believe, what was she doing there?''

''It was the closest hospital to the accident, don't forget. But she went back there to have her baby. That's the unusual part.''

Paddy continued from where she left off. ''And when she left, she paid in full, in cash, so there was no bank to trace her to, and her address on the hospital paperwork was either false or incorrect.''

''Why that hospital? And who paid her bills?''

''Why the mysterious disappearance?''

''Why no family, friends or background?''

They looked at each other.

''Evidence does seem to be accumulating,'' Paddy remarked.

''It's pretty thin, though.''

''Give it a while.''

''We need some answers.''

''Mustn't let her suspect we're onto her, though.''

A couple of days later Marielle finally talked herself into going to the hospital to visit Uncle Willy—at six in the afternoon—with an armful of fabulous purple and yellow irises. When she walked into his private room, Cedric was already there. It seemed to Marielle that she had interrupted quite a serious discussion.

''I was in the neighborhood.'' She smiled at Uncle Willy as she handed him the irises. ''So I thought I'd drop in.''

"Uncle Willy, you remember Marielle Bond?" Cedric's dark eyes smiled warmly at her. So warmly that she was sorry she hadn't come sooner.

Willy looked very thin, and he had a worried expression on his face. Fifteen years younger than his brother Paddy, Willy appeared a much weaker character, and at the moment, looked to be the older of the two. However, when he smiled, the Greenleaf charm came sparkling through.

"Of course I remember Miss Bond. How kind of you to pay me a visit. The last time we met, you were in yellow...."

Everybody laughed a little at the remembrance of their first meeting.

"I'm happy to see you're up to making fun of me—" Marielle paused to smile "—or is it those sumptuous silk pajamas that are making you feel so good? That's an absolutely lovely paisley!"

This time only Cedric and Marielle chuckled at Willy's bedridden splendor. Uncle Willy sniffed and grumbled, "It's frightfully boring in here. You've no idea! Any little thing helps to brighten up my days!"

"It's a hospital; it's supposed to be boring!" Cedric spread his hands a trifle impatiently, as though he had been dealing with gripes all afternoon.

"Well," Marielle put in, "at least you're going to come through this looking gorgeous, bored or not. I'll bet the nurses adore you!"

Uncle Willy smiled modestly. "These pajamas draw them like a magnet."

Cedric looked faintly embarrassed, and Marielle laughed again. "Is it really so dull here, Uncle Willy?" she asked sympathetically.

"Excruciatingly!" He softened quickly with a bit of attention.

"Does anyone have a deck of cards?"

"Yes. Why? I hate card games!" he announced petulantly.

"Oh, yeah? How about grubstake poker?"

"Show me the color of your money!" he chortled, rubbing his hands.

"I'll wipe you both off the map," Cedric promised, adjusting Uncle Willy's hospital table into a poker table for three. Marielle sat on one side of the bed, he sat on the other, and Uncle Willy reigned in silken magnificence in the middle.

They played until the patient was tired, which wasn't very long, and while Cedric tidied up after the game—in which his uncle had cleaned them both out of small change—Uncle Willy fell asleep. Marielle sat in her hospital chair and watched Cedric quietly put things away. Then he dimmed the lights. He walked around the bed to where Marielle was sitting. There was only one chair, and he nudged her over so that she ended up with one leg on and one leg off the chair seat. He sat down.

"Thank you for coming," he whispered.

"I enjoyed it," she whispered back.

"So did he. Thanks again."

They were close enough to kiss. In the quiet dimness Marielle thought her heart must surely be echoing against the hospital walls. She said nothing but looked over at him, scrutinizing him closely, hoping to find something she wouldn't like.

But his hair was a ripple of thick, dark mahogany, and his eyes were clear and deep. His mouth was strong, maybe a bit too strong, but it was sensual and generous, too. The chin was a bit worrisome, for it indicated certain bulldoglike qualities.

"You went to the house?" he asked her, his whispering breath warm against her cheek. She liked the way he smelled up close, clean and manly, with a touch of after-shave. Marielle wouldn't have moved away for the world.

"Yes, I saw everybody. What are you going to do?"

"There's plenty I'd like to do! But Aunt Agatha and Uncle Willy took Deirdre in, so, in a way, my hands are tied. I have since suggested to my aunt that she show Deirdre the door, but she won't. All I can do is sit around waiting for Miss Wheeler to make her next move! And patience isn't one of my strong points. I . . . hired a private detective this morning. I want to know where she comes from, and whether she's working alone or with an accomplice." He gazed into Marielle's eyes for a moment. "I hate this, Marielle. I can't think of anything that's felt as bad as this."

Marielle was sympathetic. But she also realized that right from the start he had been winning her over, bit by bit.

"That god-awful fountain!" he went on. "Do you know that water fountain has been a source of continual agony ever since I first thought of it?"

Marielle couldn't help but smile; it slipped out and spread all over her face before she could stop it. "Things that are hard to attain are usually worth it in the end."

"Please, no more wise old sayings! And don't you start sounding like my father!"

"Let me put it this way." She still hadn't stopped smiling; now it was turning into an ear-to-ear grin. "Something as idiotic as a water fountain is bound to cause you some trouble!"

"*Some* trouble?" His whisper was intense. "Idiotic? It started out as a harmless, pleasant little idea I had one day, and—"

"Oh, yes, of course, just a little idea..."

"It was!" He defended his position. "I was standing in the doorway of the shop. It was a hot, dry and dusty day, and everyone on the street looked parched. I thought, idly, wouldn't it be nice to have a cool, wet, refreshing water fountain right there in the middle of the intersection....

"It just snowballed from there. Now I've got Deirdre around my neck, worse than any millstone or albatross! Not to mention a thousand charities bewailing all the dollars being spent on the fountain—why didn't I send them the money instead? One of them went so far as to accuse me of taking food out of the mouths of the poor!

"Oh, I'm not finished yet! The specialized pump to keep the water circulating won't work in our test runs. Why it won't work is an absolute mystery. All the pieces are there, and they've been put together right. It simply refuses to work, that's all. And have you heard the latest? Some bones were found in the excavation yesterday, and the university sent over their archaeology department for a look. Wouldn't you know it...the bones turned out to be skull fragments from some prehistoric man, and while I'm thrilled, of course, the department has closed down the site. No more work can be done on the fountain until they're through with the dig!"

"We-ell, perhaps by the time the site is returned to you, the pump will be working. The situation is actually not that terrible...."

"No? There's a great big hole in the street right in front of my shop, full of dirt. On windy days it's dusty as hell, and when it rains, the whole street turns into a mud bath. And every merchant around hates me for the traffic tie-up. The construction was supposed to take one month from beginning to end. It's taken *two* so far, and now my stonemason is gone, the pump won't function, and all work on the site has been stopped!"

"Yes, but you did get your granite back." Marielle wanted to run her fingers through his hair, kiss his furrowed brow and tell him that it would all work out in the end.

"But the worst—" his whisper sank a little lower, and his eyes moved down to her mouth "—is Deirdre. I don't know when I've disliked a human being more. It's like she's shut down my life, and I can't do another thing until this nightmare is over. I can look but I can't touch, and it's killing me, Marielle!"

"You'll survive!" She laughed softly. Raising her hand, she hesitantly traced his lips with an inquiring fingertip, and when he bent his head slightly, she turned her own just the little bit required, raised her chin and kissed him full on the mouth.

Her lips were soft and inviting. For a shocked second Cedric didn't respond. And then his hands curved around her shoulders to draw her ardently against him. As she trembled, he gathered her closer yet, and she had time for only a quick breath before his mouth descended onto hers, gradually deepening the impulsive kiss she had started. He tightened his embrace, locking her securely against him. The precariousness of their position on the chair precluded struggling for release…they would have both ended up on the floor!

Nevertheless, struggling to get away was exactly what Marielle wanted to do. Cedric was burning her up with desire, and any second now he was going to win over a lot more than her mind. But she didn't dare ask him to cease and desist, and anyway, the physical rush he had set loose was too sweet and glad and feverish to give up. In the end, rather than struggle for release, she moved to get closer yet, wanting more of his hard body pressed against her.

Naturally, the chair didn't want to cooperate. When it creaked, they both sprang up in alarm. Then Marielle started giggling, and Cedric pulled her against him. Infected by her merriment, he joined in her laughter.

Not wanting to wake up Uncle Willy, Marielle smothered her giggles in Cederic's shoulder, while his fingers trailed through her loose hair. Laughing together while in a close embrace was a powerful aphrodisiac, Marielle found, a sublime new experience. His palm slowly curved along her cheek and jaw, and from there it was just a small thing for him to lift her chin so that her mouth was at the perfect angle for an indepth, no-holds-barred kiss.

Under this sort of deliberate, premeditated attack, Marielle didn't stand a chance. She froze for a fearful instant, but as their joined body heat quickly melted into erotic heat, and his mouth tenderly coerced hers into response, her body gradually relaxed against his, and she became greedy for more. She stretched up on tiptoe and wrapped her arms around his neck in total commitment to the kiss.

Together, their bodies were a matched set. Cedric's hands wafted down to circle her waist, bringing her in closer. Thrilling to his taut, hard body, Marielle opened her mouth just a little wider to the inquisitive glide of his tongue.

Kissing him was far better than she had ever imagined . . .

CHAPTER ELEVEN

UNCLE WILLY STIRRED SLIGHTLY in his sleep, and it broke them apart. Grasping her by the hand, Cedric drew her quickly out of the room into the hospital corridor. The bright hallway lights had Marielle blinking, and she had to hurry to keep up with Cedric, who was heading toward the exit. He didn't relinquish her hand.

"Will you have dinner with me tonight?" he asked quietly as they passed a nurses' station.

She shook her head.

"Damn!" he said under his breath. "You see what I mean, look but don't touch!" They passed by a few patients going for an early evening stroll.

"You're doing pretty well already, considering I hardly know you! I wouldn't complain if I were you," Marielle fired back, just loud enough for him to hear.

He stopped in the middle of hall and with his free hand brushed a strand of hair off her temple and back over her shoulder. It was a small but very provocative gesture. "So who's complaining?" He smiled crookedly.

C. E. Greenleaf was staking his claim on her, and Marielle was letting him get away with it without a word of disagreement!

"I'll wait, Marielle; darling. But you should know that one of these days I'm going to be coming for you. And there won't be anything then to stop us."

"Is that a threat or a promise?" she teased him.

"It's a warning to stay out of my way unless..."

"Yes?" she prompted curiously.

"Unless you meant what you said." His half smile was beguiling. He drew her arm through his, and they continued on through the hallways.

"But I didn't say anything!" Marielle quickly pointed out.

"The hell you didn't!"

His low, charged words told her he was referring to the passion they had just shared. The possessive glide of his dark eyes over her feminine curves reminded her of how she had pressed herself against him. His eyes finally came to rest on her cheekbones, which were, she knew, covered with a telltale pink tinge. Suddenly she was breathless.

They went out of the hospital and down the steps and were beside her car before he stopped again. Marielle was already aching for another kiss, just a little one in parting, but he just took her car keys, unlocked the door of her yellow Porsche and opened it for her. He waited until she sat down and swung her legs in, admiring her slender ankles; then he quickly shut the door. Leaning down to look closely at her, he murmured succinctly, "I could make love to you all night long,'' in a tone of voice that said he meant it.

With that he just walked away. He had disappeared in what seemed like seconds, and Marielle was left staring after him. She moaned softly to herself, wondering what kind of a fool she was to be sitting there alone when she could have been folded in his strong arms that very minute.

She couldn't sleep that night. She lay in her big, comfortable bed and wished Cedric was beside her. She rolled back and forth, remembering how he had felt against her, and hated the skinny girl who had brought them together and was now keeping them apart.

But then there was her own fear of getting too close, which bordered on the neurotic. He'd told her to stay away unless she was serious. Well, the truth was, she was already far too serious! What had started out as a simple physical infatuation was turning into a full-fledged love affair, and Marielle wasn't sure she wanted one of those.

What really frightened Marielle was the new, persistent feeling that love was the only thing really worth having. Perhaps she'd worked all her life for things that she didn't really want, after all. What she wanted now with a fierce desperation was the one thing she had always spurned. Love sweet love.

Dammit all, Marielle thought to herself. It was the one thing she had no practice at. She was no virgin, but never before had desire been so wildly exhilarating. Never before had she tried to sing while brushing her teeth or walked around all day long with a goofy smile on her face. If she couldn't have him, if he decided he didn't want her, after all, she would be devastated. When her fears ran her through at unannounced times, they cut right through her.

MARIELLE AVOIDED everything that had to do with Cedric for a couple of days, but then she felt the urge to visit Paddy. When she showed up at the mansion in Coronado, Deirdre assumed she had come to see her and fell about her neck with gladness.

Marielle carefully disengaged herself.

"Marielle is my very best friend!" Dierdre avowed to Aunt Agatha, who was pacing to and fro in front of the salon fireplace and giving the baby a bottle.

"We've only known each other two months," Marielle said dryly.

"She's the kindest person alive!" Deirdre exclaimed generously. She was wearing another new dress, and what looked like new shoes, too. "She came to visit me in the hospital when I was all alone and brought me baby clothes and blankets and things when I had nothing. She was my dear friend when I needed one most!"

"Really, Deirdre," Marielle said, squirming, "I didn't save your life; I just gave you a lift to the hospital!"

"You stood up to Cedric for her, don't forget," Aunt Agatha chimed in. She cooed at the baby, adjusted his blanket and went on. "And standing up to that particular Greenleaf is no mean feat! He was impossible when he was twelve years old, and he's only gotten worse."

"You're telling me!" Deirdre suddenly shivered, and both Marielle and Aunt Agatha glanced at her in quick alarm, hoping she wasn't about to succumb to tears. But she merely cried tragically, "He frightens me some days!"

"He frightens me most days," Marielle commented wryly. She was struggling to hide the jumble of violent emotions seething just under the surface. She wanted to rip Deirdre Wheeler to shreds to find out what lay beneath. Instead she had to content herself with leading questions.

"Have you asked Cedric for child support yet?" she queried.

"Well, I . . . I'm scared of him. . . ."

"Then get an attorney to do it for you," Marielle suggested crisply.

Deirdre looked at her admiringly. "Gosh, I wish I could be more like you!"

Marielle felt something akin to nausea rise up in her stomach.

Deirdre went on, "You're so self-confident . . . so strong. What do you think I should do?"

"What do you want from Cedric?" Marielle didn't think she could put it any plainer. "Figure that out first, toss it at him and see what happens!"

"You might as well make him pay," Agatha agreed. "He had his fun!"

"All I want is to get married, like he promised!" Deirdre burst into tears. "I want a father for my baby! I want a home! I want a husband!"

"Now look what you've done," Aunt Agatha scolded Marielle. "And just when I'd finally gotten

a smile out of her! The world just seems full of selfish people these days! There, there, poor baby,'' she
crooned, holding Ricky and patting Deirdre's head
with her other hand.

''I didn't mean to upset her, Aunt Agatha,'' Marielle commented. ''I merely wanted to know what she
was planning to do next.''

''What do you think I should do?'' Deirdre questioned eagerly through her tears.

''Nail him to the wall, darling!'' Aunt Agatha
counseled, rocking the baby back and forth. ''Take
him for every penny! Look how he dumped you.
Make him pay! It won't hurt to take that arrogant
young buck down a peg or two!''

Agatha's bloodthirsty point of view had Marielle
gazing at her in startled surprise. Cedric's triumphs
were obviously not a source of pride to his aunt; that
much was clear. Marielle said to Deirdre, ''Just do
whatever you want to do! But get on with it!''

''Yes, strike while the iron's hot, so to speak!''
Aunt Agatha urged. ''Why should he sleep in peace
one more night?''

''Er...well....'' Marielle cleared her throat uncomfortably and decided to change the subject.
''Perhaps you should invite some of your friends
over. Aunt Agatha would like to meet them,
wouldn't you?'' Aunt Agatha nodded vigorously and
Marielle continued. ''They must be wondering
what's happened to you. I'm sure you don't want to
worry them.''

Both Marielle and Agatha looked expectantly at
Deirdre while she blew her nose and wiped her wet

cheeks: Agatha with agreeable interest, Marielle with veiled suspense.

"I don't have any friends," Deirdre finally managed tearfully. "I've always sort of been alone..."

"But what about your family, dear?" Aunt Agatha probed, obviously curious. Marielle could have cheered.

"I—I'm an orphan" was the sad reply.

"Oh...." Aunt Agatha sighed, full of sympathy and concern. "You poor little thing! All alone in the world! Life can be so cruel!"

"But now that you've been so wonderful to me, Aunt Agatha, I feel like the world is a super place!"

"You've been a pleasure to be nice to!" Aunt Agatha beamed.

"Ever since you took me in, well, I've never felt wanted before, really, and it's ever so nice! You're like the mother I never knew!"

Marielle rose from her chair. She had had enough of this syrupy mutual admiration society and had the distinct feeling this afternoon's session had only just begun. "I have to run...."

"Hi, Paddy," she said smilingly a few minutes later. She had found him in the rose garden, snipping off spent roses with a set of garden clippers. A wisp of pipe smoke was curling up above his head, and for some reason Marielle felt suddenly reassured. In him, at least, was a measure of calm sanity. However, disappointingly, he had nothing new to relate about either Cedric or Deirdre.

"I think the Indians are on the warpath." She nodded back at the house behind them. "And I might have had a hand in it. Cedric's going to kill me!''

''What did you do?''

''We-ell, I'm not sure, but I think I stirred them up. All I wanted to do was get Deirdre to make a move, and when I egged her on, Aunt Agatha's response was to nail Cedric to the wall *tout de suite*! She...er...doesn't appreciate men much, does she?''

''So you've noticed.'' Paddy chuckled. ''She always did have a sour disposition, and as she got older, it settled in permanently. That's the trouble with getting old, Marielle: one can grow stiff, ideas can become fixed...fears can become paralyzing...''

''Fears can become paralyzing,'' Marielle mused.

The phrase kept running through her head, long after she'd left Paddy. She went to visit Uncle Willy in the hospital a couple of days later, eager to see Cedric. When he wasn't there, the disappointment was crushing. Uncle Willy casually remarked that Cedric wasn't coming to see him that day. Marielle pretended scant interest.

''Anything new happen between him and Deirdre?''

''No! He hasn't given her the time of day! Poor little dear, what a hard time she's had!''

''Don't you think there might be some sort of...of misunderstanding? Cedric is still denying everything.''

''Misunderstanding? How can there be a misunderstanding about something like that? That's like being 'sort of' pregnant. No, I think it's perfectly clear what's going on.''

"So you think...Cedric did it?'' Marielle couldn't help but notice that Uncle Willy looked uneasy. The subject was not a favorite with him, obviously.

"I know my nephew.'' He sighed sadly, shaking his head. "Of course,'' he amended quickly, "it's not all his fault. Women do throw themselves at his feet...lucky fella!'' He chuckled, but Marielle was not amused. She felt a sharp dissatisfaction with Willy Greenleaf on this occasion. After a short chat, she found reason to leave.

She was miserable. That sad sigh of Uncle Willy's had wrung her heart. Aunt Agatha didn't think much of Cedric, and clearly, he did not rank high in his uncle's opinion, either. Was Paddy the only supporter Cedric had? It seemed terrible that he couldn't count on his whole family to stand by him. But worse than that, his uncle and aunt were actively working against him!

When she wasn't aching on Cedric's behalf, she was fretting about her own predicament. Was she letting her fears dictate her future? Was she crazy? To let fear run the show was foolish, and she berated herself out loud. Rusty overheard.

"Now he's reduced you to talking to yourself, Marielle!'' He shook his head disgustedly. "And you're always preaching to me about hopeless entanglements!''

Rusty's remarks brought home the fact that sitting around stewing over her misfortunes wasn't doing any good. She should take some action. Of course, the only action she really wanted to take was a lot of kissing and hugging and...

In the past, Marielle had always made it a practice to outline her goals and then go after them. Well, she knew what it was she wanted now: she wanted Cedric, body and soul—not for a one-night stand, but forever. But how was she to determine that he was precisely what she wanted? When one was playing for keeps, one couldn't afford to make mistakes. And Cedric came with many problems! She would have to study him at close range...preferably right under her nose, in a place where making love was next to impossible. But first...

"Rusty! Hey, wait a minute!" Marielle, in a red Danskin and ballet slippers, went dashing after him. She caught up with him on the stairs between the studio's second and third floors. "Are you busy tonight?"

"Well, gee, not exactly." He draped a white towel around his neck. His gray sweat suit was drenched in sweat, and he mopped his face. "I just had a workout with Tanaka. I think I'm dead! I hope we can get him, boss."

"So do I." She lowered her voice. "It would be a triumph for Sun Studios! And it keeps us current."

"Yeah. And with a tie-in to the film industry like Tanaka, we could have movie stars showing up here."

"A franchise in L.A., I think...." Marielle smiled thoughtfully. "Anyway, where was I? Oh, yes, I want to go to every singles' bar in San Diego tonight. Are you game?"

"You want to *what*? Did I hear you right? What's gotten into you? What are you up to now, Marielle!" He hastened down the steps after her.

"I'm in the mood to go cruising. And it'll be my treat, because I know you're broke!"

"Cruisin'? You? Since when are you short of admirers?"

"I don't want to go out with anyone I know. I want to see if I can find something new out there in this big wide world. New and exciting."

"Uh-uh." Rusty shook his blond curls doubtfully. "I don't like the sound of this! Cruisin'! For cryin' out loud! Look, Marielle, you and I are both orphans, and so I'm your brother, father, uncle and grandfather all rolled into one, and I say, nix on it! I won't let you go *cruisin'* through the bars! If that low-down dog has driven you to this—"

"I'm only going to window-shop, for heaven's sake! That's why I'm taking you."

"Oh!" Rusty moaned. "You make me so darned uneasy when you get that determined look on your face. Okay, okay, we'll go. Just remember, *I'm* taking you home!"

"We might as well leave directly from here."

"I'm just glad I'm your family and not your husband. Your poor husband. You're going to drive him crazy."

"Huh. What do you know?" she scoffed.

"What do—" he pointed dramatically at himself, straining to keep their discussion to a low murmur "—what do I know about you? You forget the years I've been a grandfather to you." He grinned craftily, and Marielle laughed at his silliness. "You forget the years I've watched you, Marielle. I've known you from the time you were a wild kid. Now you're a tough old lady." He shuddered. "I wouldn't marry you if you *paid* me."

"Thanks a lot. You're just getting back at me for all the preaching you say I do. At eight, okay? We'll start with dinner."

"Uh-huh."

The evening turned out to be great fun, but then, Marielle always had fun with Rusty. Nevertheless, her quest for romance failed miserably. Her pulse didn't jump once in eager anticipation of a simple touch. She didn't find one pair of brown eyes whose caress bathed her in giddy exhilaration. No smile tempted her to take a chance....

The following morning, while brushing her teeth, Marielle faced the fact that she would go mad if she didn't set eyes on Cedric soon. She felt faint from missing him. The question then was, how to engineer a meeting. She was out of the red cinnamon hearts. She could always go to the shop to buy some more.... But first she would have to buy a new dress for the occasion!

She went to the newest shopping area downtown, Horton Plaza, and was going from one elegant boutique to the next when she saw Deirdre and Aunt Agatha enter a leather-goods shop across the way. Curiously, she paused to watch them.

The baby was not with them, she noticed at once. She studied them carefully through the store window, staying well back. Deirdre was shopping for a handbag, it appeared. A suitable bag was soon found and placed beside the cash register. But Deirdre had found the wallet nook, and after some deliberation, placed a wallet beside the bag. Marielle thought she saw a key fob, too, plus, at the last minute, another purse that just sort of found its way onto the pile. Out came Aunt Agatha's charge card. They came out of the shop, and Marielle saw Deirdre, with an impulsive, childish gesture, reach up to plant a kiss of gratitude on Aunt Agatha's cheek. Agatha patted her fondly, and the two merrily continued on to the next store.

Marielle hurried after them. "Why, hello!" she exclaimed a moment later, feigning the greatest surprise at seeing them. "Isn't it a lovely day to shop!"

"Aunt Agatha is just the mostest!" Deirdre gushed. "She let me come shopping with her. I've had such a good time!" She smiled prettily. "I've never seen so many lovely things, and do you know what? I'm just a little nobody, and she's treating me like I'm a princess! I can never begin to thank her enough!"

Aunt Agatha was soaking up the adulation like a sponge. She beamed fatly and complacently.

Marielle smiled blithely back. "But where's Ricky?"

"At home. With the nanny Aunt Agatha hired yesterday morning!" Deirdre kept on smiling like an angel. "She said I shouldn't be cooped up at home all the time, being so young. I should get out and have some fun, and so...well, she decided little Ricky must have a nanny."

"A nanny," Marielle echoed. "Of course, yes, I see."

"Isn't everything just ever so exciting?"

"Oh, yes, ever so," Marielle agreed dryly. "So I imagine you've decided what to do about Cedric?"

"Now don't you spoil our day!" Agatha hurriedly broke up the discussion. "My nephew's stubborn refusal to recognize his own son is a source of great embarrassment to his family."

"Not to Paddy," Marielle pointed out quietly.

"To most of his family." Aunt Agatha continued unperturbed. "He's a brute, I tell you, a brute! It's shameful how he treats his uncle! My husband has worked his fingers to the bone for him, what does he get for it? Arrogance and cheek! And taking our car! Don't you tell me about Cedric! Allow me to know my own nephew! Come along now, Deirdre! We have a great many things to do!"

"Bye, Marielle!" Deirdre waved the hand that wasn't toting parcels. "Oh, say, Auntie and I saw you and your football star last night! Aren't you lucky! What a hunk! Isn't he a hunk, Aunt Agatha?"

"One could call him a hunk, I believe." Aunt Agatha fluttered her eyelashes.

"We waved, but you two were so involved with each other that I don't think you noticed you were still on this planet!"

Marielle sincerely doubted this. "Rusty and I are the best of friends, Deirdre, and nothing more," Marielle protested mildly.

"Oh, sure! Contrary to popular opinion, I wasn't born yesterday. Come and visit soon! Pretty please?"

"Yes, indeed, do drop in for a visit, Marielle, dear. We'll be expecting you. Did you know there's a one-cent sale on dresses—"

Marielle heard all about the sale at one of the fancier department stores, and after everyone had said their goodbyes for the third time, she made her way there, thinking all the while that for a person who didn't ask for anything, Deirdre seemed to be getting an awful lot. A designer purse wasn't exactly a necessity.

The two dresses Marielle chose were not normally her style. They were made solely for the sake of romance, and it was in that adventuresome spirit that she bought them. . . .

Upon returning to her office, Marielle phoned the candy store and asked Cedric's secretary whether her employer was going to be in his office that afternoon. The secretary, Mrs. Stevens, took her name, excused herself for a moment to check, and Marielle waited, nervously tapping her pen against the scratch pad. She started doodling, wondering what was taking Mrs. Stevens so long to ask Cedric one little question. She almost expected him to come on the line, but finally the secretary came back.

"Miss Bond? Mr. Greenleaf will be in all afternoon."

"Thank you so much, Mrs. Stevens. Goodbye." Marielle hung up the receiver and eyed the two dresses draped over the chair opposite her. Which of the two delectably feminine frocks was the one to go shopping in—shopping for hearts?

CHAPTER TWELVE

"HAVE YOU BEEN SERVED, miss?" one of Cedric's clerks asked her politely, smiling rather like Marielle imagined Mrs. Santa Claus would smile, as though the clouds were made of candy floss and chocolate was health food. Marielle thought there was no way anyone would be able to leave without a bag of some sweet, not with Mrs. Santa Claus so eagerly hoping to please.

She already admired Cedric's business sense, and she suddenly realized that Cedric knew some things about marketing, too. Perhaps he would let her pick his brains one day....

"Miss? Perhaps you would like to try some samples?" the clerk suggested, smiling indulgently now, as if she suspected Marielle couldn't make up her mind.

"I'd like a bag of the cinnamon hearts, please."

"It's all right, Mrs. Whitney. I'll take this customer." Cedric suddenly materialized beside his clerk and smiled charmingly at the white-haired woman. She patted his sleeve and bustled off.

"You're popular with your staff."

"Immensely!" His smile was wide.

"But so formal! At my place, everyone's on a first-name basis!"

"It's tradition here."

"Oh." Marielle feasted her eyes on him. Among all the sweet little old ladies, Cedric looked very strong and very male.

"What would you like today, Miss Bond?" His smile was slightly taunting and very sensuous. "Peanut Butter Daisies? Amaretto Truffles? Chocolate-covered Strawberries? Tiger Butter?" Tiger Butter was layered white and dark chocolate, he revealed, cut to show the layers.

"Cinnamon hearts. I want cinnamon hearts, please." Her own heart was racing madly.

He took her hand and, catching her averted gaze, placed the small bag of candy in it. "Enjoy them, with my compliments." He lowered his voice intimately. "I hope every one of those little hearts makes you think of me."

Quickly she dropped her eyes, hoping they weren't as revealing as she was afraid they might be. She put the bag of red hearts into her purse, feeling more self-conscious, more uncertain of herself than she had for ages. There was something about him that cut right through layers of armor, the years of loneliness.

"Darling, do you have an hour to spare?" he asked nonchalantly.

"What?" she said, gasping, her gray eyes widening in alarm.

Laughing at her reaction, he added, "How about a tour of my factory kitchen? You did want a tour, didn't you?"

"Oh, yes," she replied, gulping, wishing she hadn't reacted so strongly. She probably shouldn't have come at all....

But he didn't seem to think so. He came out from behind the marble counter, and taking her arm, led her through the door she had seen him disappear through the first time she'd come to the shop. In a hallway, with the sounds of the shop fading fast, Marielle drew in a deep breath and gathered her poise.

"What's the status of that great big hole you have out in front of the shop?" she teased him while walking.

"It's now a registered archaeological dig, and my stonemason is due back next week. I don't know what to do! If I let the mason go, he may not be available by the time I need him. He's the best man for the job. I want him specifically. And yet to pay him to sit around watching that hole out there get bigger.... Stonemasons don't come cheap!"

"I'll remember that, just in case I decide to build a fountain some day. And how's the pump? Did you ever manage to get it working?"

He grinned, shaking his head ruefully. "You'll never believe what happened. You see—and you probably know this already—fresh water is in short supply in San Diego. Especially in the summer. I decided to solve the water supply problem by using seawater. There is, of course, lots of that. But seawater, being salty, is never used for fountains because the salinity corrodes the pipes and causes all sorts of problems. Well, to get around that difficulty, I had a couple of engineers design a special pump, drawing from pumps that are used in saltwater: bilge pumps, dredging pumps, and those used on oil rigs out at sea. Anyway, the pump finally arrived, and my project manager and I promptly put it together for a trial run. But, being the brilliant types we are, we hooked it up to a system that was designed for fresh water use."

Marielle laughed. She could well appreciate his chagrin. "That reminds me of the time a special kind of exercise bike arrived from the factory in a kit of labeled pieces. Rusty and I tried to assemble it. We must have put it together and taken it apart at least six times before we finally figured out that what we had wasn't an exercise bike at all, but a box of spare parts for a paper press conveyor belt! And we only figured that out when we finally looked at the picture on the front of the carton!"

"Now I don't feel quite so bad."

"Neither do I." Marielle changed the subject. "D'you know who I saw this morning? Deirdre. And Aunt Agatha, of course. Deirdre told me your aunt hired a nanny for the baby yesterday."

"Yes, I know. I'm getting used to hearing bad news."

"It struck me that your aunt might be doing it just to get back at you. She's still sore over losing the Rolls."

"Uncle Willy could have had one of his own if he'd gotten off his—" Cedric stopped abruptly. "Dad would have given it to him, had he only taken care of it,'' he finally said, a bit tiredly, Marielle thought.

"Have you heard anything from that private detective you hired?"

"Not yet. He's still trying to trace Deirdre's background. But just the fact that she appears to have none is in itself noteworthy. There isn't much I can do until she makes a move. Things would be a lot easier if I didn't have an aunt tripping all over herself to help a con.''

"It's the baby more than Deirdre. Your aunt is nuts about that baby. Maybe things will get better once Uncle Willy is back home. He should be released soon, shouldn't be?"

"That's another thing. I don't think he wants to leave the hospital. I know it sounds crazy, but his doctor told me two days ago that he's well enough to go home right now. He just has to take it easy."

"And he won't go?"

"Let's just say he's stalling, inventing new aches and pains every day."

"But *why*?"

Cedric shrugged an elegant shoulder. He was conservatively dressed that day, in a black suit, white shirt and royal-blue tie. Marielle thought he looked divine.

"Maybe he knows he should ask Deirdre to leave,'' Marielle suggested, "but he doesn't want to have a row with Aunt Agatha."

"I don't know. It's not like he's henpecked. He and Aunt Agatha just don't...relate, that's all. They don't spend a lot of time together. She's always at home in front of the TV, and he's always out, at his club or in a bar with one of his cronies.''

Opening the door at the other end of the hall for her, Cedric ushered her into what he called his factory kitchen. The aroma of chocolate and hot roasted nuts had Marielle's mouth watering instantly. It smelled even better than the shop; the aroma was much more potent here.

On a small table was a pile of pamphlets and paper hats. Cedric took two of the hats and gave her one. ''For cleanliness standards I must insist you wear one of these.'' He explained, ''If just one long blond hair fell in the strawberry fondant....'' Showing her how to unfold her expanding chef's hat, he placed hers on her head and then put his on. ''Now don't touch anything, and don't wander off.''

''No, sir!'' She smiled at him. Suddenly a thought occurred to her. ''It must have been pretty awful growing up in that big old Coronado mansion,'' she said quietly.

He glanced sharply at her then paused before replying, ''It wasn't that bad. Aren't you forgetting? I was the kid who had everything!''

''We—ell, you did have Paddy. You were lucky there.''

''Yes,'' he agreed simply. ''He wasn't home much in those days, though, and I sure missed him when he was away. My aunt didn't exactly dote on me. I used to think she hated kids.''

''Maybe that's because she couldn't have any of her own.'' At Cedric's questioning glance, she explained, "Er . . . Paddy mentioned something about that."

"Now, Miss Bond, are you ready for your tour?"

"Lead on!"

But they had to wait for an official tour to pass them by first. One of Cedric's staff, with a long white smock over her dress and a white hardhat placed jauntily over her bright red curls, was heading a group of about ten Japanese businessmen.

"You wouldn't believe the demand for tours," Cedric explained in an aside to her while the men were fumbling with their hats. "Every one of my factory kitchens has a full-time tour guide. It's an expensive service that I don't have to provide, but...say, I don't have to explain public relations to you, do I, darling?"

Every time he used that endearment on her, Marielle felt faint. "No," she managed breathlessly, wishing they were alone so that she could throw her arms around his neck. "Can you give me an outline of your history?" she requested instead.

"My great-grandparents came here from England, where they had made candy. Some of their recipes are still used. Mrs. Greenleaf started by making chocolates in her kitchen, with Mr. Greenleaf as her taster. Every batch of chocolate is still tasted today, by the way."

"By whom?"

"Me, of course!" He smiled. "It's the best job in the place! Do you think I'd give it to someone else?"

"I suppose it's just like tasting wine."

"Exactly. So, my great-grandmother made the chocolate, and my great-grandfather would pack it in a wheelbarrow and sell it on the streets. He touted them as 'the best chocolates in the New World!' Eventually they opened a store."

"This store, right?"

"Yes, except the original store was just a little clapboard shack. It was all they could afford, at first. Ten years after they built the first store, they started construction on this building, and it has remained virtually unchanged since, except for some modernizing. And that's basically it. The business has always been in the family, and today there are forty-five stores across the country."

"So what's this place for?" Cedric had led her away from the tour into an empty room with store display cases at one end, blackboards and stacked chairs at the other.

"Training area for the staff. Every new member goes through a thorough two-week training course, learning about our products, our ingredients and our customers. Ask anyone who serves you about the place: if they can't give you a good answer, I'll be surprised."

Marielle was impressed, but she couldn't help asking, "But why do you go to such lengths?"

"Say a customer comes in with an allergy to milk. Naturally he's going to want chocolates containing no milk, and my staff have to know enough not to sell him something that is going to make him ill—and very angry, too."

"Ah, yes, the disgruntled customer." Marielle smiled in quick sympathy.

"Next, we have the boiler room."

"No kidding!" It was full of vast boilers reaching far up to a very high ceiling.

"We use enormous quantities of hot water," Cedric explained. "Everything must be kept scrupulously clean, and only boiling water is used, no detergents whatsoever. Detergent leaves behind residues. The factory is actually constructed inside the brick building you see from the outside, and between the two buildings there's an asbestos liner to control the humidity. Chocolate must be kept dry."

The factory kitchen was completely white—floor, walls and ceiling. It was brightly lit and spotless. All the staff wore long white smocks, white hair nets, hard hats, and some of them, white gloves.

"Nothing shows up dirt like white," Cedric told Marielle, taking her hand to draw her arm through his. "Okay, all nuts come cleaned and sorted, but they're sorted once more on this broad conveyor belt, to pick out any shells that might have been overlooked and to separate the broken nutmeats from whole nuts. I like to sell only whole nuts out of my stores. If you buy a bag of cashews, and they're all broken into little pieces, they're not nearly as appetizing, and the customer feels cheated. By the way, did you know cashews aren't really nuts? They grow on the end of what's called a cashew pear, and therefore are not true nuts at all."

Marielle smiled at Cedric. It felt terrific to be walking around arm-in-arm with the master of the establishment. But beyond that, the place really was fascinating.

"Now over here the nuts are roasted in coconut oil, one kind at a time to preserve their unique flavor. In total, twenty-five thousand pounds of nuts are roasted in the same oil before it's changed. But the used oil isn't thrown away: instead, it is bottled and sent to Europe to be used in perfume."

"Perfume?" she exclaimed.

"Yes, darling. It has a very soft but sensuous aroma." He studied her profile as she peered into the vast cauldrons of coconut oil. "Two hundred pounds of nuts are roasted at a time, from a half a minute for soft nuts like cashews to twenty-two minutes for hard nuts, like Spanish peanuts, for example." He bore her onward.

"These slab tables are used to set up the caramels and fudges. There are copper pipes running beneath them that carry water, either hot or cold, depending on what's on top—hot for peanut brittle, cold for caramel. That slab of toffee you see there is about three feet by six feet in size. We make six different flavors of toffee alone."

Next they came to large round stoves that Cedric called furnaces. Indeed, they were huge, bearing copper pots three feet across. Copper, Cedric explained, conducted heat evenly and extremely well. In several of these pots cream centers for chocolates were being heated. Others had whipping machines attached to them that beat the fudge and toffee while it bubbled and boiled away.

Then there were the "cream beater" tables, six feet across. Runny syrup was poured from the copper pots, was left to cool and then beaten around and around until it was firm. It was then put through a round press and separated into pieces. Then all the little pieces were arrayed on a long conveyor belt, where liquid chocolate was poured over them and sprayed up from underneath. This process, Cedric told Marielle, was called enrobing. While the chocolate was still warm, each piece was hand-marked to identify the type of cream inside.

The filled cream chocolates were then zapped with cooling rays to firm the chocolate and sorted for imperfect specimens. Then they were packed by hand in what Cedric called stock boxes. Marielle wondered whether this was the job Deirdre had performed.... These boxes were stored for ten days while the cream centers aged. Caramels, however, didn't have to age.

They ducked into the warehouse area to let the tour bypass them. The area was huge and cool. High up, fans rotated in the air ceaselessly. What had Marielle enthralled were the blocks of chocolate stacked almost right up to the forty-foot ceiling.

"How much chocolate is there in here?" she asked in awe.

"Well, I'd have to check the books to be certain, but we go through forty thousand pounds every two months, so that should give you some idea.... We manufacture thirty thousand pounds of finished chocolate per week. Out of this factory alone. Those stacked pails there hold peanut butter—twenty-five pounds in each.''

''Wow!''

''Coconut and cordial cherries come in five gallon pails. But it's mainly the chocolate that makes Greenleaf products distinctive. We use our own particular blend of Belgian and American chocolate, and nothing but the finest quality.''

''What on earth are those weird-looking things?''

''Molds, for the chocolate. Don't you recognize Santa?''

''But how on earth do they work?'' Marielle turned the mold over from side to side, puzzling over it.

Cedric smiled at her frown. ''Only one side is filled with warm chocolate. Then the mold is clamped shut, put in a wooden brace and simply shaken like mad or put through a centrifuge so that the chocolate coats the whole interior.''

''So that's how hollow Easter eggs are made! I always used to wonder about that!''

The last area Cedric showed her was the place where the blocks of chocolate, weighing ten pounds each, were broken into smaller chunks with a big rubber hammer. These smaller chunks were then mixed in huge blenders that melted and stirred, or conched, the chocolate, for literally hours on end. Marielle was amazed at seeing that much chocolate swirl around and around in the enormous vats. The temptation to stick a finger in for a taste was very difficult to resist.

"From the blenders the chocolate goes into holding tanks. Those overhead pipes then deliver it to wherever it's needed, to the enrobing area, to the molding area, and so on and so forth...."

They paused for a moment to watch some staff demolding Easter bunnies. The flexible plastic molds popped right off, and any rough edges of chocolate were brushed away with a white-gloved hand or dexterously pared with a sharp knife.

"It's a labor-intensive industry," Cedric commented. "Every single box of chocolate that goes out of any Greenleaf store is entirely packed by hand, too. That's why I have so many employees. They're treated well, though. In all our years of business, we've never had any labor problems. Now, Marielle, I've saved the best for last. Come and meet my hand-dippers. Peggy's worked for us for fifty-three years and refuses to retire, and Lila has been with us for thirty-three years in all."

Cedric introduced her to the two women who were up to their elbows in chocolate. They sat side by side in front of marble slabs on which were pools of warm chocolate.

"They each dip approximately thirty-two hundred cordial cherries every day."

"Oh, my God!"

"Exactly. Peggy and Lila are treasures!" The women beamed fondly up at their handsome young employer, neither one missing a stroke. "The marble slabs are kept warm from below to keep the chocolate workable."

"But their hands!" Marielle protested, "Don't their hands get sore covered in chocolate eight hours out of every day?"

"Oh, no! They probably have the softest hands in the world. It's the cocoa butter." In silence Marielle watched as Lila took a cherry—it looked like a little pink snowball to her with its sugarcoating—rolled it in her pool of chocolate and dropped it in a small frilly paper cup. Her finishing touch was a swirl on top, executed with a practiced fingertip. And she was on to the next.

"These brandied cherries are aged for two weeks, during which the sugarcoating and the brandy turns into the syrup that runs down your chin if you don't pop the whole thing in your mouth."

"I've never had one."

"What?" He was amazed. "Never? Oh, Marielle!" He looked as though he didn't know whether to feel sorry for her or scold her. "Don't you know chocolate is good for you?"

"So your father tried to convince me. I don't believe it, though. I mean, all those calories!"

"Well, yes, certainly, there are many calories. But everything in moderation, eh? And besides, the calories aren't *empty* calories, like...like the ones in potato chips. Some day, when we have plenty of time, I'll tell you all about chocolate. It's an interesting subject. For example, cacao beans were once used by the Aztecs as currency. About one hundred beans bought a slave. Who says money doesn't grow on trees! Then the Spaniards took the beans with them to seed 'money plantations' in Trinidad and Haiti.''

''Granted that it's a fascinating subject, but why is chocolate supposed to be good for me?'' Marielle persisted doubtfully, eyeing the racks of exquisite chocolates.

''Chocolate itself is low in saturated fats and salt. It's actually high-energy food. Didn't Sir Edmund Hillary eat chocolate all the way up Mount Everest? Why do you think our astronauts always carry chocolate aboard their spaceflights? The Soviets do, too. Research has even found that there's a substance in cocoa powder that may inhibit tooth decay!''

''In that case, give me some chocolate, please, right away, before I die on the spot! The last thing I want is another cavity!''

Cedric divested them of their hats and then led her through a maze of doors, hallways and stairs, and into his own office on the second floor. He closed the door behind them.

''I had a box specially packed for you.'' He smiled, nodding toward his desk. A gorgeous pale gray satin box was the only thing on it. ''When you phoned this morning, I had a feeling you were going to show up.''

With a sparkling smile at him she went over to his desk. He didn't move but stayed by the door, watching her.

''Oh, thank you, Cedric!'' Marielle brushed her fingers over the box before carefully opening it. ''They're too pretty to eat....'' She picked out a cordial cherry and looked at it. ''The whole thing?''

"All at once," he said, nodding. He watched her pop the chocolate-covered, brandy-soaked cherry into her mouth. She closed her eyes in sweet delight.

"Oh, dear!" she exclaimed a moment later. "I'm afraid I love it!"

"Maybe I should tell you—" he had been leaning against the closed door, but now he came slowly toward her "—that research has also revealed that chocolate contains small amounts of phenylethylamine."

"Um...what?" She was studying her box of chocolates, trying to decide on the next treat. "Pheny-what?"

"It's thought to be an aphrodisiac." The faintest of smiles began to lift one corner of his mouth. "That's why the custom developed of giving a lady chocolates."

Marielle's mouth formed a soundless O. She looked at him then quickly placed the beautiful box back on his desk. She had no need for aphrodisiacs; she was quite ready for making love without one. And if she had another chocolate, there was no telling what she might do. As Cedric started to come toward her, she began to edge around his desk. It was a lovely desk, an antique like hers, but his desk wasn't what was on her mind right then.... "But, Cedric," she quavered.

"Yes, darling?"

She trembled at the soft, beguiling quality in his deep voice. "Is...is the tour finished? Have you covered everything?" She kept on edging around the desk, and he kept on coming closer. "What are you called? I mean, there are farmers and bankers and lawyers, but what are you called? You're not a candy man, are you?''

"I'm a chocolatier, darling.''

Three seconds more and he caught her. She was wrapped in his strong arms. "I've been dying for this ever since you came into the store! You should have sent your pet gor—Rusty for those cinnamon hearts if you didn't want to get kissed!'' And then he kissed her. It was all that she had been waiting for, and more.

Deep and definite, his kiss curled her toes and banished her fears. Within his tight embrace she shivered in ecstasy. "Oh, Cedric,'' she breathed, sliding her arms over his shoulders and her fingers into his dark hair. He crushed her against him, and the feel of his body was a balm. "Oh, Cedric!'' she whispered and held up her mouth to be kissed again and again....

CHAPTER THIRTEEN

AFTER THE NOISE of the factory kitchen downstairs, Cedric's office seemed a restful, quiet oasis. The overwhelming aroma of roasting nuts, simmering mocha cream and rich bittersweet chocolate was only a warm, lingering presence there.

Assured of her willingness to be in his arms, Cedric gently sought out her sleek curves. His careful, sensitive touch was far more tantalizing than a more demanding approach might have been. In return, her response was eager, and she melted in his embrace.

Softly, slowly, their lovemaking continued uninterrupted and held them spellbound. The inquisitive glide of his tongue coaxed her lips apart to admit a deeper, more intimate, questing glide just inside her upper lip. The slow roaming of his hands discovered that all she was wearing under her dress was a pair of lacy bikini panties.

With many small kisses Marielle outlined his mouth, and then her lips wandered farther across his cheek and chin, luxuriating in the taste and feel of his skin.

One of his hands pressed her tightly to him with passionate desire, and the other slid down the outside length of her thigh and back up again, taking her dress along with it. He continued his leisurely exploration around the elastic band atop her panties and moved down to cup her firmly rounded bottom, breathing a throaty sigh of contentment.

Her fingers rested on the lapels of his suit, wanting to caress him but thwarted by the layers of clothing—suit, vest, shirt, tie. She moaned in faint frustration. Through the layers of material she could feel the iron-hard muscles that the black belt in karate had formed.

She slid her hands up over his shoulders and combed her fingers through his hair. She then ran her fingers along the line of his sizable jaw and kissed him with delicious dedication. But as soon as she tipped her head back, his lips sought the pulse point below her ear. It was all she could do to cling to him. His arms were wrapped around her tightly, and she let him carry her weight as she concentrated instead on another kiss....

Nestling closer yet, she wished the moment would last forever. When he swung her right off the ground, her arms were already around his neck. He effortlessly carried her the few feet to where a huge and inviting couch beckoned.

It was a large, plush, plaid couch. Cedric tenderly lowered her down onto it.

In her mind's eye Marielle suddenly saw Deirdre, lying in the hospital bed, clutching her newborn baby and tearfully telling her about the fateful seduction on the plush plaid couch in Cedric's office.

Marielle went totally numb. Reality hit her like a pail of icy water. She struggled against the cushions to sit up, pushing against Cedric's broad shoulders. Wildly she searched her mind for an excuse to tear out of the room as fast as possible. It occurred to her that she'd left work hours ago.

"What's the time?" she gasped.

"What's the matter, Marielle? It's...quarter past four, darling."

"What?" she squeaked in disbelief. "Do you realize I have an aerobics class in fifteen minutes? I'm not even changed yet, and...I still have to get there first! Oh, damn, and I haven't a hope in hell of getting there with your great big hole in the middle of the street tying up all the traffic! You and your stupid fountain!" There was a lot more she wanted to say, but she left it at that.

"Don't go, Marielle," he said quietly, his voice devoid of any particular expression, his jaw settling into a very determined jut. "The phone is right there. Call your—call Rusty and tell him to find a substitute because I doubt you'll get there in time to do much more than wave goodbye to your class. Rush hour has started, and—" he had gone to a window, and looking out over the intersection below, he predicted "—it's going to be as bad as ever."

"Damn, damn, damn! This has never happened to me before! I must have lost my mind! Where is my purse? Egad, I've lost a shoe! How could I have lost a *shoe*?"

A quick scout found her sandal nearby, just underneath the dreaded couch. All the while Cedric watched her as though he, too, believed she had lost her mind.

She didn't care. Grabbing her purse from his desk, she headed for the door. It was locked.

Coming up behind her, Cedric grasped her by the shoulders, spun her about and gave her a little shake. "Marielle, calm down! What's the matter with you? What did I do? I know things got out of hand, but I didn't plan it that way! It just happened!"

"Did it just happen with Deirdre, too?" she cried, looking past him at the couch.

He turned to stone. Then a muscle in his jaw flexed, but that was all the reaction her tortured cry received. She couldn't meet his eyes, couldn't look at him at all. She felt mortally wounded. In silence he unlocked the door, and she slipped out.

She was dazed. She knew she had to get to work, but what she really felt like doing was throwing up. Though it was warm out, she felt freezing cold, and she wrapped her arms around herself forlornly and tried to remember where she had parked her car. But then it occurred to her that she had better get word to Rusty....

Eventually she found a phone booth. But Rusty reported that Cedric had already called him with her news. What in the dickens was going on? "You don't sound so good," he finished.

Marielle hastily cleared her throat. "I'll be in shortly."

"Listen, if you're not feeling good, maybe you should take the rest of the day off—"

"I can't sit home alone!" Marielle immediately realized how she must have sounded. There was a pause on Rusty's end.

"What's he done?" he growled.

Marielle shook her head. "Nothing, nothing, leave it alone, Rusty. He really didn't do anything to me that I didn't do to myself!"

"Uh . . . could you repeat that?"

Marielle hung up the phone.

A half hour later she was back at work in a lilac Danskin, heading an exercise workout. It felt good to be busy, to be active, to be in control. Whenever she thought of Cedric, she felt violently sick, so she tried not to think of him—or what had happened— at all.

"Up, down, up, down, reach for the sky, stretch, stretch!" The music played happily, briskly, and her class reached for the sky. When Rusty poked his head through the door, she was able to smile quite brightly at him and cheerily wave. Reassured that she was okay, he smiled, waved back and disappeared. Marielle felt suspiciously like bursting into tears. "Spread your legs and touch your toes, down to the left, down to the right, come on, left, right. . . ."

A little later, Marielle saw Deirdre walk in the door of Sun Studios with the baby in her arms. Her bad day wasn't over yet. Marielle quickly finished conferring with the carpenter and went to greet her. She wondered, in passing, why Deirdre hadn't left the baby at home with the nanny. Was she using her infant as a prop to gain sympathy?

"Why, hello, Deirdre," she said casually. "What brings you here? Are you and Aunt Agatha going to enroll in time to get fit for the summer, or is this a social visit?"

"Well, actually..." Deirdre licked her lips uncomfortably, quickly glanced at Marielle and then down at the baby in her arms. "I, uh...just had to see you...."

"Why don't we go to my office. We can talk more comfortably there." On the way Marielle made small talk, mostly concerning the baby. Deirdre kept taking sidelong glances at Marielle's lilac Danskin and matching tights. Marielle couldn't imagine why. Not wanting the girl to get the idea that it was going to be a long visit, she sat her down in a chair while she remained standing, casually leaning against her desk.

It struck her that here was her opportunity for the private chat she had been wanting. Here was the chance to find out a few things, like how Deirdre managed to pop up from nowhere, disappear and then pop up again. But Cedric and the girl *were* lovers, or at least, they had been lovers; that much was painfully evident now. Marielle didn't care anymore about anything. All because of one blasted plaid couch....

She didn't care where Deirdre had come from nor where she had gone, and she didn't give a damn who had paid her hospital bills. What she had once thought a niggling coincidence, namely, Uncle Willy and Deirdre being in the same hospital, didn't bother her at all anymore. In fact, it seemed too insignificant for words. She could see now that she had been grasping at straws, trying to twist the facts to clear Cedric. And why shouldn't Deirdre keep on going to Coronado even though Cedric lived in La Jolla? It was a free country, wasn't it?

But Marielle's violent distaste for the girl surprised even her. By nature she wasn't a jealous woman, and yet just the sight of the helpless twit in front of her was enough to set her blood seething.

Deirdre was looking around. "Why...you don't have a couch in your office," she noticed.

Marielle did not jump or scream or throw a heavy brass bookend at Deirdre's head. She just smiled. She didn't say anything about the chaise lounge in her boudoir. "What is it you wanted to see me about?"

"Well, gee, I don't know how to say this. I'm ever so sorry, and I know you're one of the only friends I have in the whole wide world. I know you wouldn't do anything to hurt me or, um...little Ricky...." She looked down at the baby fast asleep in her arms. Marielle felt a pang for the unwanted child. "I promise I won't cry—" But she sounded very close to it.

Marielle groaned inwardly, already dreading the coming scene. Should she get her tissues out now, or should she wait until the tears actually began to fall? One good thing was that seeing Deirdre made her feel less like crying herself. Be thankful for small favors, she joked sourly to herself, suddenly remembering the picnic in Balboa Park under the gum trees. Her heart was disintegrating into small pieces within her breast. . . .

Deirdre sniffed loudly in the quiet.

"Yes? Go on, please."

"Well, I don't want you to think I've been spying on you—I haven't! It's just that, well, Cedric mentioned to Uncle Willy that you've been seeing each other, and Uncle Willy told Aunt Agatha, and Aunt Agatha told me. I don't know why you've been seeing Cedric; maybe it has just been to argue my case, for which I'm eternally grateful . . . but you're so awfully beautiful! And I'm so afraid that, oh, how am I going to say this?" She sniffed again, and Marielle went for the box of tissues.

"Thank you! Thank you! Oh, I'm sorry to be such an awful nuisance. But I just had to c-come!" She wept into the tissue. "Please, please, don't take Cedric away from me! Don't you see? I need him so desperately! With a new baby and all! There's *two* of us who need him, me *and* little Ricky! You've got so much already: you've got your fantastic job and your super car and, um, you have Rusty, too. Can't you please leave Cedric alone? I know it's just awful of me to come here and beg like this, but . . . honestly, Marielle, I'll get down on my hands and knees if I have to!"

"That won't be necessary!" Marielle hastened to say. She felt about two inches high and frightfully embarrassed. "I certainly have no interest in him!"

Deirdre was effusive in her thanks. Marielle felt totally ill. How could she have been so naive? Worse even than Deirdre, now busily blowing her nose. Easy pickings, indeed! How could she have been so idiotic as to get involved with someone who went around donating fountains! She should have known right from the start.... But she had known. That was the cruelest irony. Even Rusty had tried to warn her off....

Deirdre wanted a tour of the spa, but, gritting her teeth in a supreme effort to keep on smiling, Marielle suggested that another time would be more suitable. She saw to it personally that Deirdre exited the spa.

OVER THE NEXT FEW DAYS, all Marielle did was work, work, work, with the sort of zeal that left her with no time for anything else but eating and sleeping. She didn't do a lot of eating, however, and she didn't sleep very well, either.

Tanaka was now on her team, and four other martial arts champions assisted him in the new karate department. The restaurant was almost finished, too. She would be able to open it soon. And she had found a use for crystal and sunlight in the restaurant. She had installed intricately-cut glass in the windows, and the sunlight that radiated through the patterned panes made the windows into crystal jewels. The restaurant was already a popular item of gossip, and it wasn't even open yet!

Despite all the reasons she had to be happy, she wasn't. Rusty tried to get her to confide in him, but she was a very private person. He knew that, and so he didn't persist. But when she went home in the evenings, he was always there to keep her company. She was immensely grateful for his silent comfort and impressed that he was forfeiting dates.

Exactly a week later, as she was going up to the fifth floor, she found Rusty barring Paddy Greenleaf's way in front of her office. She arrived just in time to hear her sidekick emphatically state, "If she won't see Cedric, I hardly think she'll see his father!"

Rusty looked relieved to see her. "You tell him!"

Paddy also seemed relieved to see her. "Hello, Marielle," he greeted her in a mild tone of voice. "I hope I haven't upset your partner—"

"It's all right, Rusty. Thank you, I'll take it from here."

"Okay. But if you need me, you call."

"I will. Thank you." She smiled at him as he stomped off down the hall. "Come in, Paddy." Opening her office door, Marielle motioned him in. "Have a seat.

"You've no couch in your office?" he remarked.

Marielle thought that she'd shriek. "No," she snapped. "There is no couch in my office. This is an office! It's not a...a...a bedroom!"

"No, no, of course not." Paddy looked at her wonderingly, and she felt foolish. Releasing a shaky breath, she went to sit behind her desk to keep the meeting formal. Paddy continued gently, "I haven't seen you for a while, and I was downtown so I thought I'd pop in. You have a wonderful place here! Cedric told me how lovely it is." He paused. "You know, I've missed your visits."

"I've been busy." Her voice was cool.

But Paddy cut right through to the core. "What's gone wrong between you and Cedric?"

"Did he send you?" she spat.

"Heavens, no!" He laughed at the idea and took out his pipe. Marielle relaxed a little. "No, he's as taciturn as you are, and about ten times as grumpy. He has his poor secretary treading on her tiptoes and talking in whispers." Very carefully he tamped the tobacco down in the bowl of his pipe. "If it's just a little quarrel—"

"Little quarrel?"

"I know my son, and—"

"No, you don't!" Her careful control suddenly exploded. "Cedric lied to me, Paddy! And to you! And to everybody! He *did* do it!" To her horror her bottom lip trembled, and tears seemed frightfully close. She bit on her lip between ragged gulps for air. "He…Deirdre…she told me about the couch a long time ago! And I—and he . . . that damned couch!"

"What couch are we talking about?" Paddy asked curiously, lighting his pipe. The smoke curled up above his head.

"That god-awful one in his office! That big ugly plaid thing!"

"I see...." He looked as if he really didn't, though.

"Oh!" Marielle sighed exasperatedly. She got up out of her chair and walked over to the window. "Deirdre told me that Cedric seduced her on that couch in his office! *Now* do you see?"

"I'm sure I do."

"No, you don't!" Marielle paced agitatedly. "Cedric had convinced me that everything she said was a lie. And then, last week, I, er, had occasion to be in his office, and ... *there it was*!"

"What?"

"The *couch*!" Marielle cried, raking her hands through her hair.

"Oh, yes, yes, of course, I see now." Paddy's blue eyes were twinkling at her, but she was too upset to notice. "Tell me if I have it right. This, er, couch is your evidence for finding Cedric guilty?"

"*Yes*! What more do I need? How could she have described the thing to me if she hadn't been in his office? How would she know it was soft if she hadn't tried it out?"

"Ah! But one can judge a sofa's softness by looking at it, and since she worked at Greenleaf Sweets, she could have seen this plaid monstrosity from the doorway, just passing by."

Marielle gazed at Paddy, stunned by his calm logic. She realized at once that what he was saying was entirely possible.

"Deirdre was hired, and laid off, by my brother, I've discovered. Willy's office is right beside Cedric's. She was hired for exactly one month's duration to replace someone with a badly sprained ankle. So, you see, Deirdre would have had reason to be up in the office area at least twice, once when she was hired and once when she was let go. Cedric's door is usually open. It strikes me that no jury would convict Cedric on your evidence.''

''But I did,'' Marielle murmured to herself, feeling a wave of keen regret. But she felt confused, too. ''But...but...if Deirdre really is a con, why doesn't she ask for money and go? Why is she still hanging around? What for?''

''That I don't know. It may be part of her game. She's wearing everybody out, though; I can tell you that much! If it weren't for the baby, I think even Agatha would have liked to suggest at times that she move on. No one can take all that weeping and whining indefinitely. And Willy's home now, too, and that has made a difference.''

''He's better, then?''

Paddy shook his head doubtfully. ''He seems to be doing a lot of moping about.''

''Maybe he doesn't like sharing Agatha with Deirdre and the baby.''

''Hmm. They never spent much time together, anyway. But Willy never could keep a secret, so we'll find out what's eating him up before long. Of course, he could be upset over all the money Agatha's spending on Deirdre and Ricky. He could also be grieving over the Rolls-Royce that now belongs to Cedric, especially if Agatha is giving him a hard time about it, and I think she is. Had he taken care of it, he would still have it! However, that's neither here nor there. Did you know Cedric hired a detective?''

''Has he come up with anything?'' she asked eagerly.

''We-ell, if you call coming up with nothing, something, then he has! Now wait, hear me out. People like you and me, Marielle, have backgrounds. We can be traced. We pay bills, we use banks, and we have homes. But Miss Deirdre Wheeler never existed, according to the record books. That's downright suspicious! No accomplice has been found, so it's the detective's opinion that she's working alone. That could account for her lack of good judgment. Any experienced con knows enough to get in and get out quickly. Or so the detective pointed out. The longer a game takes, the greater the risk of making a slip. And she's made several.''

''For instance?''

''Getting too comfortable, wearing out her welcome, helping Agatha spend her charge card right through the roof. The other day, she said at breakfast that children were tax deductions, so why didn't Cedric spend the money for the fountain on Ricky. Now that's a rather curious thing for an innocent little scrap of a girl to say, isn't it? And that fountain is worth a lot more than fifty thousand dollars! That could have been a clue as to how much she's really hoping to get out of Cedric. And then, too, she overdoes the young and helpless bit. And I think she tries to play down her looks. I know Cedric is no saint, but he has no need to go seducing shop girls on his couch!"

Marielle could see what Paddy meant. She absentmindedly helped herself to some cinnamon hearts.

"Put some makeup on her, a different style of dress, a pair of high heels, and she doesn't look like a kid anymore. She proved that when she and Agatha went out on the town one night. Now, that *was* a mistake! Cute little girls don't go to singles' bars . . . they don't even know about singles' bars!

"But," Paddy continued, "there is not one thing that makes for overwhelming evidence against her . . . not yet. I mentioned your coincidence to the detective, you know, about Uncle Willy and Deirdre being at the same hospital. He agreed with your view that it could be an important noncoincidence. In fact, he thinks that she knew our family physician was located there and booked herself in there purposefully to make it look as though Cedric had placed her there and had paid for the bills."

"Um-hm. That's probably what happened. I don't suppose there's any way to check, though." Marielle frowned. "Is the detective still working on it?"

Paddy nodded, taking a puff on his pipe. For a short while he smoked in silence. Then he commented, "I'm too old for such excitement."

Marielle just smiled at that remark. "Paddy, I hope you don't think this is too personal, but it's something that has always piqued my curiosity. You and Willy are both fair, and yet Cedric is so dark...."

"His mother was Mexican. I met her on the Baja one summer. I had pulled into a little cove to spend the night. In the morning when I went for a swim, there she was, just out past the rocks, spearfishing. Ah, I remember it as if it were yesterday.... He looks a lot like her. She was such a beauty. Spirited and yet so...gentle. How I loved her! I don't think I ever really recovered after her death. It was shortly after Cedric was born. Of cancer. In those days, there was nothing that could be done."

"I'm sorry. Now I've made you sad!" Marielle touched his blue-veined hand fleetingly in genuine regret.

"No, no, my dear, the memories of her are very dear to me. Now, do you think I could prevail upon you for a tour? Cedric tells me you've hired his karate partner. Tanaka, is it?"

After Paddy had gone, Marielle sank her face into her hands and stayed that way for a long time. She wished she could cry over Cedric. Anything would feel better than the awful, aching certainty inside that she had made a terrible error in judgment.

How many times she had let him down...how many times she had been rude! She must have driven him mad, seeking him out one minute, only to spit in his eye the next! He had been willing to trust her, yet she'd never completely trusted him. How that must have smarted, over and over again. And then, finally, the ultimate insult, running out on him the way she had.... When she remembered how he had looked, the taut jaw, the stony calm, she writhed in her chair.

He was probably convinced by now that she was completely neurotic. He had probably decided to wash his hands of her, would probably never, ever, talk to her again! However was she going to bear that?

CHAPTER FOURTEEN

As THE MINUTES AND HOURS AND DAYS passed, Marielle gradually became convinced that she had ruined whatever chance she had had for happiness. Just when she finally realized she loved Cedric, she had brutally pushed him away. Their relationship had been so fragile, hardly old enough to weather such a blow.

Another whole week went by, April turned into May, and Marielle became sadder and more heavy of heart with each passing day. There was no word from Cedric, of course....

Marielle didn't make a return visit to the candy store, and she didn't drop in at the mansion in Coronado anymore. Deirdre called her one morning to ask hesitantly why she hadn't come to visit. The baby was growing bigger every day, she reported, adding that Aunt Agatha had asked her to extend an invitation to come around for dinner that evening in the hope that it would cheer up Uncle Willy.

"We don't know what's the matter with him. Maybe his heart attack has made him feel old and useless. That's what Auntie thinks. Anyway, I thought I'd better call. After coming to see you, I feel it's my fault you haven't come around, and we all miss you terribly! Please come, pretty please? Oh, and of course Rusty's invited, too! As your beau, Aunt Agatha would like him to feel welcome—''

"Rusty is not my beau," Marielle insisted quietly. "He's my dearest friend and a valued business partner, but that is all, Deirdre."

Marielle didn't know why she agreed to go to dinner. It would be nice to talk to Paddy, of course. As for Aunt Agatha and Uncle Willy, while she liked them well enough, their standpoint concerning Cedric would make the evening terribly hard for her. She certainly had no wish to see Deirdre, and while the baby was cute, there wasn't much one could do with him at this stage. Still, she agreed to go. It was, after all, the only link she had with Cedric, and while it was a tenuous link at best, it was better than nothing.

Several hours later, Rusty and Marielle walked up the narrow lane to the Greenleaf mansion. The unkempt garden had Rusty bemused.

"You'd think they could afford a gardener!" he said, puzzled.

"I don't think anyone cares. Paddy stays in his wing of the house, and all Aunt Agatha does is watch TV and eat candy. Uncle Willy...well, I get the general idea he's not very good at taking care of things. Paddy keeps his area up. Gosh, you should see it. It's the most perfect rose garden I've ever seen. It's almost too perfect. I have this sneaking suspicion its based on a mathematical equation. He's a matnematician, did I tell you that? And a bit of a recluse, I suspect."

"I wonder what we're going to get for dinner," Rusty grumbled. "If the yard is this bad, what's the kitchen like?"

"I'll take you out for dinner afterward if it's anything like this," Marielle placated him, looking around at the gloomy tangle.

Marielle was glad she'd prepared herself for an ordeal. Paddy was pleasant but mostly quiet and watchful. Uncle Willy was morose. The hired nanny, who joined them at the dinner table, was a homely, sourly disposed individual. Aunt Agatha and Deirdre ruled the conversation, which was fortunate, for it appeared no one else felt like talking much. Marielle certainly didn't feel like making merry, and Rusty was fully occupied digging into the absolutely scrumptious dinner.

Eyeing Aunt Agatha's two hundred pounds, it occurred to Marielle that she should have known a good cook would be of the utmost importance in this household!

As she had promised, Marielle did her best to cheer up Uncle Willy. She hardly knew him, but even she could tell that he wasn't well. While his doctors had pronounced him physically fit, he was uncommunicative and preoccupied. She studied him surreptitiously.

One elaborate course followed another, and Marielle choked down a few mouthfuls of each. She wished she hadn't agreed to come, and that it would all be over soon. It was a beautiful, warm spring evening, but inside the dining room it was too dark, too crowded and too stuffy. And while the company wasn't the most congenial, she could have suffered through it all, even the nanny's dreadfully long face, had Deirdre not been so gushing and syrupy.

She thought at one point that she would run screaming from the room or else toss her potato mousse in the girl's lap. Paddy's blue-eyed twinkle kept her from doing either of those things. Finally it was time for dessert to be served, and Marielle breathed an inward sigh of relief. If she could just endure another hour....

But Aunt Agatha announced that dessert was going to be served in the salon that evening and that she was giving everyone a half an hour to get hungry again. The cook had been working on a special treat all day. Marielle's heart sank.

She decided to take a badly needed breather in Paddy's rose garden and slipped away as everyone else meandered in the direction of the salon. Rusty followed her. "Phew," he muttered under his breath as they went out. "Wasn't that awful! You owe me for this favor, Marielle! You talked me into coming!"

"Come on, you tucked away a mountain of food!"

"Yeah, dinner was great. But it wasn't good enough to make up for that crowd! Nothing could be that good! And now we have to stay at least another hour!"

"Probably more like an hour and a half," she mourned.

He groaned. "That dessert had better be the best one I've ever had. I don't even like dessert. No wonder Uncle Willy didn't want to come home! And did you get a load of that nanny?" He shuddered. In companionable silence they walked along the flagstone path, and Marielle took deep breaths of the sweet, rose-scented air. "Say, Marielle," Rusty began, his tone of voice making her suspicious.

"No, Rusty."

"Aw, c'mon! Listen to me first! All I want is a measly two hundred dollars!"

"I gave you two hundred dollars the day before yesterday!"

"I know, but there's this bra I want, and—"

She gaped at him. "A bra? You want a bra? A two hundred dollar *bra*?"

"Dammit, Marielle, it's for my car! It's a thingamajig that fits around the headlights and the nose to protect it against chips and paint scratches and that sort of thing!"

"Oh, thank God!" She was immensely relieved. "For a second there, you had me worried. I thought that with your thumping around on the mat with Tanaka these past few days you might have bumped your head. But Rusty, you have a trinket fixation. You'll buy anything as long as it costs enough!"

"Aw, geez! Not a lecture, not now! It's on sale, Marielle! It's beautiful! It matches my upholstery and—"

"Wait for your paycheck and buy it then, if you must! You already owe me three hundred eighty dollars. You can't spend money like it grows on cacao trees, Rusty."

"Huh?"

She could have explained that remark, but instead she just wondered why she always had to think of Cedric. "Never mind. Forget I said that! Where were we?"

"You were saying I can't have my bra," he mumbled dejectedly, shoving his hands into his pockets.

"Now, Rusty, you do understand, don't you? I don't want to come across like the heavy, but you simply have to learn to live within your means. You must curb your spending. You have just so much money, and once it's gone, it's gone. I won't allow you to blow every penny you make on toys. At least, not the pennies I give you! Where would we be if I gave you money every time you asked for it?"

They had been so involved in their quiet argument that when Cedric walked right by them with a curt "Good evening," they were both totally surprised. He had come from the direction of Paddy's wing. Marielle spun around to stare after him, shocked and hurt. Without stopping, without once looking back, he stalked on to finally disappear into the house. Uncharacteristically, he slammed the door shut behind him.

She felt faint suddenly and put a hand to her forehead. Rusty didn't say a word; he simply put an arm around her and started patting her back as though she were a little girl with a stubbed toe. Somewhere a door opened and shut again.

Finally she pulled away from her friend. "You were right about that dessert." She was composed now. "It had better be the best this planet has ever seen!"

Marielle and Rusty entered the salon just in time to see Aunt Agatha fluttering agitatedly about, instructing Sylvester to bring another plate and another fork for her nephew. Uncle Willy looked downright gaunt, as if the last time he'd eaten was a month ago. Deirdre was staring at him speechlessly. Only Paddy looked comfortable.

"I thought I'd drop in for dessert," Cedric announced coolly. He didn't sit down but leaned against the piano. "Didn't you say, Aunt Agatha, that you were serving my old favorite, Sacher torte?"

"Oh, Cedric, you naughty boy, now you've spoiled my surprise," Aunt Agatha twittered.

Marielle tried to block him out, but his image seemed to be burned into her consciousness. Closing her eyes only had her remembering what it had been like to kiss him.... Startled by the clarity of the vision, her lips parted for a long intake of breath.

When she opened her eyes again, he was looking straight at her. For a second she thought she glimpsed volcanic anger in his eyes, but in the very next instant the ferocious heat was gone, and he was looking at her as though she were a total stranger. It had happened so quickly that she wasn't sure it had happened at all. Was it a trick of the light, she wondered.

"And why did you two disappear?" Deirdre asked Rusty coyly. "Did you have a little dessert of your own out in the garden? I was going to join you, but when I saw what was going on.... Oh, have I said something I shouldn't?" With round eyes she turned to Marielle.

The hair on Marielle's nape prickled with outrage. Rusty was too embarrassed to rescue them. She had to say something! "I've told you before, Deirdre, Rusty and I are...friends."

"Yes, I know. Didn't you tell me he was your *dearest* friend?" She smiled innocently. "I think it's absolutely wonderful!"

Aunt Agatha chuckled. "Now, Marielle, don't protest too much!" She winked conspiratorially.

Marielle clenched her teeth in helpless fury. Any number of colorful expletives were battling for release.

While Sylvester provided some distraction with his serving trolley, Marielle took a peek at Cedric to see what effect Deirdre's little ploy had had on him. He was looking at Rusty from under half-closed lids with violent antipathy. Marielle's heart leapt into her throat. He ended his scorching perusal of Rusty and switched his gaze to Deirdre. In his look now there was only a certain distaste. He glanced Marielle's way, and she couldn't help but shiver under his cool regard.

The tip of her tongue moved out to wet her lips, in an unconscious reaction to him. His dark eyes fell briefly to her pink lips, and her breath became shallow and quick. Then Sylvester handed Cedric a cup of coffee, and he turned away.

The air was tense. Somewhat nervously, Aunt Agatha served the torte, putting a triangle of cake on each plate and handing the plates to Deirdre to pass out. Deirdre, the ingenue, was smiling and fluttering her eyelashes a lot. Coffee was then dispensed. Conversation was scarce.

The Sacher torte, layers of cake and apricot jam, covered with chocolate, was really delicious. But Marielle hardly tasted hers. Her nerves were stretched almost to the snapping point. She wanted to take her plate and hit Deirdre over the head with it, and then she wanted to go to Cedric and—

"Thank you, Aunt Agatha." Cedric put down his plate. "I enjoyed that." He smiled faintly. The hawk being kind, Marielle thought, watching him fixedly. "I'm glad we're all together, actually..." Casually he glanced around the room, taking everyone in. But he looked right through her as though she weren't there. Marielle's heart ached. "Because I have something to say to Miss Wheeler that I want everyone to hear." Everyone seized up and nobody moved. "I have waited, Miss Wheeler, with exquisite patience, for you to realize you're making a serious mistake. However, since you're incredibly slow at coming to that conclusion yourself, let me make it for you."

There was a general stir. But Cedric didn't allow anyone else to get a word in.

"It's time to pack up all your newly acquired belongings *and* your child, and go! You'll never get so much as one dollar from me!"

Deirdre burst into tears. Aunt Agatha rose from her chair in a flurry of excitement to snatch the baby from the nanny. Ricky woke up and started screaming....

"Are you going to throw a mother and child out on the streets?" Aunt Agatha said accusingly over the baby's wailing. She shushed him and jiggled him up and down in her arms. "Have you no conscience? Have you no decency? Where do you expect your child to sleep? Under a newspaper in a gutter? You monster!"

Cedric replied with remarkable calm, "That baby is not mine. I repeat, I have never touched Miss Deirdre Wheeler, therefore that child cannot possibly be mine. You are sheltering an ordinary criminal, Aunt Agatha. If you want the baby so badly, why don't you adopt him? I'm sure a single mother of Miss Wheeler's ilk would be only too happy to have him off her hands. I don't think I've ever seen her near him."

Deirdre, sobbing, cried out in a pitiful voice that she would never give up her baby, never, and then Aunt Agatha started crying, too. Uncle Willy just sat huddled in his chair, looking very pale.

"Get me out of here," Rusty hissed at Marielle under his breath. But she wasn't going anywhere, not now.

"If you have any sense at all, you'll go before you're locked up in jail!" Cedric's ruthless voice cut through all the noise. "I've run out of patience with your charade! I've had enough of your false accusations. Pack up, Miss Wheeler, and go!"

"You can't make her go! You have no right!" His aunt was screaming. "This is my house!"

"I have every right! That woman is trying to ruin my life! If you keep her here, you be prepared to see me in court! Because I have finally had enough! I'll sue her for slander and anything else I can think of! If you're prepared to hire a lawyer to back her, you do it!"

Aunt Agatha wept harder, Ricky wailed, and Deirdre sobbed into a tissue. Rusty nudged Marielle then poked her in the ribs. "Get me the hell out of here," he pleaded.

Paddy spoke up. "Nanny, for heaven's sake, take Ricky back to the nursery! The poor little tyke is probably scared to death with all this racket!"

Nanny had a bit of a struggle getting Ricky away from Aunt Agatha. But she prevailed. No one could stand up to that dour face for long. Away she marched.

"I don't believe you can be so, so brutish!" Aunt Agatha was really crying now, great fat tears coursing down her cheeks.

"Watch me. As for you, Miss Wheeler—" Cedric snarled, and even Marielle was taken aback by his grim demeanor "—you prove that baby is mine, or get out!"

And then he left.

There was a moment of catatonic quiet during which even Deirdre made no sound. Marielle rose, glanced around at everyone and then bolted out after Cedric. Rusty said a hurried goodbye and thanked Aunt Agatha for dinner. Then he, too, bolted out the door after Marielle.

But Marielle didn't know that. She was intent on catching up with Cedric. Since he had originally come from Paddy's wing of the house, she dashed off in that direction. But Rusty, thinking that Marielle was headed for his car, which was parked at the curb, went that way.

Marielle found Cedric in the rose garden. "Wait, Cedric!" she cried, running after him. She had never run after a man before. He kept right on going. "Wait...please?" She caught up with him, and in an effort to make him stop, she put her hand on his sleeve. He stopped abruptly. He looked pointedly down at her hand, and she hastily withdrew it, feeling as though he had slapped her. "Cedric, I'm sorry! Won't you listen to me just for a minute? I know I—"

"Good night, Marielle," he said distantly. "Actually, I think goodbye would be more suitable." And with that he simply walked away.

Hurt and shocked, Marielle could only stand there staring after him. Anger would have been preferable to his cold indifference. Soon he had disappeared from sight. Pressing her hands over her heart—her pain was so great it seemed physical—she stood there in the moonlight, quivering.

Rusty found her there. "What the hell happened to you?" he blazed, thoroughly irritated. "Great leaping lizards, can we get the bloody hell out of here?" Taking her arm, he promptly led her away.

Marielle followed him automatically. Rusty steered her back inside, through the whole length of the checkered hall. "If I see another Greenleaf tonight, I swear I'll smack him—or her," he affirmed under his breath. "Even that downright creepy butler of theirs! And I thought only cats were called Sylvester!"

Ordinarily, Marielle would have at least chuckled at that remark. But not so much as a shadow of a smile curved her mouth. Rusty searched her face anxiously and started swearing under his breath. "Crazy family! You and I are lucky to be orphans. What a madhouse! Stupid bunch of insane crackpots...."

Rusty helped her into his Corvette, buckled her in and then started driving. He kept up a running commentary the whole time. Marielle just gazed out the window passively. She was exhausted and brokenhearted.

He took her keys from her gently and opened the door of her condo. He then sat her down on the couch in her living room and started rummaging through her liquor cabinet for some brandy. He poured two stiff drinks and planted one in her hand.

"Drink it!" he ordered. He sat down, with a groan, on the matching chair. "That's the last time I go there for dinner!"

Marielle sipped her brandy, letting the fiery liquid slowly burn all the way down to her stomach. She felt numb, dazed, incapable of functioning correctly.

"You know," her partner started off in his most philosophical tone of voice, "I don't think he did it. I mean, up until tonight, I did. I thought he was just a rich spoiled kid who always got things his way. Just a scumbag, you know, treating everybody like dirt. But he isn't really like that, although he is arrogant, in a way. King of the castle, and all that. But he's pretty much a regular sorta guy, isn't he? I mean, I'll bet he played football. Yeah, he's got the build for it. He could have played football. . . .

"You know, I finally figured out why he dislikes me so much. He's jealous. Yep, that's it. He's been jealous all along. For a while there tonight, I thought he was going to knock my block off. I don't mind telling you I was actually sweating a bit. I mean, he can take Tanaka! And I don't think Tanaka would lie about a thing like that. . . . I'll tell you, Marielle, if looks could kill, I'd be missing some mighty important parts right now. But that's why he kept putting me down all the time. Here I thought he figured he was too grand for the likes of me, but he was just plain old jealous. Bites us all, sooner or later. . . .

"That Deirdre is a nasty little piece of work, isn't she? All cutesy and smiley—so . . . sticky. Brown-nosing all the time, it kinda gets on your nerves, doesn't it? The poor guy. She's putting him through hell. And his lousy family doesn't help. The poor guy. . . ."

There was a thoughtful lull in his musings.

"Aw, Marielle, don't cry! Hey, stop that!" Aghast, Rusty stared at her tears. "C'mon, now! Stop that, Marielle, you never cry!"

But she was crying, and she couldn't stop. A flood of scalding tears rushed down her face.

Rusty started swearing again, and then, rather awkwardly, he sat down on the couch beside her and gathered her into his arms. As she cried into his muscular shoulder, he patted her back and muttered curses against C. E. Greenleaf, chocolatier.

"I told you he was trouble, baby." Pat, pat, pat. "I told you not to mess with him." Pat, pat, pat. "I could always punch him out for you, baby," Rusty suggested doubtfully. But she only cried harder. "Just a little tap on the nose, baby, that's all I'd do. Just to let him know what's what. But now see here, you have to tell me what he did because I can't very well hit a man without telling him why first. It wouldn't be fair."

"He didn't do anything," she managed to say through her tears.

"But he must have done something!" Pat, pat, pat.

"No. It's all my fault. Everything is my fault. I can't blame him for not wanting to have anything more to do with me!"

"I don't believe that. When a guy is as jealous as he is, he wants plenty to do with you."

"You don't understand, Rusty. I've been awful! You can't punch a guy for not loving me enough! Oh, Rusty, I've been so stupid!"

"Never!"

"I've been so selfish!"

"I don't believe it!"

"It's true! And then I let my fears paralyze me!"

"You? Afraid?"

"Positively riddled!" She sobbed.

"That's a new one, baby." Pat, pat, pat.

"What am I going to do, Rusty? Whatever am I going to do?"

Pat, pat, pat.

His presence was comforting, but it didn't ease the desolation within her. She would never feel Cedric's arms around her again, never feel his mouth on hers, never be loved by him again. . . .

"Baby, I think you're taking this too hard."

Sobs racked her slender body. "I don't think so, Rusty. He said goodbye, and he meant it."

Pat, pat, pat.

CHAPTER FIFTEEN

NOW THAT IT WAS REALLY ALL OVER between her and Cedric, life seemed to lose its sparkle. Marielle began to hate Cedric a little for taking so much away from her.

Up until she had fallen in love, her happiness had revolved around her accomplishments, around solid, real things she could see and touch, like her condo, her car and her business. But now life seemed to be thumbing its nose at her; now her happiness depended on capricious whims of the heart. She hated to be dependent on something that was as illogical and insubstantial as love.

Now that it was too late, she knew she should have stayed away from him in the first place. They really had nothing in common. He was old money; she was new. He was elegant; she was casual. He was educated; she had street-smarts. Heavens, even their professions were diametrically opposed! While he sold candy, she preached vigorously against it!

The days crept up on her unawares. Marielle was shocked to discover that she was due to fly to Paris in precisely three days. In a last minute flurry, she prepared for the trip, not at all sure she wanted to go anymore.

It seemed sinful to feel so unenthusiastic about going to Paris. And considering the amount it cost, it seemed almost criminal not to be eagerly anticipating the trip. She toyed with the idea of not going at all, but could she really just throw away all that money she had put down? And what did she have to do instead? The sad truth was that there was nothing to stay home for. Had there been, she would have tossed the money out the window in an instant.

She told herself sternly her holiday had come at a good time. She could probably use the time away to think things out. Different surroundings might throw a different light on things. In Paris, her life might not seem so tragic. . . .

She didn't contact any member of the Greenleaf family during her remaining three days in town, not even Paddy. She couldn't bear the thought of seeking out reminders of the ghastly night Cedric had said goodbye. Had she thought there was even a remote chance he would be interested in her leaving, she would have swallowed her pride and gone to see him. But his almost bored dismissal of her had cut deeply. The glimpse of volcanic anger she had seen that night had probably been a delusion. Had he shown anything for her at all, she would have had some shred of hope left. But indifference? She just couldn't force herself on someone who viewed her with such abysmal contempt.

At the airport Marielle bought a San Diego paper to read during the flight. Rusty was there to wave her off. Trying to look as though she was having a good time, she waved back....

Several minutes later, buckled into her seat, airborne, Marielle opened her paper. She had no desire to converse with fellow passengers. On the bottom of the front page of the *San Diego Union* was an article about the prominent businessman, bachelor, and chocolatier, Cedric Evelyn Greenleaf. He was being sued for child support by a Miss Deirdre Wheeler. Marielle couldn't stop a whimper from escaping her lips.

The man beside her gazed at her curiously, signaling with his attention that he could be talked into enjoying a little chat. But she rustled her paper and buried her nose in it.

Avidly she read further, noting with great relief that the initial court date was set for two weeks after her scheduled return home. The paper went on to say that the paternity suit was being contested by Mr. Greenleaf. There was an accompanying article that included the latest news of the fountain. The dig had turned up a few more bones, but these were only of minor importance. It was thought that the university would soon return the by now huge hole in the middle of the intersection to Cedric, so that work on the elaborate plumbing could continue without further delay.

Absently Marielle thought that Cedric's stonemason must have arrived back from Italy. She wondered why the granite couldn't be sculpted in a workshop, to be moved to and assembled on the site once it was ready. That would save the stonemason's having to sit idly by, costing Cedric megabucks, while.... Marielle sighed impatiently at herself. She was supposed to be forgetting Cedric's problems, not sorting them out!

But her thoughts couldn't help but move to the paternity suit. If she could have, she would have turned the plane around and gone straight back home. Cedric probably had need of some friendship right now. She could have offered hers....

But she went to Paris and on her educational tour. She climbed up the Eiffel Tower, saw the Louvre, sampled the city's culinary delights and visited the couturiers. Every time she saw something particularly intriguing, she wished Cedric were by her side so that she could point it out to him. And every time some fellow smiled at her, she remembered Cedric's velvety brown eyes and despaired of ever feeling whole again.

But when she stepped on the plane back home two weeks later, she was a little more poised, a little more polished, and a lot more elegant.

"You look fantastic!" Rusty breathed when he set eyes on her. He was at the airport to collect her and all her new luggage. He gave her a lovely welcoming bear hug.

The first few minutes all they talked about was business. But then, unable to contain herself, Marielle asked whether the Greenleaf water fountain was finished. Rusty informed her that although the hole was finally filled in, and the pipes were in place, and the paving around the fountain was completed, there was now some hitch concerning the granite. But at least the traffic was flowing again.... And then she asked whether he knew anything about the paternity suit. She hardly realized she was holding her breath for a reply.

"What a mess that is! Of course, the whole town's buzzing with it. I wasn't born yesterday, Marielle; I know people can be damned unkind, but geez! They're crucifying him! They figure he's got to be guilty, or she wouldn't have had the guts to take him to court. They're taking bets on who will win the case. It's sick! And little Miss Innocent Wheeler is playing her part to the hilt. That stupid fountain of his sure doesn't help matters. It makes him look like a rich creep. You know, spending piles of dough yet not sparing a penny for his son. A cartoon in one of the rags had a throne built on top of the fountain, with him sitting on it way up high, eating chocolates, and Deirdre and Ricky begging on the street below. Guess what the caption said..."

"I don't think I want to."

"Let them eat cake!"

"Oh, no!"

"Yeah! The very people he's building the fountain for are crapping all over him! I mean, I'm not exactly crazy about the guy myself, but to assume he's guilty just because he's male, and just because he's got a few bucks...well, it's damned unfair!"

Marielle couldn't agree more. "Never mind about them, Rusty. They're going to have to 'eat crow' before too long. It does seem that the laws are rigged against men as far as this sort of thing is concerned, though."

"I'm just glad I don't have any money!" Rusty grinned at her.

She had been meaning to tell him that some stock market commodities she had taken a rather big gamble on had paid off, and he had a lot more money than he thought he did! She said casually, "Say, Rusty, remember that bra thing you wanted for your car? Well, you can buy it now, if you want."

"Naw. I've been really good while you were away, you know. I haven't bought one single thing. Payday is coming up, and would you believe I haven't spent my whole check already? 'Course I owe petty cash a hundred because I got hungry one night . . ."

Rusty drove her home to Pacific Beach, and since there was no reason for her to hurry back to the spa, she let him go back to work while she stayed home to unpack and rest after her long, tiring flight. Although the trip had been refreshing, it was wonderful to be back in her very own place.

She wandered around a bit, becoming reacquainted with all her things. Her equilibrium had been somewhat restored by the trip, she realized. She didn't feel quite so stricken anymore. She knew she wasn't going to die of a broken heart, although, like Paddy, she, too, might never completely recover from her lost love. But she consoled herself that at least she had a lot of other things to fill up her life....

Marielle tried to take a nap, but she was too restless, and so she unpacked her fabulous new wardrobe instead. Then she tried to eat something but found that she was too tense for that, too. The only thing she had a craving for was a certain somebody's chocolates, but there was no way she was going to step inside the venerable edifice of the Greenleaf Sweets Company, Incorporated 1883!

On the spur of the moment Marielle decided her car needed a drive after sitting in the garage for two weeks, and she set out for the Greenleaf mansion in Coronado. She could hardly get there fast enough, but she took a small detour past the half-finished water fountain. It was a mass of bare piping, and what looked like spigots glinted in the hot sun. Scaffolding surrounded the site.

As soon as Aunt Agatha offered her chocolates, Marielle dug out a cordial cherry. The older woman seemed pleased to see her. The house was even gloomier than usual; Deirdre had gone and taken the baby with her.

"Where did she go?" Marielle asked, refusing a second chocolate and sitting down.

"I don't know; nobody knows. She's even got an unlisted telephone number, it seems. I feel sick about little Ricky! Deirdre's so young and ... well, a little irresponsible. She really doesn't know anything about caring for a tiny baby...."

"But she learned a lot from you and the nanny, I'm sure." Marielle tried to console her.

"I'm afraid not." Agatha shook her head. "She ... well, to be truthful, she wasn't terribly interested...." Cedric's aunt looked somewhat shamefaced. "She was a lot more interested in shopping."

"So she's basically disappeared again. Doesn't she call or anything?"

"Oh, yes, now and then." Aunt Agatha sighed sadly.

"But surely she could at least give you her address and telephone number!"

"She won't. She says—" embarrassed, Aunt Agatha cleared her throat "—she says she's afraid Cedric would beat it out of me. She says he's threatened her, and she's terrified of him. Believe me, Marielle, Cedric is no innocent, but he's no woman-beater, either! He is not a violent person." Sighing and shaking her head, Aunt Agatha said, "She went a little too far there."

Marielle's resentment against the young mother flared. Belatedly she wished she *had* cracked her dessert plate over the girl's head....

Then Uncle Willy wandered into the salon. Marielle, trying not to stare, thought he looked dreadful. He no longer looked haunted, he looked hunted! Whatever could be the matter with him? She wondered whether she should suggest to Aunt Agatha that perhaps it was time for him to change doctors. But glancing in her direction, Marielle saw that she was already thinking the same thing. Uncle Willy soon left them alone again.

"I do wish he would go back to work!" Aunt Agatha exclaimed. "It's not good for him to mope all the day long. He won't do anything: he won't go out; he won't take me away for a holiday; he won't even talk! And he's been drinking far too much!"

"Er..." Marielle was really more interested in Deirdre at the moment. "So what else did Deirdre have to say when she called? Did she happen to mention who's paying for her lawyer? Are you?"

"Heavens, no! I am not going to pay to take my own nephew to court! She said it was the sort of deal where her lawyer will make his money by getting a percentage of whatever he manages to get out of Cedric. Sounds like one of those vile ambulance chasers to me!"

"And how's her apartment? Or is she living in a house now? Who's paying her bills?"

"I don't know. She won't say. I can't get a thing out of her! It's most annoying. Well, she did say she was near a park.... I asked her whether Ricky was getting any fresh air."

"Speaking of fresh air, do you think we could open a window?"

"But it's so hot out . . . and I don't—"

"Only one little window," Marielle coaxed. Hurriedly she pulled the heavy drapes wide open, whisked aside the lacy sheers, and with a feeling of glee, opened one of the many-paned windows. "There! Isn't that better! What park did she say?"

"Balboa. Yes, I'm sure it's Balboa, because she mentioned the zoo."

"Anything else? Tell me everything you can remember." Marielle hated herself for doing it, but she picked up the bowl of chocolates and urged Aunt Agatha to take one, trying to help her to relax and remember. It worked. The woman sat back in her easy chair, munching on the candy, and stared contemplatively out into space.

"There was the park, and she said something about a grocery store being right across the street where there were lots of fresh flowers.... Oh, I do recall she said once she was on the fourth floor, so it must be an apartment. I remember because I was worried that Ricky could fall out the window! It gives me palpitations just thinking about it!"

"Aunt Agatha, you're a hopeless worrywart. He's not even crawling yet!"

"I know, I know, but he will be soon, and then what?"

When Marielle mentioned on her way out that she was going to stop in to see Paddy, Aunt Agatha informed her Paddy was downtown at the shop. He was managing it for Cedric, who was away in New York to oversee the opening of the Greenleaf's newest candy store, the forty-sixth. He would be gone until the day before the court date, a whole two weeks away. Marielle's heart dropped all the way down into her shoes. She thought of the one bright spot: Agatha seemed to be wavering in her loyalty to Deirdre . . . a good sign for Cedric.

Later, Marielle assembled her few facts: Deirdre lived in an apartment building, on the fourth floor, somewhere close to Balboa Park. And across the street was a grocery store with fresh flowers for sale daily. It struck Marielle that it might be handy to know exactly where Deirdre was living and who was paying her rent. Whoever was signing her check could be either the father of her baby or another blackmail victim.

Marielle went to the spa every day and worked diligently. There was the grand opening of the new restaurant to plan, so she scarcely had a minute to herself. Yet on more than one occasion she came close to hopping on a plane to New York. She had a mad desire to see Times Square, she kept telling herself.

What did Cedric do when he wasn't working, she wondered. How was he spending his evenings? With whom was he having his dinner? Did he give gray satin boxes of chocolates to other women?

During the few hours that she wasn't either working, sleeping or eating, she scoured the areas around Balboa Park in search of Deirdre's apartment. The task had sounded so easy when she had thought of it, but there seemed to be thousands of blocks with four-floor apartment buildings, and of those, there were hundreds with grocery stores that sold flowers across the street. Deirdre had really not let much slip.

Although Marielle kept in contact with Aunt Agatha, she never did learn anything more. Agatha couldn't worm anything else out of the girl. Marielle had, however, made an interesting discovery. The residential areas around Balboa Park weren't exactly cheap. Whoever was paying Deirdre's rent was putting her up in style!

She spoke with Paddy several times during the following two weeks. He was as calm as ever. He wasn't privy to any information garnered by Cedric's detective, however, so although he could report that his son was just fine, and that the new store was coming along as expected, he had no other news with which to cheer her up.

The evening before the court date, Marielle was at home, thinking that Cedric had come home from New York earlier that day. He was so close . . . just a mile down the beach. She could scarcely believe it, and her eyes filled with tears at the mere thought. She was as blue as could be and sick with worry about the following day.

All her searching for Deirdre's apartment had been for naught, though she still had several areas left to check out. Her quest had begun to seem somewhat foolish. For all she knew, Cedric and his detective had already discovered Deirdre's address for themselves.

Too exhausted to do much else, Marielle lay on her couch and watched TV. And she thought fruitlessly about Cedric. When her front door buzzer went off, announcing company waiting to be let in at the downstairs door, she sprang up like a shot. Living just downstairs, Rusty naturally had his own key, so she knew it wasn't he.

"Hello!" Her voice wavered hopefully into the intercom. She had only the one thought in mind that it might be Cedric. He had come to see her!

"Marielle? It's, er, Willy Greenleaf." He sounded very apologetic, as if he knew he wasn't the person she had wanted to see.

She was so surprised that for a couple seconds she said nothing at all. Then she gasped out a startled welcome and pushed the button to let him in. By the time he arrived at her door, she was able to greet him as though he dropped in to visit her at ten o'clock in the evening on lots of occasions.

"Come on in, Uncle Willy!"

He stepped in her door but stopped there. He shifted his feet uneasily. "I can't stay. I just popped in for a second. Is Cedric here?"

"Cedric? No. Should he be?"

"Well . . . he did return from New York today, but he's not at his home. He's not in Coronado, either, or at the shop. I thought he might be here."

"Sorry, no."

His disappointment was intense. His thin shoulders sagged down even farther. None of the sparkle that had been present when she had visited him in the hospital was present now.

"Uncle Willy? Are you all right? Are you sure you won't come in for a minute?"

"No, no, thank you, my dear. I'll just roll along."

With a puzzled sigh Marielle watched him go.

It took a huge amount of determination not to go to the courtroom the next day to watch the events for herself. She waited on tenterhooks for Paddy's promised call.

"Nothing happened," Paddy reported. "Cedric's lawyer delayed the case for two months."

"What?" she squeaked in disbelief. "But why?"

"To put pressure on Deirdre. Now she'll have to wait even longer for the money she expects to get."

"What was he like in court? What was Deirdre like?"

"Cedric wasn't there. Deirdre looked about twelve years old."

"Cedric wasn't there? But he came home yesterday from New York . . . didn't he?"

"He's back. Marielle? Don't be too hard on him. He's a proud, lonely man in some respects. He's a bit of a recluse, like me, I suppose, and finds it difficult to trust people."

"Don't you mean women?"

"Well, you really can't blame him too much, can you? The media has been awfully hard on him. Deirdre is being treated as though she had nothing to do with getting pregnant!"

"Oh, I know it's rotten. But what he's doing is throwing out the baby with the bathwater!"

Paddy chuckled. "You have a point there."

"Well, what's his detective up to?"

"Cedric isn't telling anyone anything. The whole case has become highly secretive."

"Oh." She sighed despondently. There didn't seem to be anything else left to say. She thanked him and hung up the receiver.

So her love was back in town. And he hadn't come to see her. Fervently wishing that she had never met any of the Greenleafs, she berated herself for having hoped that Cedric would forgive her for doubting him.

One endless week ground by. She'd given up trying to find Deirdre's apartment; the search seemed pointless. She wasn't too surprised that Deirdre had given up seeking her out, though, for the girl had probably come to the conclusion that Marielle was no longer sympathetic to her cause. And while Deirdre called Aunt Agatha occasionally to report on Ricky's progress, even those calls were becoming fewer and far between.

Marielle was therefore somewhat surprised to pick up her phone one evening to Deirdre's tearful hello. She returned the hello but was utterly stumped as to what to say next.

"Oh, Marielle, I knew I could depend on at least you to be my friend!"

"But ... er, Deirdre—"

But Deirdre interrupted. "I've always been alone, with nobody to care for me, and you've always been so kind! I don't know how I'll ever be able to thank you enough!"

"But Deirdre—"

"God knows I need somebody to stand by me now!"

"What do you want, Deirdre, money?"

"You ... you sound strange, Marielle. Different, somehow. Or maybe it's just that I'm not feeling too good. I've been worrying terribly, you know. I've been so upset over everything that I can hardly eat. That's probably a good thing, seeing as my fridge is bare. Baby food is awfully expensive, and little Ricky is gobbling it up like a vacuum cleaner. Honestly, I don't know where it all goes! Do you know how much a quart of milk costs these days? And formula? And cereal? And strained peas?"

"Ah. You do want money."

"Oh," she whimpered, "I try so hard, but I feel like the whole world has turned against me! What did I do wrong, Marielle?"

"First off, you allowed yourself to become pregnant. You should have known better than to—"

"Oh, it was an accident!" Deirdre cried. "Babies sometimes show up whether you want them to or not! I was unlucky! I'm always unlucky! In everything! I have nobody and nothing. Even when people say they're going to love me, they don't! Cedric lied to me! He made a fool of me. And now look what he's done! Thrown me out of the only real home I ever had!"

Marielle sighed in acute frustration. "I'm only surprised he didn't do it sooner," she said succinctly.

There was a long startled pause and then a sniffle and a ragged gulp. "He's turned everybody against me...even you! My only friend! Oh, Marielle, how can you, too, turn your back on me?"

"How?" Her voice was cool and contained. "Because I think this is just a money-grubbing paternity suit, Deirdre, just like Cedric once said. Only then I didn't believe him. I wish I had.''

"Oh!" Deirdre sobbed. "He's poisoned your mind against me!''

"No, you've done that all by yourself," Marielle answered dryly.

There was another startled pause. "Oh? What on earth have *I* done? I've been patient and kind and nice to everybody, and in return, I get stomped on! Just what is it that I did?'' she demanded angrily.

"You use people, Deirdre. You used me. You used Rusty at that dinner party. You use Aunt Agatha shamefully, not to mention Cedric—even his name, for heaven's sake.''

"It's my right!" She was shouting now.

"I don't think so," Marielle continued calmly, but her hand was sweaty on the receiver. "You seem to think whatever you want is your right. You're constantly making people feel sorry for you. And then you guilt them into doing whatever you want. You're a manipulator and an exploiter. And that innocence is all an act, isn't it?''

"I don't know what you're talking about!"

"I think you do. All that cuteness is hard to keep up *all* the time, isn't it? Every now and then it slips a little, doesn't it? Like when you try to tell people that Rusty and I are lovers. You know very well that isn't so. Then why do you persist? I'll tell you why. Because it suits your plans for Cedric to believe Rusty and I are having an affair.''

"Ah-ha! I see what's gotten into you! You're not satisfied with what you've got . . . you want some of mine, too! You want Cedric! You're just jealous of me!" There were more sniffles and gulps. "But I'm nothing. A nobody. A plain, ugly nobody, who's only good for a quick f-f-fling!"

"Deirdre, it's wearing thin! Why don't you give up, while you still can. Get out of this before Cedric really does have you thrown in the clink!"

"He wouldn't dare!"

"Why not? I would, if I were being falsely sued, slandered and embarrassed."

"But he's not! It's all true. Everything!"

"Oh? And I suppose Cedric made love to you many times and not just that once in his office?"

"Of course he did," Deirdre returned haughtily.

"Where? In some scummy little motel?"

"Of course not! At his house! He invited me to his house lots of times!"

"Oh? Then why doesn't Schwartz know you?"

"He was never there. Cedric always cooked dinner for me himself. He said it gave him pleasure to do little things like that for me!"

"Uh-huh. And so why were you on your way to Coronado the night we met?"

"What do you mean? I was going to see Cedric, like I told you!"

"Why?"

"What do you mean, *why*?" Deirdre was losing her patience. Not only that, her voice was losing its sweet, innocent tone. . . .

"Why go to Coronado when Cedric doesn't live there?"

"Well," Deirdre said hurriedly, "he—he took me there once. When nobody else was home. And, um, he had said he was going over there that night."

"Oh? Didn't you tell me in the hospital that you hadn't seen him for six months?"

"I hadn't! He called me on the phone!"

"Oh? What was your phone number?"

There was another abrupt silence. Then she said hastily, "Well, actually, I think I called him."

"Really?" Marielle was relentless. "But how could you have, when you didn't know his telephone number? You told me the night I gave you a ride to the hospital that he had an unlisted number, and that you didn't have it."

"Well, uh, I—I called him at the candy store."

"Are you sure?"

"Of course I'm sure! I called him at the store!"

"Did you? Then why did you tell me that Cedric never answered your calls?"

"Well, um . . . he did that once."

"I see. Isn't that strange. Where did you call him from?"

"Well, from my place!" Deirdre snapped, getting flustered. "What does it matter!"

"What place was that?"

"Why?" Now she sounded suspicious.

"Because you didn't have a place. You didn't have a phone number. In fact, before that night, you apparently didn't exist. There are no records."

"Don't be stupid. I—I was sharing a friend's apartment. Everything was in her name."

"My, my, my. I thought you said you didn't have any friends!"

There was a sharp intake of breath followed by a shocked second of quiet then the abrupt slam of the receiver at Deirdre's end. Marielle winced at the bang and rubbed her ear as she hung up the receiver.

She went out to the balcony and looked pensively over the ocean. How she wished she had confronted Deirdre months ago! Dammit all, anyway! She had finally pinned the girl down, but when it didn't matter, when it was already too late. That awful, wretched girl!

Marielle began to genuinely hope that Deirdre would be thrown in jail, for she was most likely very dangerous. There would be another victim, certainly, whose life she would attempt to destroy. And to think how easily she had taken everyone in! Marielle could hardly believe how thoroughly she had been duped. It all went to show that appearances were deceptive. With sour humor she thought that there had to be a wise old saying to apply to this situation. Indeed there was! She said out loud to the waves crashing below, "Never judge a book by its cover!" And then, after a moment's reflection, she went to telephone Paddy to apprise him of this latest development. He would probably find it rather interesting. . . .

THE SECOND TIME Uncle Willy dropped in to see Marielle late in the evening, she wasn't too surprised. Again he just stood inside her door and refused to come any farther.

"Forgive me, Marielle, but—I have to find Cedric. It's most urgent. Do you know where he is?"

She gaped at him uncomprehendingly. "Isn't he at home?"

"No. The house is locked up, and Schwartz is gone. There's only a caretaker who comes by once a day to water the plants, or some such thing."

"At the shop, then?"

"No. He hasn't shown up there. His secretary keeps on saying he's away indefinitely."

"I haven't a clue where he is."

"You . . . haven't see him?"

"No. Not for, well—" She didn't want to admit exactly how long it had really been. "Not for ages. Ask Paddy. He'll know."

Uncle Willy rubbed his forehead. "Paddy hasn't seen him, either. He told me to try you."

"But—but—surely somebody must know where the head of the Greenleaf Sweets Company is! This is insane!"

Willy shrugged miserably. "He seems to have disappeared."

CHAPTER SIXTEEN

PADDY INFORMED HER that there was nothing to worry about. Cedric was in the habit of going off by himself whenever he felt like it. And he would simply reappear when he felt like it, too. His lawyer and detective were handling the case. As for the candy store, it was running just fine without him.

Marielle worried, anyway. Pacing around her living room, she said to Rusty, "What if something awful has happened to him? He could be in trouble! And nobody is doing anything about it!"

"Now, Marielle, Cedric is a pretty tough cookie. What kind of trouble would he be in? You've lost all your common sense over the guy!"

"Rusty, Deirdre is a crook! She's probably got friends who are crooks, too. Crooks have been known, on occasion, to have guns! What if he did some investigating of his own? And found more trouble than he had bargained for.... What if Deirdre and her unsavory friends hit him over the head and dumped him in a dirty gutter somewhere? What if they shot him in the back and dumped him in the ocean? I'm worried sick!"

The next morning one of the first things Marielle did was telephone the candy store and ask to speak to Mrs. Stevens, Cedric's secretary. She knew secretaries were often privy to information others weren't. If Cedric was just off having a bit of a rest—and who could blame him—Mrs. Stevens might know how to get in touch with him.

"Hello, Mrs. Stevens?" Marielle identified herself and then said, "Perhaps you can get a message to Cedric for me. I would really appreciate seeing him if it's at all possible. It's fairly urgent."

Marielle rather doubted Cedric would answer her plea. Why should he? But Uncle Willy had asked for her help, and she was doing her best. Of course, under the circumstances she probably should have instructed Uncle Willy to give the secretary his message. However, what was done was done. If her call brought forth no result, Uncle Willy could make the next attempt.

That same night, Marielle had only just stepped out of the Jacuzzi when she heard a short rap on her apartment door. Since there had been no call from the downstairs intercom, she expected Rusty to be on the other side of her apartment door. Wrapping herself in a huge, fluffy terry robe, she dashed down the hall, tying the sash. She opened the door to the second knock to see Cedric standing there, large as life, tanned and handsomer than ever. She stared at him in shocked amazement.

He was dressed in a pair of narrow, faded blue jeans and an old roomy white shirt. His collar was open, and his sleeves were rolled up. A pair of scuffed leather sandals were on his bare feet. He took her breath away. She was rooted to the spot and stared helplessly at him, wordlessly clutching her thick terry robe.

"You wanted to see me?" he asked, with the faintest of smiles.

With a heart-wrenching cry she lifted her arms around his neck just as his strong arms encircled her. He held her so tightly that she could barely breathe, but it felt like heaven! "Cedric, oh, Cedric!" Her whisper was tremulous: she could have wept with happiness.

"I missed you, Marielle," he murmured huskily. Dexterously he maneuvered them inside the door and kicked it shut, not letting her go all the while. Then, leaning back against the closed door, he studied her upturned face and the masses of blond hair she had piled up on top of her head. Gentle fingers drifted across her cheek. "I've missed you so much!"

"Me, too, Cedric. Every minute of these past five weeks!" Winding her slender arms around his neck, she hugged him ecstatically. But a moment later she loosened her hold to look up into his beloved face. "Do you mean to tell me that I could have asked for you to come at any time, and you would have come?"

He thought about it for a moment, holding her so close that she felt like the most desirable woman on earth. It was a wonderful, heady feeling. "Yes, I'd say so. I don't think there's much I could refuse you.''

She could have hit him. "Oh!" she exploded. She didn't know whom she was angrier with—him, or herself. "You mean to tell me that I suffered all this time for nothing?"

He said quietly as he began to take the pins out of her hair and deposit them in his shirt pocket, "I suppose we both did.'' Her hair cascaded down over her shoulders. Threading one hand through the loose tresses, he bent his head and kissed her carefully, evocatively, on the mouth.

When he raised his head she was breathless. For a dreamy moment she simply gazed back into his eyes. "But where have you *been*? Oh, Cedric, I was so worried; I was ready to call the police. I was sure you were dumped in an alley somewhere or half eaten by sharks and...." She tightened her arms to cling to him. It was frightening and yet exquisite to feel so dependent on someone else. But love was a gamble, and she was now fully prepared to take the risk.

He pressed her against him, and his arms cradled her. His body offered solid support. "I have a small cabin on the Baja where I go sometimes...." His hands slid slowly up and down her back, gentling her fears and easing out all the knots and anxieties of the weeks she'd been without him. "I went there to think. There's nothing there but a few palm trees, a sandy beach and the ocean. It's very private. This cabin is...a cabin. No plumbing, no electricity, no phone. But the village across the bay, where I get my supplies, has a telephone in the square, and that's how I received your message.''

"But . . . I only called Mrs. Stevens this morning! Your jungle telegraph must be remarkably efficient!''

"It is—but it's more desert than jungle. And Mrs. Stevens is a highly paid professional. It's only a half an hour across the bay by motorboat. If a call comes for me, one of the villagers brings me the message right away.'' His touch was soft and warm as it slid around her nape and underneath her hair. "My little cabin is the perfect place to think because there's nothing to do there. Do you think you'd like it?''

"It sounds like paradise to me. So what did you think about?'' She linked her hands behind his neck. In her happiness Marielle had forgotten all about Uncle Willy and how badly he wanted to see Cedric.

"You. I thought about you, Marielle, morning, noon and night.'' He gathered her closer and bent his head to capture her willing pink lips beneath his.

His kiss was tender yet shockingly erotic. His mouth was hot, his body hard, his arms strong; his cheeks and chin were unshaven and rough on her skin, and he smelled of sun and sea. The wealth of sweet sensations was overwhelming. She lost her head and kissed him back with all the yearning of five long weeks.

Immediately returning her caresses, he quickly discovered she wasn't wearing anything underneath the robe. And as the warm soft swell of her breast filled his hand, she snuggled closer yet, desiring both to give and to have. His hands moved down her ribs to the neat indent of her waist and the feminine curve of her hips. Slowly he savored what he had only been able to look at for so long. He went on to trace the curving line of her hipbones, and all the while his mouth devoured her soft and eager lips, further inflaming the feverish need surging through her veins. His heart was pounding against her breast; she could feel it pulsing, or was that her own mad heartbeat?

Then, for a moment, there was nothing but the heightened rhythm of their breathing and the thudding of their hearts. And finally it filtered through Marielle's consciousness that they were still standing just inside the door.

"Won't you come in?" she invited belatedly.

They started laughing. Her robe was undone, her long blond hair was already tousled from his caresses, and her lips were stung red. Laughing while locked in such a close embrace was just further inducement to greater intimacy. . . .

Deft fingers opened the buttons of his shirt, and she laid her cheek against his bared, furry chest. He buried his face in her hair and then wrapped the long silky mane around one hand. Softly, he tugged her head back. He claimed her mouth again, and she continued undoing his shirt buttons. Carefully she pulled the shirt out of his jeans and then, with a satisfied low sigh of contentment, she slid her hands up his tightly muscled stomach and into the dark tight curls ranging all across his chest.

But as soon as he released her mouth, she broke away from him. She cupped his face in her hands and, standing up on tiptoe, kissed him quickly, promising more to come. His hands settled around her waist to pull her against him again, but before he could, she slipped away.

"You haven't been in my home before, Cedric. Please come in." She started down the hall, with him right behind her. "And you've just had a long trip. Are you thirsty? Hungry? I make a mean French omelet! I learned how on my holiday!"

He reached for her, and she danced just out of reach, teasing him with a radiant and highly provocative smile. "Follow me. This is your second tour... aren't you lucky! This is my hall closet, that is the guest bedroom, there's the linen closet, and that's the bathroom." Her quick dispatch continued, and sailing onward, she hardly gave him time to poke his head in anywhere. "This is my bedroom, and here's the den. The kitchen's through there... and this is the living room."

Swiveling, she feasted her eyes on him, from his bare feet in the scuffed sandals to the long, lean legs and the trim male hips, up to the broad, powerful shoulders and then the thick, mahogany hair with the slight wave to it.

He was studying her, too, the slim temptress wrapped in the oversize robe. One tantalizing curve of breast was partially visible in the V of her robe. Her golden hair shone, and the big, gray eyes sparkled like diamond fire.

For a moment the only sound in the room was the crashing and pounding of the surf just outside her wide-open windows.

Then she suggested with a smile, "We could have a picnic right here on the rug, in front of the fireplace. It just so happens I stocked up on wood today...." In a reminiscent tone, she said, "Did you know that was the first real picnic I had ever been on? You know, I was terrified you'd kiss me that day."

"What worried me was that once I started I wouldn't be able to stop. Marielle, I'm not thirsty, and I'll take a rain check on that omelet. There's nothing I want but you." He came toward her then leaned past her to switch off a bright reading lamp. Her living room was plunged into semidarkness. "You're not afraid any longer, are you?" he murmured.

"Certainly not!"

"I'll just light that fire...." He left her and got down on his knees in front of the fireplace. Expertly he arranged some old newspapers, kindling and wood, while Marielle curled up on the soft white sheepskin rug behind him. An ocean breeze wafted in through the open windows and lightly stirred the blond tendrils at her temples, still damp from her recent sojourn in the Jacuzzi.

"Cedric," Marielle said, and she she ran her fingers delicately over the breadth of his shoulders as he leaned forward to light the crinkled newsprint, "do you still have that box of chocolates you gave me? I want it. I've never received candy from anyone before.... I'm sorry I left it behind.''

The tiny flame from his match caught and ignited the whole works. Cedric turned to catch the look in her wide, beautiful eyes. He took off his sandals, tossed them aside and sprawled comfortably down on the rug beside her, taking her down with him.

"Why did you leave it behind?" he asked, propped up on one elbow, looking down into her face. With his free hand he started to search out her alluring curves, his touch gliding slowly over the robe. He took his sweet time, roaming at will wherever he pleased.

Marielle luxuriated in his slow-motion caresses. She loved the way he touched her. "Because of your plaid couch." His quizzical expression had her melting into giggles.

"You have something against plaid?" he asked uncertainly. He pulled a little of the white terry robe aside and lowered his head to take the tip of her breast into his mouth. His wet, hot tongue teased her nipple into a hardening response. A sensual wave of pleasure engulfed her.

"No, and I'm sorry I said it was ugly," she gasped, her whole body tingling from his deliberately slow, wildly arousing action. "It's not a monstrosity at all. It's only that Deirdre had told me in the hospital that you'd made love to her on a big plaid couch, and then when you laid me down on it...." She groaned as his seductive lips trailed over her skin, leaving a line of fire. "I—I guess I went crazy, thinking that you were planning to make love to me where you had made love to her." Small kisses meandered over her chin, and at last he sought out her mouth. "I didn't stop to think. I ran out of there like a screaming idiot. Cedric, I'm not used to dealing with jealous demons!" Her fingertips trailed down his cheek. "And oh, God, was I jealous!"

Capturing her hand, he kissed her palm. "You don't know how much it means to me to hear you say that!" His lips brushed lightly across hers. "It seems we've both been going a little crazy, lately. I've been fighting my own demons...."

He took her chin in his hand and held her steady so that he could look directly into her eyes. "Speaking of which, I have to hand it to Rusty! He doesn't exactly head the list of my favorite people, but when I met him just now he was on his way out, and he let me in the building. I can tell you one thing for certain; I wouldn't have let him in, and I sure as hell wouldn't have been so...decent about it."

"So that's how you got past the security door downstairs! But Cedric, Rusty's on your side, too. He told me so. And I didn't talk him into it; he came to that conclusion all by himself."

"I appreciate that, believe me. But I still wouldn't have let him in!"

Marielle slid her fingers delicately through the dark hair at his temples, her heart overflowing with simple joy at his nearness. She loved the feel of his arm around her shoulders, his warm body aligned with hers. "Cedric, darling, I adore Rusty, I really do. He makes an excellent friend and business partner. He's all the family I've ever had. But never, never, never have we made love. Or wanted to! How many times do I have to tell you that?''

"But when I came across you two in Paddy's rose garden, you were having the kind of argument that.... A man and woman don't argue over finances unless they've set up house together—''

Marielle pushed Cedric down and placed her hands on his shoulders to keep him down while she spoke. "I'll explain all about Rusty, okay? But don't interrupt. Rusty lives in the condo below mine. That's why you ran into him downstairs. No, no, stay there, Cedric, until I'm finished. And don't do that,'' she said, laughing, wriggling out of his easy reach, "or I'll forget what I'm trying to say! Where was I?

"Oh, yes. Rusty is good at some things and really awful at others. He can't handle money, so I'm his financial adviser. I dole out what he can spend, and when he overspends, which is practically all the time, I read him the riot act. So that's what you overheard.''

He reached for her, and she moved to escape him. "And about what Deirdre said about us in the garden…well, yes, he did have his arm around me, but it was only because he's my official comforter, and he was comforting me just then because *you* were being so damned obnoxious! And when I left for Paris, he hugged me, and when I came back, he hugged me. When I cried, he held me, too. But that's all, Cedric.'' She came closer again. Her fingertip drew circles through the short curls that ranged across his chest.

"You were crying?" He pulled her down on top of him. "Oh, darling, why? Tell me what happened, Marielle.''

"You said goodbye. That's what happened," she whispered. "You broke my heart! And it's never been broken before!"

He rolled over, pinning her underneath his weight, which was considerable. But when he touched her face, his hands were as gentle as a butterfly's wings. "If I broke it, I'll put it back together again, I promise." He kissed the tip of her chin then her nose and then ravished her mouth with his. "I *was* mad. I just barely restrained myself from brawling with Rusty like a drunken sailor. I thought you had made a fool of me with him.''

"Deirdre's been trying to link Rusty and I for ages! But I would have expected you not to believe anything she said!"

"Yes, but you forget I was already jealous of Rusty. He was with you every day, while I couldn't even get you to come out for dinner with me!" His lips settled for a hard second on hers. "And while we're on the subject of broken hearts, you destroyed mine by going away when I needed you most. I couldn't believe it!"

"But I thought I had no reason to stay!"

"Because I said goodbye. Damn. Do you suppose we have trouble communicating?" he asked with a wry smile, sliding an arm underneath her.

"Considering the mess we had to fight our way through...Deirdre, et al...." Winding her arms around his neck, she smiled and murmured, "I really don't think we have any trouble at all!" In the fire's warm glow she kissed him lengthily. "Do you?"

"I see what you mean," he whispered, his lips on hers. As she arched her body intimately against him, his narrow hips pressed into hers, and the buckle of his belt was a cold shock on her bare skin. She gasped and wriggled beneath him. Her fingers slid down the length of his chest and the stretch of bare stomach toward the offending buckle. Of course, once she had the buckle open, she didn't stop there but worked his zipper down and then slid her fingers inside his jeans. To her delight he didn't have anything on underneath them. She was on fire.... Finally they were intertwined on the deep sheepskin rug with nothing between them but their love and endlessly sweet desire.

The firelight provided illumination; the pounding of the breakers on the sandy shore was all the romantic music they required. The cool ocean breeze blew over them now and then, causing them to shiver.

He kissed, touched and tasted her all over. He wanted to be sure she understood that he had never loved anyone else like this. And she, who had never loved before, gave all she had to give in willing and deliciously wanton abandonment. She had so much stored up in her to give him, and there was so much more to explore. . . .

The June moon had risen and set before they lay in sweet and sleepy satisfaction in each other's arms, their bodies drenched from the torrid heat of their fusion. Satiated by desire, Marielle had never felt more relaxed or so supremely lazy.

The fire in the grate was only an ember's glow, a faint blush of winking red. The ocean breeze had died down. But the breakers pounded on and on ceaselessly, accompanying the beating of their hearts.

IN THE MORNING they enjoyed Marielle's promised omelet; creamy eggs lightly browned and folded over melted brie and fresh watercress. Hot croissants were the perfect accompaniment, and the breakfast was topped off with a bottle of dry California champagne.

"I didn't know you could cook!" Cedric was surprised, and Marielle laughed. They were on the private patio off her bedroom, bathing in the early morning sunshine. She had already arranged for the day off. Rusty had been remarkably understanding. He seemed to know not to ask any questions.

"I had to cook for myself for a lot of years, and I learned a few things, but only very simple things. Like eggs. I know ninety-nine different ways to prepare eggs! I'm also big on macaroni and cheese."

His deep brown eyes avidly studied her. She was radiant. All she had on was a pale yellow silk teddy;

it covered all that had to be covered, yet it revealed the supple perfection of her shape. "You're beautiful, Marielle. Have I told you yet that I love you?" His deep voice was soft and husky. "I know ninety-nine different ways I'd like to make love to you. And ninety-nine ways to kiss you. Right now, I'll settle for a kiss...."

He was showing her some of those kisses a bit later, having pulled her down onto his lap, when her telephone in the bedroom rang. With a reluctant sigh Marielle went to answer the persistent ringing.

"Oh, hi, Paddy!"

"You sound so cheerful, Marielle. I hate to have to be the bearer of bad news—"

With a quick intake of breath she broke in, "But what's happened? Oh, no. Uncle Willy. Is he all right?"

"Why, sure. At least, I think he is. No, this is about Deirdre." There was a short but ominous pause.

"What's she done now?"

Paddy sighed. "Deirdre tried to commit suicide last night. In Cedric's house in La Jolla. According to her, what happened is that around six o'clock last night she quarrelled with Cedric, and he stormed off. That's when she took an overdose of sleeping pills. But apparently she didn't take enough to do herself irreparable harm. Had no one found her, she would have lived."

Marielle had sagged down weakly to sit on her bed. Her heart ached for Cedric, still sitting out in the warm sunshine, happy and unaware of this calamitous turn of events. Paddy went calmly on.

"Cedric's neighbors to the left are retired and at home most of the time. They have already told the police that they heard the loud argument. And they're certain it was Cedric's voice they heard. Not long after the argument, Deirdre thrust her baby at them over the garden gate, pleaded with them to look after Ricky and ran back into the house, sobbing that life was cruel or some such thing. Not knowing who she was, they called the police. Upon arrival at Cedric's house, they found Deirdre in Cedric's bedroom, on his bed, in a nightie, fast asleep. The spilled bottle of sleeping pills was on the floor."

All Marielle did was moan.

"It looks pretty bad," Paddy continued.

"That's the understatement of the year!" She tried to catch Cedric's attention, but he was feeding some sparrows who had come to clean up after breakfast. And Paddy was talking again.

"As soon as Agatha heard about this latest catastrophe, she rushed over to Cedric's neighbors and demanded Ricky. So the baby's back here again. Deirdre is in the hospital, and the police are looking for Cedric. They want to question him about the argument. You wouldn't happen to know where he is, would you?"

"Yes." She swallowed. "As a matter of fact, I do. I'll, um, have him go home. I mean, to Coronado. You can tell the police that, okay? That he'll be over there soon."

"Yes, my dear. Tell him not to take too long, though...."

Slowly Marielle hung up the receiver. In utter dismay, she walked slowly back to the patio door.

"Cedric, darling, sit down, please. I've something to tell you."

The sparrows fluttered away. Cedric could tell by the serious look on her face that the phone call had not been a happy one. "Let me guess," he said dryly, setting his jaw. "Deirdre. There's just no getting rid of her! If it didn't go against everything I believed in, I would just pay her off. She's worse than the common cold!"

Marielle merely nodded, too distressed to appreciate his humor. She repeated, almost verbatim, what Paddy had related. "And now the police want to ask you a few questions. They are looking for you, darling."

CHAPTER SEVENTEEN

"OH, GOD, I'M SORRY, Marielle! So sorry I dragged you into all this!"

"It's not your fault, darling! Paddy said your lawyer had the paternity suit delayed to force her to show her hand. Well, it seems she has, so don't waste time feeling sorry!"

He raised her hand to brush his lips across the inside of her wrist. Then he held her eyes an intimate second longer before she turned to pour them both a fresh hot cup of coffee.

Cedric rubbed his nape. "But, Marielle... suicide!"

"It's a logical step when you consider her scheme. It's the big shocker, the sympathy grabber. After all, nothing else worked. And don't forget, she didn't take enough sleeping pills to do any real damage. Who's to say she didn't know exactly how many pills to take in order to stage a realistic scene? If she's cunning enough to launch a blackmail plot, why not a relatively simple 'pretend' suicide? At least this time she made it to the right house." Marielle smiled.

Her attempt at levity didn't succeed. Cedric looked miserable. With a sigh she rose and walked over to stand behind him. She put her hands on his shoulders and softly caressed them then pulled the collar of his white shirt back to place a small kiss on his nape. He leaned back against her, and she slid her hands down his chest. He sighed, some of the tension leaving him, and took up from where they had left off.

"I came straight from my cabin on the Baja Peninsula to you. I haven't been home in a week. And Schwartz has had the past three weeks off. How could she have gotten into the house? There's a burglar alarm. And when Schwartz and I are both away, a caretaker comes by once a day. He makes sure that the alarm is working and that the house is secure. And how could she have rigged an argument between us when I wasn't there?

"One thing at a time! Maybe she learned something about that burglar alarm from Aunt Agatha or Uncle Willy. Do they know how to shut it off?"

"Well, of course, but—"

"That must be it, then. Don't forget how sneaky she is. I'll bet she wormed that information out of Aunt Agatha without her being any the wiser! And don't you see? She had to do it when the house was empty! Schwartz would have turned her away."

"That's true enough...."

Her hands flexed and kneaded his taut shoulder muscles. "Cedric, darling, do try to relax a little bit." Pulling his collar aside, she kissed his nape again and then bit him lightly, making him jump. "Now. About that argument. That's tougher, because the neighbors said they recognized your voice. Whew, it's her style, isn't it? I mean, think about it, Cedric. The baby over the back fence bit! It's rather too dramatic! She went out of her way to make sure she was found. I think we can rule out that she had any intention of committing suicide."

"But that argument!" He swore under his breath.

"Yeah." Marielle frowned. "I think Paddy said that your neighbors pegged the argument as happening around six. Where were you at around six yesterday? Do you have an alibi? Somebody who might have seen you enroute? In a restaurant? A gas station?"

"I was in a hurry to get to you, Marielle. I didn't want to stop anywhere. My Jeep has two saddle tanks, so I didn't need to refuel, and I had packed a light dinner and some fruit. I ate that on an empty stretch of beach at around five, five-thirty."

"And there was nobody at all who might have seen you?"

He shook his head. "A couple of sandpipers." He caught her hands and turned the palms up then kissed each one. Swiveling in the chair, he pulled her down to sit on his lap. "You're a good woman, Marielle."

She kissed him tenderly. "Yes, I am, and try to remember that the next time you get mad at me."

"I'll never be angry with you again."

"Are you kidding? We'll have the odd argument now and then, I'm sure." She grinned at him, not caring that she'd voiced the assumption that they would be spending a lot of time together. Anyway, the way he held her signified more plainly than words that he wanted her for good! "And you should know right now that I'll only let you win about half of the time."

He nuzzled her soft skin and the thick silky hair at the side of her throat. "I have this paternity suit hanging over me," he muttered thickly, "and Deirdre around my neck like the proverbial albatross...and I still feel like the luckiest man on earth! Marielle, you're the best thing that has ever happened to me. I can't believe you'd stick by me like this! If we can get through this god-awful mess, we can get through anything, can't we?"

She kissed him full on the mouth with all the loving care she had to offer. When at last they broke apart, his breath was uneven. The way he was pressing her against him had pagan fires running rampant through her blood. "Oh, Cedric," she breathed weakly. "We shouldn't have done that; we have business to attend to!" His roaming hand on her bare thigh had her pushing against his chest, trying to gain the safety of a couple of inches. "Cedric, where were we?"

"The argument, I think." He dropped a kiss on her bare shoulder.

"Right. We know she rigged it; now all we have to do is figure out how. She might have smuggled in some friend of hers to play your part. He could have left right after they staged the fight."

"A friend who sounds just like me?" Cedric shook his head. He gathered her comfortably against him, and she didn't protest this time. It was a good thing she had chosen sturdy wooden patio chairs!

"If only we knew who was paying for her apartment! I've looked and looked for her place. She told Agatha there's a grocery store across the street that sells flowers, and—"

"You've been looking for her apartment?" Cedric looked at her incredulously.

"Oh, for ages! Whoever is paying for it is probably another blackmail victim of hers! Coming up with another victim would be just the sort of proof we need to get her off your back."

"Darling Marielle. That you would actually go looking for her apartment—"

"I love you, Cedric Evelyn," she explained simply with a lilting smile. "I couldn't find her place, though. I was hoping your detective had come up with something."

"He did. Uncle Willy is signing the rent checks. My detective discovered that soon after she moved out of Coronado. I figured as much. The way Aunt Agatha feels about that baby, she wouldn't just let Deirdre slip off into the blue."

"Then Aunt Agatha was having me on all this time!" Marielle was furious, and she told Cedric all that Agatha had told her.

"It's been clear from the start whose side she's on." Cedric shrugged, dismissing his aunt's deceitfulness. Marielle thought, small wonder he didn't trust women! She was beginning to admire his restraint. Most people, had they gone through the trial he had, would have taken their anger out on those around them. But not Cedric. She began to suspect he was really a big softy underneath his sometimes surly demeanor. She gave him a sudden bear hug.

"What was that for?" He smiled crookedly at her and ran an appreciative hand up and down the length of her trim, tanned, bare thigh again.

"Just for the hell of it." She smiled back. It would never do to tell him that she thought her tough cookie was a cream puff! "About that staged argument...."

"You know, she could have used a tape recorder. I gave her plenty of opportunity to record me at my angry best: in the hospital after she had the baby, for instance, or in Coronado the night I booted her out of the house. She could have had all of that."

"That's right!" Marielle exclaimed excitedly. "Oh, Cedric, I bet you've hit on it! Sure! Even an amateur splicing job could cut out Aunt Agatha's part and anyone else's, and she'd be left with a lovely tape of you in a rage telling her to get out! It's perfect! She wouldn't even have had to do too good a job on the tape.... The neighbors were supposed to hear a muffled argument! If she can hand her baby over a garden gate to strangers, she can splice a piece of tape! It's... it's frighteningly simple, actually."

"It is, isn't it. There's just one hitch, though."

"What?"

"She needed two pieces of equipment: the tape and the recorder. After all, she couldn't be certain I had one at my house. While tape would be fairly easy to get rid of, the recorder wouldn't. An ambulance took her to the hospital, so she couldn't have taken it with her, and she didn't hand it over the gate with the baby. So—"

"So maybe the recorder is still in the house?"

"Maybe she hid it somewhere," he suggested.

"But that's not a hitch! That's a blessing! It's proof. Real, solid, three-dimensional proof to put her right in jail where she belongs!"

"We have to find it first."

"What are we waiting for?"

Marielle changed into a shirt and jeans and then, against Cedric's wishes, phoned Rusty and asked him to join their search party. After just a bit of grumbling, Rusty agreed to help. She explained to Cedric, "Darling, that recorder could be anywhere. I've only seen your house from the street, but it looked awfully big to me! If we're going to find that thing in less than a week, we need help. And you have to go to Coronado and talk to the police before they come looking for you. While you're there, talk Paddy into joining us, too."

"I can see why you make such a good business woman, Marielle! If Napoleon would have had you organize his campaign, Elba would never have happened! Okay. Let's go."

Cedric's house in La Jolla was a rambling Spanish adobe villa with a red tile roof, gorgeous ceramic tile floors and a stunning view of the ocean. It stood on a little promontory by itself. The garden was huge and very private, with a high adobe wall surrounding three sides. The fourth side was open to the ocean, but still private, for a rocky cliff dropped down to the creamy sand beach some twenty to thirty feet below. Marielle didn't understand how Deirdre could have handed the baby over the ten foot high adobe wall, however, until she realized there was a small gate between Cedric's property and the house next door, where the retired couple lived. On the villa's other side, of course, was where her own banker resided.

She and her sidekick had only just arrived when Schwartz returned to resume his duties as general factotum about the house. The task fell to Marielle of explaining recent events to him while she searched. Soon Schwartz was diligently searching, too.

She paused sometimes to look around, to absorb the ambience of Cedric's home. It was very nice, she thought; plain and simple, not the slightest bit ostentatious. Beautiful things were there in abundance, yet they didn't overwhelm. There was a basic feeling of comfort about the place. It wasn't just a showpiece.

Windows were many and multipaned. The ceilings were high and the rooms spacious. Sunlight poured in and glistened on the cool tile floors, and Mexican and Indian rugs added color and texture. The adobe walls of pale, creamy pink complemented the busy tiles and carpets. He liked art, she realized. Everywhere she looked there were pieces he must have collected over the years. As for the furniture, there was an eclectic mix.

Rusty, Schwartz and Marielle had all chosen separate rooms to search. It was a tedious, painstaking process. A tape recorder was very small indeed, but in a single room there could be literally thousands of places to hide it. As she poked and pried and lifted, Marielle muttered all kinds of nasty things under her breath about a certain Miss Deirdre Wheeler.

What she really wanted to do was wander about at will and examine everything. She wanted to browse through Cedric's bookshelves and curl up in every chair. And she wanted to watch the people strolling on the beach below and explore the garden and wait for the sunset. Most of all, she wanted Cedric's strong arms around her....

A couple of hours after their arrival, Cedric and Paddy turned up. Cedric didn't look too much the worse for wear. The police had questioned him, taken his statement and then let him go. He had spoken with his lawyer and the detective in the meantime. With any luck, the whole nasty business might soon be over....

The juicy news he revealed concerned a series of capers in Los Angeles and San Francisco undertaken by someone called Darlene Wiley and/or Dora Wilkins. The private detective thought Deirdre Wheeler was just another alias. Her real name hadn't come to light yet, but the law was starting to close in.

Marielle ended up searching the same room as Cedric, and he pulled her close to him, hungrily covering her face with kisses.

"Darling—" he began to say hesitantly once they had broken apart.

"Um-hm?" Smiling up into his face, she linked her hands behind his neck. Then she ran a fingertip between his brows, smoothing out the worried frown there.

"Are you going to be upset that Deirdre used my bed for her staged suicide?" He glanced over his shoulder at the king-size bed, still rumpled from its encounter with the petite con artist.

"No, and I have nothing against plaid couches, either!"

"I'll have Schwartz strip the bed right away."

"Why don't we do it. We have to turn the room upside down, anyway."

Working together, they quickly divested the big bed of its blankets and sheets and dumped them near the door. Together they heaved the top mattress aside to check whether Deirdre had jammed the recorder into the springs. Nothing. For a solid half an hour they worked on taking the room apart. It was a particularly pleasant room, Marielle thought, though perhaps a little too plain. They didn't find a thing.

The sound of the breakers penetrated here just as it did at her place. The sea breeze wafted in the wide expanse of windows, and she thought to herself that she could be very comfortable here. Of course, as long as Cedric was beside her, she would be happy anywhere.

"Damn!" he said, sitting down dejectedly at the foot of the bed. "I thought for certain it would be in here!"

She sat down beside him. "You have one huge house, Cedric!"

He looked at her for a moment then tipped her back on the bed. "And I have one huge desire to peel off these tight jeans of yours!" A possessive hand ran along her hip and thigh.

Laughing, she circled her arms around his neck. "I like your house, Cedric."

"I was hoping you would." Lowering his head he kissed her softly, savoring the warmth of her embrace and the growing tightness in her arms as she held him fiercely all of a sudden. In immediate response his arms lifted her against the muscular breadth of his chest, and when he claimed her mouth again, it was with a kiss so ferocious and utterly divine that she quite forgot what it was they were supposed to be doing. She opened her mouth to accept the thirsty questing of his tongue and gloried in the crushing weight of his body.

"Oh, Cedric, I wish..." She looked toward the partially closed bedroom door, and following her glance, he chuckled and with one more hard, quick kiss, he sat up and lifted her, too, so that they were once more sitting decorously side by side.

"We'll make up for this later. Marielle, it's not official, but the cops don't want me to leave town—"

"How dare they!" she broke in. "Why? What have they accused you of doing? Do they figure you told her to jump off the cliff, and she took the sleeping pills instead?"

"Darling, hold on; they're not accusing me of anything!" He laughed. "But since I'm her latest victim, I'm supposed to be available to sign complaints against her, identify her, etcetera. I guess they figure they're pretty close to nabbing her, and they don't want her slipping through their fingers at the last minute. Anyway, what I wanted to ask you was... as soon as we can get away, will you come to the cabin with me?"

"I was hoping you would ask me!" Her shaky smile had him taking her back into his arms.

But there was a slight noise out in the hall, and they reluctantly parted and stood up to resume the search.

A little while later Marielle thought to herself worriedly that they could turn the house upside down and still miss an obvious place. If she were Deirdre, where would she put the recorder? Concentrating, she tried to imagine how she would pull off such a stunt. She would have to be careful about every detail. She would have to put the tape recorder where it would never be found....

"Cedric! Oh! Listen to me for a minute." He was checking the underside of some drawers, and a pile of socks already lay on the Persian carpet. "Wait, before you dump every drawer out on the floor! I don't think she would hide it. I think she would try to destroy it. Don't you?"

He stared at her for a startled moment and then agreed. "I think you're on to something."

Rallying their search party, they discussed these new implications and tried to think of all the places where one could destroy or dispose of something. The fireplaces were discounted; for while the tape would burn, the machine would leave charred remains. They poked about in the fireplaces, anyway, and Schwartz checked all the outside trash cans. No luck.

"She could have just thrown the damn thing off the cliff," Marielle complained disgustedly. Then she brightened. "The trash compactor! Cedric, the trash compactor!"

They all charged for the kitchen. Schwartz pushed a few buttons, and out of the bottom of the appliance came a very small, neatly wrapped package of trash. Carefully Cedric slit the plastic wrapping. There before them were the remains of a tape recorder, smashed into pieces, in among the crumpled tin cans. The recording tape was mangled, but it looked as though large strips of it might still be intact. And it wasn't difficult to see that the tape had been spliced and patched back together in numerous places.

"Whoopee!" Marielle cried and threw her arms around Cedric's neck. His answering grip lifted her right off the ground.

"Well!" Paddy beamed. "I'll call the police! Don't anyone touch it! Deirdre's fingerprints are probably all over it, and we don't want anyone else's on it."

"How about some nice tall icy glasses of lemonade?" Schwartz suggested, wiping his forehead.

Rusty said nothing. He just stood there grinning from ear to ear.

The ringing of the doorbell interrupted their activities. Everyone stood around apprehensively. Finally Schwartz said, "It could be good news!" And he headed for the door.

Schwartz returned to the kitchen with a police detective in plain clothes and a uniformed cop. Marielle instinctively clutched Cedric.

"Deirdre Wheeler's real name is Darby Walters, and she's got a criminal record as long as my arm," the police detective informed Cedric. "Now that we know just who she is, our job's a lot easier! Actually, I came to check your trash compactor. That's usually where she disposes of items she doesn't want found. Everyone turned to look at the opened drawer of the compactor. His eyes followed theirs.

The detective whistled upon seeing the smashed tape recorder. "Bingo!" he exclaimed. "What did I tell you!"

He went on to say that Deirdre had been released from the hospital and was already booked on charges dating back to three years ago. She used to work her "marks" with her husband, he told them, who was the mastermind behind their joint capers. They had separated a year ago, however, and since then, Miss Wheeler, or rather, Mrs. Walters, had been working alone. And not too brilliantly.

Cedric's private eye was already at the police station issuing his sworn statements as to his role in the whole affair. Cedric, after a cursory trip down to police headquarters to sign some documents, would be free to come and go as he pleased. Marielle was asked to join him in issuing a statement regarding Mrs. Walters. The paternity suit would naturally be dismissed. The nightmare was over.

The uniformed policeman wrapped up the package of trash and the detective chitchatted on a bit longer, telling them that Deirdre—or rather, Darby—had already admitted that it had been the initial article in the newspaper about the water fountain that had convinced her Cedric was a worthwhile "mark." And she would likely give up the baby for adoption. Aunt Agatha might get to keep little Ricky, after all. In any case, at her request, Mrs. Agatha Greenleaf was going to be appointed the child's temporary guardian by the courts. He added that the baby's real father would probably never turn up. Not that it really mattered. And then he left with the uniformed policeman and the package of trash.

"Well!" Rusty shook his head. "Thank goodness that's all over! When I think of how she took me in, I could just—" He stopped and shook his head again. "I'd like to see what all those lousy gossip rags will have to say now!"

"Since it's a happy ending, they won't print it," Paddy predicted. "They're already onto someone else...."

"I'm sorry for whomever they pick on next, but all I can say is, thank God!" Cedric smiled at Marielle beside him, who smiled back, too happy to say anything.

"I'd better be going back to work," Rusty proclaimed cheerfully. "Bye, folks! See you later, Marielle. Don't worry about anything; I'll take care of things at the spa. Oh, and, congratulations, Cedric." He offered his hand, not in an overly friendly manner, but quite civilly.

"Thanks." Cedric took the proffered hand a trifle warily, but he was also prepared to let bygones be bygones. "And thanks for helping with the search. I really appreciate it."

Marielle beamed her thanks at Rusty, and he left feeling pretty good about the world in general.

"I suppose I should be getting back to Coronado myself...." Paddy smiled gently at them both.

As soon as Paddy mentioned Coronado, Marielle, with a pang of guilt, remembered poor Uncle Willy! "Oh, Cedric, Uncle Willy is simply dying to talk to you, and I think it's urgent...."

It was decided that Paddy and Marielle and Cedric would all go to Coronado. Paddy left in his car, and as Marielle dug in her purse for the keys to her Porsche, Cedric suggested they use the Rolls instead. Schwartz was happy to drive them, and off they went.

In the spacious back seat of the old car, unmindful of the world around them, Cedric went about showing Marielle some of the ninety-nine ways he'd said he would have liked to kiss her....

"Seventeen...eighteen...nineteen..." At number twenty he nibbled on her earlobe, and at twenty-one, he started down her throat. The darkly tinted windows shielded them from curious eyes, and Schwartz, up front, was invisible behind an old-fashioned velvet curtain with a pretty fringe of cream tassels. "Twenty-two, twenty-three." Softly his wandering hand caressed a firm, round breast, and his fingertips coaxed the tightening tip to harden and push against the fabric. "Twenty-four...twenty-five, twenty-six..."

His lips rested provocatively in the hollow of her throat, where a thin gold chain momentarily caught his attention. He slid the tip of his tongue along the chain, and she quivered, dizzy with the erotic sensation he aroused. "Twenty-seven...twenty-eight." With a nudge of his chin he pushed the collar of her shirt aside just a little, and his mouth imprinted sweet smoldering kisses on her bare flesh. His mouth skimmed over her cotton shirt down to where the tip of her breast rose. He paused, and the heat of his breath through the shirt had Marielle wriggling out of his arms and pushing against him, struggling to sit upright. Her blond hair was wildly tousled, her cheeks were flushed, and her were lips parted. Her breath came in quick, shallow pants.

"Oh, Cedric, do you think we should?" she gasped, her gray eyes big and round in protest, looking around to see who might be watching.

Laughing under his breath, he threaded a hand through her hair to cup the back of her head and brought her closer once more. "There's nobody in the world but you and me, darling. Twenty-nine…"

But as they were going over the Coronado Bay Bridge, he abruptly halted his caresses and simply held her close for a long moment. Then, after taking a very deep breath, he said in a low voice, "Darling, that police detective was probably right about the fact that we'll never find out who the baby's father is…." He took another deep breath. "What I want to know is…will you marry me, anyway?"

CHAPTER EIGHTEEN

"I WOULD BE DELIGHTED," she assured him politely. "When? It's likely to be a bit of a fuss, you know. Invitations and flowers and all that."

"Um-hm.... What do you say to having a little peace and quiet first? After everything that's been going on, I think we deserve it. So... let's have the wedding when we get back from the cabin."

"Okay."

"Where do you want to live once we're married? Your place, my place or a new place?"

Marielle didn't even have to think about it. "Your place. It's more of a home. Mine was always more of an investment."

Then she slid her tongue into his mouth and ran the tip just inside his lower lip. With one hand moving over the breadth of his shoulders and the other delicately stroking his nape, she arched her back, curving her body against him. As she nestled into him, his arms encircled her. His returning kiss liquified her desire into a sweet fever.

Cedric groaned and put her safely from him. "Marielle, how soon can we leave for the Baja? I can be ready almost anytime." Unable to resist her, he pulled her right back into his arms.

"Me, too," she breathed happily. "I can leave Sun Studios in Rusty's capable hands. We could leave, well, probably as soon as we've seen Uncle Willy. Oh, no, then we have to go sign our statements down at police headquarters."

"After we take care of that, you wrap things up at the spa, and I'll go to the candy store and do the same there, and then . . ."

He would have kissed her again, but they had arrived. Schwartz drove the gleaming Rolls right up to the door of the stone mansion.

With a creak of the massive front door, Sylvester let them in. His slippers slapped against the marble floor as he followed them down the hall.

"I truly think he's escaped from a horror movie," Marielle whispered to Cedric.

"He's been like that for as long as I can remember," Cedric whispered back with a grin. "We happily dislike each other. I used to terrorize him when I was a kid. He'd chase me with the rolling pin, but I could always run faster. Honestly, I tormented him. It's a wonder he didn't quit. I've no idea how old he is, but he must be over ninety! He won't say, though, and he refuses to retire."

Aunt Agatha was in the salon. She had Ricky in her arms and a delighted smile on her round face.

And, wonder upon wonders, the window Marielle had once opened stood wide open once more, allowing in fresh air and a rather depressing view of the tangled garden. Paddy and Uncle Willy were with Agatha, duly admiring the baby and commenting on how much he had grown during the weeks of his absence. Paddy had already enlightened Aunt Agatha and Uncle Willy about what had happened earlier at Cedric's place.

The baby chortled, playing with his pacifier, and Agatha proudly bubbled, "Isn't he a good little boy! He hardly cries at all! And he knows me...see how he's holding on to my finger? Isn't he just the cutest little darling you've ever seen?" she demanded of no one in particular. Everybody agreed that he was.

Abruptly Uncle Willy stood up, upsetting the ubiquitous silver bowl of chocolates. The candies rolled everywhere, scattering on the carpet. Sylvester came out of a shadowy corner and, sourly shooing everybody away, laboriously began to pick them up.

Appearing more drawn than ever, Uncle Willy cleared his throat as though he had an important announcement to make. However, when everyone turned from the baby to eye him questioningly, he just licked his pale lips and turned away. Then he blurted out, with his back to the room, "Ricky is my son."

The shocked silence in the salon was palpable. Everyone stared speechlessly at him. Even Sylvester stopped in his pursuit of the chocolates to stare.

"I can't keep it a secret any longer. It's killing me!" Willy Greenleaf turned to face his paralyzed audience.

"It's killing you!" Cedric flared, coming to life. "I'll kill you!"

"Now, son—" Paddy interjected mildly.

"I'll kill him! Please let me kill him! Do you have any idea what you've put me through?" he raged at his cowering uncle as he began to stalk him. "You're...you're...beneath contempt! Dammit! And I suppose you and she—on my plaid couch—" Cedric smacked one fist into the palm of his other hand, and Uncle Willy winced. He circled to stand behind the love seat.

"Well, er, she's tricky; she, she, er, she had me. I was so flattered that she'd like an older man like me—it just happened," he said quaveringly.

"And you let me take the rap all this time?" Cedric ground out. "You said *nothing*? You just stood there and watched while she put me through hell? You let people call me all sorts of unmentionable things, and you...you..." Cedric raked his hands through his hair. "You let Marielle think the worst of me, when you *knew* I was in love with her?"

"I—I—I was hoping Deirdre, I mean, Darby, oh, hell, whatever her name is, I was hoping she would realize her game was fruitless and just go away." Uncle Willy was next to tears. "She bled me dry, and you weren't coming across. I really thought every minute that the next minute she'd be gone. I can never tell you how sorry I am, Cedric! I guarantee you, nobody could despise me like I do!"

"Right now I despise you pretty damn much!"

"I'll second that!" Marielle put in. Paddy was pulling out his pipe. Aunt Agatha was still staring, open-mouthed, the baby in her arms forgotten.

"I'm sorry, I'm sorry. I know there's no excuse, but I was so confused, so upset that I couldn't think straight! And she...she's very good at twisting things around. Deirdre's been blackmailing me ever since... well, ever since she worked at the shop last June. It was more and more money all the time. But once she read about the fountain, she was relentless. She wanted everything. I told her I had no money. I told her you had control of the business. I told her that all I had in the world was a half ownership in this property. And I couldn't sell it without my brother Paddy's signature and—"

"Sell the house?" Aunt Agatha whispered, dazed. "Sell the...the house?"

"And you knew I wouldn't agree to that," Paddy remarked, lighting his pipe. "I would have wanted a full explanation."

"Of course!" Uncle Willy shrugged sadly. "There was nothing I could do, nothing more I could give her. She had already taken all my savings. When I tried to sell the Rolls, Paddy put a quick stop to that!"

"You meant to sell the Rolls?" Aunt Agatha gaped.

"I even pawned some of my jewelry—"

"The diamond cufflinks I gave you our fifth Christmas together and that you said you had lost, you gave to *her*?" Aunt Agatha yelped.

Miserably shuffling his feet, Uncle Willy nodded. "I had to. She threatened to tell you everything! I couldn't bear to have her do that. She would have been so...cruel. I thought you'd leave me. I panicked. I even borrowed money to keep her quiet." He hurried on, "But always she wanted more and more. Then that article was in the paper, and she decided to go for your throat instead, Cedric. I was small potatoes for her. I could keep giving her most of my paycheck, enough for a luxury apartment and some nice clothes, but not—not the kind of money she wanted. I begged her to leave you alone, Cedric, but...."

Marielle was relieved to know that Aunt Agatha hadn't been lying to her about Deirdre's apartment, after all. By this time, however, Agatha had collapsed into her chair. She looked dumbfounded.

Marielle said, "No wonder you had that heart attack when Deirdre showed up on the doorstep!" She ran a hand up Cedric's arm, and he responded by sliding it around her shoulders. She leaned against him a little. Some of the anger was draining out of Cedric. She could feel the tautness leaving his body.

"I wanted to die when I saw her there," Uncle Willy said quietly.

"I see now why you let her stay here!" Cedric said wryly. "You had little choice."

"And she went to that particular hospital to have her baby because you were paying the bills—right?" Marielle added.

"I'm afraid so."

"I knew that wasn't a coincidence! But why did she involve me?" Marielle mused quizzically.

"Probably because you drive a Porsche." Uncle Willy shrugged. "She attached herself to money, period. Didn't matter who had it. Possibly she thought you would help her, too, by taking her part against Cedric."

Marielle glanced apologetically up at Cedric, and he, with a faint smile, murmured for her ears only, "I'll collect on that later...."

"I bought her all those dresses," Aunt Agatha said, stunned. "And shoes and purses and..."

"And I suppose Deirdre gave Marielle this address that first night instead of mine in La Jolla because she assumed I lived here, too." Cedric sighed.

"Yes, she did. I had refused to give her any information about you whatsoever. Since you have an unlisted phone number...." Uncle Willy shifted from one foot to the other in great discomfort. "Cedric, I never *meant* it to happen like it did. Things got out of control. Every time I turned around, things were ten times worse, and I was in ten feet deeper. I didn't know what to do. I'm sorry; so sorry, you'll never know. I'm such a...a coward. I couldn't stop her, and I couldn't tell anyone because then everybody would know what a fool I'd been. The really sad thing is that I knew she was no good right from the start. When little shop girls start making eyes at old married fogies like me... You see, one night I was working late—"

"You? Working late?" Cedric interrupted incredulously.

"I had, er, sort of let things go. I was catching up, and she . . . she came into my office. I told her to go home, but she persisted. And finally she seduced me, she really did, with your brandy, on your couch."

"That does it!" Cedric exploded. "That couch has got to go!"

"I'll be so happy never to see it again!" Uncle Willy hastily exclaimed. "You've no idea!"

There was a tiny whimper from Aunt Agatha's direction. She had been all but forgotten in the turmoil.

"I'm sorry, Agatha," he said now. "It only happened the once. I have no excuse to offer, I know. But . . . when she was so interested in me, I *was* flattered. I know it was foolish and silly. But we haven't really been getting along; I haven't heard a kind word from you in years! We haven't been man and wife ever since we learned we couldn't have children together. How was I to know that our body chemistries aren't, well, compatible? Everything else was! At one point, anyway. . . ."

Aunt Agatha had started to cry. She held the baby and rocked him and herself back and forth in woe.

"What was I to do?" Uncle Willy asked his wife pleadingly, spreading his hands in emphasis. "I tried everything to reach you, but you'd locked yourself away from me and . . ." Then he shrugged, and sighing tiredly, he turned away. "Maybe I didn't try hard enough, long enough. Maybe I was too impatient. If you would have at least *talked* to me! After a while I gave up. Completely. My pride was hurt. Agatha, we loved each other once, but at the time I didn't realize having children was so important to you. You could have divorced me and married someone else. You were always free to go. But I didn't really care whether we had children or not, so I didn't understand how you felt.''

"But it was *my* fault we couldn't have babies, and I felt half a woman!'' Cedric's aunt sobbed. ''I couldn't bear to think what you were thinking when you touched me!'' The baby didn't know quite what to do. Barely three months old, his little face buckled up, and he started to howl.

"But it wasn't your fault, it was my fault!'' Uncle Willy protested over the wailing of the child.

"No, no, it was my fault!'' she insisted stubbornly. ''Don't you remember what the doctor said? My system is too acidic and—''

"Yes, but I'm the one with the low sperm count!''

"But if I were different, that wouldn't matter!''

"Well, true, but if I were different, it wouldn't matter either, would it?''

The argument seemed to have reached an impasse. The baby screamed his annoyance at having his pleasant afternoon interrupted, and Aunt Agatha wept.

Uncle Willy ran his fingers through his graying hair. ''I can't undo the years, Agatha, but I can promise it won't happen again.''

"But you didn't . . . why, you haven't knocked on my door for all these years! I thought you had lost interest!"

"I lost my courage, never my interest!" Uncle Willy admitted, looking at his shoes.

"Oh, dear, and now I've lost my figure!" Agatha mourned.

Marielle had to smother laughter. Raising her voice to speak above Ricky's howls, she said, "It's not really lost, Aunt Agatha; it's still there underneath. Come to the spa, and I'll soon have you fit and slim. That's a promise, as long as you do your part. You'll have to ration the chocolates, I'm afraid."

Sylvester had just managed to pick the last one up. He had made a rather long job of it. Now he stood up, holding the silver bowl and looking doubtful.

"Take it away," Cedric ordered.

Irritated at the thought of possibly missing some further development, he scowled and left. Very slowly.

"Please, Agatha, I'm sorry about Deirdre. I'll make it up to you, I promise! I'll do whatever it takes! I'll be a good father; you'll see. Little Ricky will be our son. I'm sure we'll be able to get custody of him and . . . somehow we'll learn to be happy again together, for his sake. *And* ours."

But Agatha cried, blowing her nose noisily into a tissue. "I'm not speaking to you ever again!" And then she busied herself with the child, shushing and rocking and cuddling him lovingly.

Uncle Willy looked as though he'd been dealt a fatal blow. He gazed longingly at his wife and the baby. Paddy drew him aside a few paces. "Give her time," he suggested gently. "She'll come around; I'm sure of it."

Uncle Willy wiped his forehead with trembling fingers. He looked dejectedly at his wife and the child in her arms. Ricky was starting to quiet down. He glanced shamefacedly at Marielle and then at his glowering nephew. "If you can't forgive me, Cedric, I'll understand," he said hollowly. "And now if you'll all please excuse me...."

Quietly, head bowed and shoulders slumped, he left the room. The rest of them watched him go and then looked at each other in amazement.

"I won't speak to him for at least a week!" Aunt Agatha snapped, wiping up her tears.

Relieved that Uncle Willy was not going to be made to suffer forever, Marielle left Cedric's side to open another window, saying that it would be good for the baby. Aunt Agatha agreed that perhaps some small changes were overdue about the place. "I guess I sort of lost interest gradually, over the years...." She sighed sadly. "There didn't seem to be any reason to keep things nice. Willy was never home."

"There's plenty of time and plenty of reasons to change things now," Cedric pointed out in a tone of voice kinder than he usually used with his aunt. "What about a gardener?" he went on to suggest hopefully, looking out the window Marielle had just opened.

Then he turned to Marielle and took her hand. "Dad, I have some good news. You'll have to pass it on to Uncle Willy, Aunt Agatha. Marielle and I are going away for a few weeks for some peace and quiet, and when we return, we're going to be married!"

Congratulations were hearty. Paddy's blue eyes sparkled brightly, and Aunt Agatha came alive with excitement. As odd as Cedric's family was, Marielle thought, she liked them just fine and was delighted to be so warmly included. Even Schwartz was beaming. As they walked toward the front door, Paddy remarked contemplatively, "In my day, we used to have the honeymoon after the wedding...."

"We're having one before, Dad, *and* one after!" Cedric grinned. Schwartz opened the car door for them with a grand flourish, and Cedric helped Marielle in. As the car took the curve in the lane, they both turned to wave out the window—at Paddy, Aunt Agatha, Ricky, and now Uncle Willy, all grouped in the big stone portico.

Cedric pulled Marielle into his arms eagerly. "Oh, Schwartz? Drive past the fountain!" Then he pulled the curtain shut, closed the window and gave her a very gentle kiss.

"Well, Cedric, we know who the father is, after all." She smiled into his dark brown eyes. "What a day it's been!"

"It's been absolutely terrible, and absolutely terrific!" He smiled back. "You know, I never knew what the trouble was between my uncle and aunt. I always assumed they had never liked each other, and

I couldn't understand why they had ever married in the first place. Their argument—over whose fault it was—has made me think...darling, do you want children?''

"I suppose so. I haven't really given it much thought. But, yes, now that I think of it. Not right away, but in time."

"That sounds good to me. But, darling, what happens if something goes wrong...as it did for them? We can't let that destroy what we have. Promise me right now that you won't lock me out of your life."

"I do, I promise! And if we can't have children of our own, we'll adopt some. You've a big enough house, and there's plenty of children in the world who need a happy home, and Cedric, we'll have a very happy home. I feel it with every breath I take!"

"Promise you'll always talk to me."

"I will. Sometimes more than you might want," she said, laughing.

"If that happens, I'll just start kissing you, and that'll solve that!" Sliding a hand around her throat, he tilted up her chin and settled his mouth softly over hers. He kissed her slowly and thoroughly. The lovemaking lasted until Schwartz, up front, delicately cleared his throat.

Against the backdrop of the venerable old Green-leaf Sweets building, the new Greenleaf fountain sprayed water sky-high in a glorious display of modern ingenuity. In pink-and-green-shaded granite, crafted to represent a cluster of water lilies floating on a lily pad, the fountain was resplendent.

"But how—"

"—did I manage to get it done so quickly?" Cedric grinned, obviously pleased by her reaction. She couldn't take her eyes off it. "You know my stonemason is Italian?"

"Uh-huh." Marielle just stared.

"Well, he has a lot of brothers and uncles, all stonemasons. Under his supervision, they all worked on it together, practically day and night. I just couldn't wait any longer. Do you like it?"

"*Like* it? Oh, Cedric! I take back every awful word I ever said about it! It's beautiful. How can stone look so ephemeral? It's exquisite! Look, everybody else likes it, too."

San Diegans were clustered all around it. Some had begun to relax on the shallow gray stone steps that led to the black granite pool.

"I used to think you were crazy for wanting to build a fountain. Now I think you're brilliant! I'm so proud of you, darling!"

"I'm glad you like it, because I've called it the Marielle Fountain."

For a bare second she stared at him in total amazement. "I knew it!" She started laughing. "You really are sweet underneath it all. Cedric, I love you."

"Three times around the fountain, Schwartz, for good luck," Cedric requested.

"Yes, sir! You betcha! Say, boss, I found this lovely little violin concerto the other day...."

"Fire away." Cedric grinned at Marielle. Sure enough, within seconds a lovely romantic rhapsody was pouring forth from the back speakers.

With a few dexterous moves Cedric had Marielle in his lap, lying in his arms. "Next thing you know, he'll be taking violin lessons," he murmured, dropping a kiss on the tip of her nose. "I think Schwartz likes his new boss-lady. Now let me see, where were we? I think we were up to thirty-five kisses, so this is number thirty-six...."

Harlequin Superromance

COMING NEXT MONTH

#222 THE LONG ROAD HOME • Georgia Bockoven
Jennifer Langley becomes Craig Templeton's link to
the prominent Kentucky family that had long given
him up for dead. Suddenly love and destiny conspire
to change their lives forever....

#223 CHOICES • Jane Worth Abbott
In this spin-off to Superromance #192, *Faces of a
Clown*, Sara Fletcher finds herself falling in love with
a younger man. And the unexpected object of her
affection is Evan McGrath, the man who is turning
her workplace upside down!

#224 MEANT TO BE • Janice Kaiser
When Diana Hillyer attempts to rescue a teenager
forced into prostitution in Honduras, she discovers
that an American soldier, Cleve Emerson, holds the
key to the girl's freedom. His stubborn refusal to
help infuriates Diana, but she finds his allure
irresistible....

#225 UNTIL NOW • Sally Garrett
Old maid schoolteacher. That's how Kathryn Keith
figures the townsfolk refer to her. All except John
Brasher, that is. The towering lumberjack is out to
change her reputation—with a marriage proposal.

Shay Flanagan is Gypsy,
the raven-haired beauty who inflamed passion
in the hearts of two Falconer men.

Carole Mortimer

GYPSY

Lyon Falconer, a law unto himself, claimed Shay—when he didn't have the right. Ricky Falconer, gentle and loving married Shay—when she had no other choice.

Now her husband's death brings Shay back within Lyon's grasp. Once and for all Lyon intends to prove that Shay has always been—will always be—*his* Gypsy!

Harlequin "Super Celebration"
SWEEPSTAKES

NEW PRIZES—NEW PRIZE FEATURES & CHOICES—MONTHLY

1. To enter the sweepstakes, follow the instructions outlined on the Center Insert Card. Alternate means of entry, NO PURCHASE NECESSARY, you may also enter by mailing your name, address and birthday on a plain 3" x 5" piece of paper to: In U.S.A.: Harlequin "Super Celebration" Sweepstakes, P.O. Box 1867, Buffalo, N.Y. 14240-1867. In Canada: Harlequin "Super Celebration" Sweepstakes, P.O. Box 2800, 5170 Yonge Street, Postal Station A, Willowdale, Ontario M2N 6J3.

2. Winners will be selected in random drawings from all entries received. All prizes will be awarded. These prizes are in addition to any free gifts which might be offered. Versions of this sweepstakes with different prizes may appear in other presentations by TorStar and their affiliates. The maximum value of the prizes offered is $8,000.00. Winners selected will receive the prize offered from their prize package.

3. The selection of winners will be conducted under the supervision of Marden-Kane, an independent judging organization. By entering the sweepstakes, each entrant accepts and agrees to be bound by these rules and the decision of the judges which shall be final and binding. Odds of winning are dependent upon the total number of entries received. Taxes, if any, are the sole responsibility of the winners. Prizes are not transferable. This sweepstakes is scheduled to appear in Retail Outlets of Harlequin Books during the period of June 1986 to December 1986. All entries must be received by January 31st, 1987. The drawing will take place on or about March 1st, 1987 at the offices of Marden-Kane, Lake Success, New York. For Quebec (Canada) residents, any litigation regarding the running of this sweepstakes and the awarding of prizes must be submitted to La Regie de Lotteries et Course du Quebec.

4. This presentation offers the prizes as illustrated on the Center Insert Card.

5. This offer is open to residents of the U.S., and Canada, 18 years or older, except employees of TorStar, its affilliates, subsidiaries, Marden-Kane and all other agencies and persons connected with conducting this sweepstakes. All Federal, State and local laws apply. Void where prohibited or restricted by law. Winners will be notified by mail and may be required to execute an affidavit of eligibility and release which must be returned within 14 days after notification. Winners consent to the use of their name, photograph and/or likeness for advertising and publicity in conjunction with this and similar promotions without additional compensation. One prize per family or household. Canadian winners will be required to answer a skill testing question.

6. For a list of our most recent prize winners, send a stamped, self-addressed envelope to: WINNERS LIST, c/o Marden-Kane, P.O. Box 525, Sayreville, NJ 08872.

No Lucky Number needed to win!

Explore love with Harlequin in the Middle Ages, the Renaissance, in the Regency, the Victorian and other eras.

Relive within these books the endless ages of romance, set against authentic historical backgrounds. Two new historical love stories published each month.